MERIDIAN 12

Surfing's Lost Outpost

QUINN HABER

Interior Illustrations by VShane

ISBN-13: 978-0-578-86897-4

Library of Congress Control Number: 2022923070
PhantaSea Books, Honolulu, HI

Cover Design by VShane @ https://vshaneart.wixsite.com/mysite
Typeset by Amnet Systems

Pouring forth its seas everywhere, then,
the ocean envelops the earth
and fills its deeper chasms

—Nicolaus Copernicus

TABLE OF CONTENTS

Chapter 1
WATER TABLES

Monstrous swells are sweeping in from the mist and crashing down along the beach with unrelenting power. I'm standing knee-deep in the violent flow of water, cradling my big-wave gun firmly beneath my arms as I try to time my entrance. With a slight break in the wave activity, I plunge headlong into the surf zone.

I'm halfway out to the lineup when a rogue wave looms up out the mist and starts exploding down the sandbar with the report of rolling thunder. I stroke desperately across the impact zone, trying to dodge the falling lip, when suddenly, a gust of wind blows against the wave face, slowing it for the split interval I require to gain the wave's shoulder. I paddle up the breaker at an angle and then pivot around at its crest, catching the wave from the top, from where I jump to my feet and go shooting back down into the trough. As I'm going to bottom turn, I get clipped by the lip, sending me teetering willy-nilly into a humongous barrel. But I'm somehow able to exit the tube, straight out of the front, whereupon it implodes behind me with a blast of spray so ferocious that I'm nearly blown off the front of my board.

Turning shoreward again, I lay prone over my board and go riding alongside the avalanching whitewater. Alas, the torrent overtakes me from behind, tumbling me headlong with my board in several full revolutions underwater. In time, I crawl back onto the beach, utterly demolished and coughing up saltwater.

Barely revived, I hasten toward the southern tip of my island, nigh stepping into quicksand on several occasions, but I soon find my target, floundering around offshore.

"Umukoro!" I holler out. "Don't fight the current!"

Flinging myself over my board, I begin paddling hard toward my luckless charge, who is flailing his arms wildly about. Suddenly, he disappears beneath the surface.

I stop down-current of his last position and dive off my board. Sounding the depths in search of him, the pressure in my ears grows painfully taut and I can hold my breath no longer when suddenly I latch on to his arm. *Got him!*

After wrenching the bumbling grom back to the surface, I toss him over the deck of my board and demand in a scolding tone, "Where's your stick?!"

"Gone," he wheezes. "It's gone, Xavion."

"But where, Umukoro? Where is it?!"

"Busted into pieces."

A triangular-shaped fin suddenly cuts the surface, curves around us and then submerges again.

"Grab my shoulders!" I order, throwing the prince over my back.

"It's coming!" he gasps while latching on to my collarbones. "It's right behind us, Xavion!"

I dig an arm into the water and swing us rudely about, just as the shark lunges at us with open jaws. I deliver a powerful punch to its snout.

The beast sounds abeam, the slipstream begot by its descent pulling us askew in the undertow.

Wresting the totality of myself, my board and the prince back into position, I start stroking hard toward the shore once more.

But the shark emerges anew, making several close passes on either side of us.

I redouble my effort shoreward, and we make the sugary strand.

Curling the grom under an arm, I march up the beach before throwing him rudely down upon terra firma. "Your board, grommet!" I reprimand again. "Where'd you lose it?!"

"It <*cough!*> it broke up in the surf on the windward side. Three pieces, Xavion—it's gone, man."

I scan the water from South Point clear up along the eastern lee and soon gain a visual of the board remnants. The tail portion is lapping onshore to the north, and so I send Umukoro there to retrieve it while I reenter the water to fetch the other two segments, which appear to be drifting out to sea. As is common during a strong northwest swell, the surf breaking along the opposite side of the island from where we are now is terminating far beyond South Point, but the floodwater created by expiring waves is swinging back up this leeside in a ferocious littoral current. While Prince Umukoro, aged fifteen summers, is too shaken by his brush with death to be clear in mind, it's no surprise to me that his board wreckage is adrift in a mass of foam moving northward with the rip. My benefit of summers, at forty, affords me the experience to know all there is to know about Meridian 12 and its surrounding waters, while my gun's length overall enables me to make headway through these worst of currents, where with a shortboard such as Umukoro's one wouldn't stand a chance.

I make good time retrieving the remnants of his thruster from the flotsam. Without doubt, bull sharks are still patrolling beneath me, and so I quickly sandwich his board pieces betwixt my gut and gun and then go stroking eagerly back toward the shore, soon passing his shoreward position as he stands on the beach, clutching the tail end of his board. I don't fight the rip to meet him directly, but instead continue in a wider angle toward the beach, for my goal is to minimize my time on the water as well as my splashing, which with a direct shoreward strike through the riptide would increase in both measures, attracting the beasties. The bull that'd made a

charge at us earlier is the least of my worries. There's a much larger shark, a tiger called Okonkwo who sometimes patrols North Point. He's three times the length of my big-wave gun and is known for surprise attacks. As such, he's the most feared shark in the remaining Meridian Islands.

It comes with great relief, then, to finally make landfall, where I start marching back down the beach with my gun tucked beneath one arm and the grom's board fragments sandwiched beneath the other.

The boy is nonplussed when I get to him, staring at me blankly with nothing to say. That he's still alive and safely ashore is one miracle; that his three board pieces have also been retrieved can only be to his embarrassment. I toss the broken jumble before him, ordering, "Let's move!"

I lead him over the south-central portion of the island, where not long into our march we encounter another major impediment. The large swell and king tide, as they often conspire, have seeped into the lowland sands, turning the way ahead into a great bog of quicksand.

We double back and continue southward along the leeward shore. There's slightly better terra firma there due to the coralline composition of the beach, which acts as a sort of atoll surrounding the saturated interior.

"Why don't we just cross at the village juncture?" Umukoro asks.

"Do you really want everyone including your father to see you so defeated? It's better we repair to my abode and stash our boards there first."

He puts up no further protest to our southbound heading.

Alas, South Point is completely awash with the flood tide, forcing us inland again over the perilous quicksand bog. I do my best to stay upon the low hogbacks—those narrow veins of coralline sand webbing across the mud pots. While these slender paths are easily identifiable due to their lighter color, their more granular composition and slight rise above the quicksand, they, too, can be traps, for

some of the paths extend over the bog without sufficient underfoot, like the crusty surface of a fried coconut pudding, easy to crack. After moving from one weak and disappearing vein to the next, we finally stop upon a solid coralline mound roughly a third of the way across the interior.

"We wait out the king tide here," I deem, dropping my equipage. "Terra firma will be firmer once the tide subsides."

"Okay, man," the grommet says. "I'm worn out too, and thirsty. Got any water?"

Opening a compartment in the deck of my board, I procure a small plastic vial and sip enough water from it to clear my throat before handing it to the prince. "Sip slowly," I advise.

He puts the container to his lips and cocks his head far back, causing him to cough up most of the drink.

I wrest the near-empty container back and stow it in my water-craft. I admonish the prince, as the rain begins to fall, "You acted stupidly today. You entered the water when the waves are too big, and now look where you've gotten us. What would your father say?"

"I just wanted to surf the big waves like you, X, and like Nyoto and Yang Ming."

"You know we don't do that anymore—not unless we have to, like today when I was forced to find you before you drowned."

"Well, what if I also have to surf them one day? How am I sup-posed to prepare?"

"It is not the fate of the prince to drown while surf-riding. The Ocean Masters are tasked with the necessities of our survival, not you. You see this sharks' teeth necklace?" I remove it from around my neck and hand it to him. "An Ocean Master must be able to kill a shark with his bare hands. This memento is one of many I own. You can keep it as a reminder of what separates you from me. Your duty it to ensure that M-12 remains a sovereign island, and as heir to the throne, you can only do that by remaining safely on land."

He lowers his head dejectedly. "The land that is quickly disappearing," he mumbles, motioning toward South Point, where a large ridge of wetsand is lopping off into the raging torrent.

"This is the trouble, Umukoro; the problem lies both with the land and the sea. But you must leave such challenges to the Ocean Masters and focus instead on how you plan to rule the dynasty."

"Why can't I do both?"

"Because your father has directed otherwise, which you know, troublesome one. When the Meridians began sinking, he outlawed free-surfing so that we could focus all of our energy and resources toward our survival. Need I remind you we're the last island situated in the chain? Landholding is our priority now, not surfing."

"But if I can better learn the ways of the surf," he rejoins, relentlessly, "maybe I can help figure out how to better save our landholdings, just like you Ocean Masters!"

"And this is how you better learn the ways of the surf? By paddling out on a quadruple-overhead day, during a gale, I might add, and getting totally creamed? Where is your observation from land? Could you not see the double-up sections pushing far across the bar? How could you even expect to catch a wave on a day like this without being swept into the southern transept?"

"That's why I rushed it at first light, man! I hiked north to get the edge on the tide."

"A lucky thing for you, not that you avoided your father's waking eyes, but that I happened to see you as you went scudding by. Otherwise, you would've perished, and who would take your place?"

"Nsia."

"The sixth-born princess? *Pfft!* She's much too young, should island rule suddenly befall her. Even you aren't ready, judging from your actions today."

"But I made a wave out there, X!"

I eye him skeptically.

"*Ya, ya, Xavion, I did!* I caught a medium one between sets, but it was still super big, like quadruple overhead. It was a double-up, just like you described it. I was way deep when I took off, but pulled the drop and stuck a sharp bottom turn just as the barrel started shooting past me. This monster was so steep, X—I could barely pump my rails along the face! But I held my line and kept jamming through this heavy, warping tube until I finally made it out. By then I was already near South Point, so I just kicked out. That's when I got hammered by a huge set that followed, which broke my board and pushed me into the transept."

"If such was the case, Umukoro, did you anticipate what would happen next?"

"Honestly, I thought I'd get washed out to sea."

"And that's where you failed in your attempt at surf self-schooling. Had you been paying more attention to the tide, the swell angle and most importantly the predominant wind direction, which is dictating the windward current today, you would've known you'd be driven back up the leeside and into bull shark territory. So, either way, it was a stupid day to go surfing—even for Ocean Masters such as I. We never would've attempted it because we would've known the consequences of the slightest mishap. You know how many seasoned riders have met their untimely fate in precisely the same manner you almost did?"

He shakes his head glumly.

"Your surf history is also direly lacking, grommet. Too many lives lost then, and an even greater loss to us today now that we're down to just fourteen islanders. For this reason, your father must *never* know about your folly today, or my punishment as your protector will be even worse than yours."

"But you saved my life, Xavion! He'd praise you for that. But, yeah, I guess you're right. We better not tell him. I don't wanna be grounded."

"Better to be punished by the king," I snicker, "than the tiger. But at least you've learned your place today. If you really want to learn the ways of the Ocean Masters, you must start by observing them and the sea. Don't ask questions or say a thing until you've thought thoroughly about ocean dynamics and the way you see us dealing with it. You've surfed enow in small waves to know a comely sea, aye, but when it comes to storm surf, *keep out*! *If* and when the time comes for you to learn such hazardous measures is not your determination. Your duty now, as determined by your father, is as our landholder in preparation for future king."

"But my dad used to surf too."

"Aye, back when all twelve Meridians were still above the water. That was a time or normalcy, of trade, of interisland peace, free-surfing and the interisland games. But now that the chain has been reduced to just two islands, it's wartime, Umukoro, and so stop playing naive. Meridian Eleven is falling, and they'll erelong seek to overthrow us here, on the last outpost in the Mothersea."

"But why, Xa-Xavion? *<coughing dryly>* Why must there be war? Our island is so much bigger than theirs. Surely, we can accommodate them."

"Stop talking, spiny one, and save what water your throat still produces. But to answer your question, look again." I point toward South Point, where another large cord of sand succumbs to the ocean torrent, removing a significant swath of ligature from our southern landholding. "There's your answer, grom: our island is also disappearing and erelong there won't be enough space for even us to live, let alone other-islanders. It is owing to the lee of M-11 that we're still larger, but as M-11 falls, our sand will wash away even more swiftly than this. Our priority is not in growing our population, but in keeping others away until we can better stabilize our landmass."

"But by then it will be too late, Xavion. The inhabitants of M-11 will all be dead."

"Their fate is not our making, young'un, just as the fate of Meridians 10, 9, 8 and all those who've fallen before them was out of our hands. Remember that M-11 was the only island besides ours to instigate a no-immigration policy, once they saw the annihilative effect of the archipelago-wide leapfrogging down the chain to M-10. M-11 is even smaller than M-10 was, so how could they expect to support hundreds of new refugees while their island is forever shrinking?"

"But we barred immigration first, Xavion. We forced M-11's hand by setting the precedent."

"Perhaps, matey—but we did so for our own survival. I regret that M-11 will erelong fall, and unless we can shore up our own landholding, we shall founder shortly thereafter."

"But <cough!> but they're only twelve in number. Surely we <cough!> can support them."

"Stay your tongue, grommet! That's enough talking for now, if you wish to survive the ordeal at hand. I'm low on water, you know. The water in these bogs is too salty to drink and will only kill us quicker. But I will say, regarding the Meridian 11 contention, they claim that they're but twelve, but how can they be trusted? They practice different ways."

I stay my tongue and set to work making a small teepee from Umukoro's surfboard pieces in order to shelter him from the incessant rain; then with my big-wave gun, I fashion my own lean-to by burying the nose into the sand at an angle, beneath which I sit, making the most of the narrow but effective cover. "We must wait for the water table to drop," I instruct as I collect the rainwater dripping from my skegs into my vial.

———

After a long interval, the water is still high, for the tempest is pushing a storm surge in with the waves, delaying the tidal drop. What's

worse, the rain is growing heavier by the interval, and so it will serve us little good to delay further only to have the downpour saturate the quicksand surround.

"Let's move!" I order. "Follow in my path, but not in my footsteps. Proceed as quickly and as gingerly as you can."

We break camp and begin traversing the perilous sand flats at a speed that the prince can keep up with, which ends up not being very fast. I keep close over the coralline veins, which resemble the fingers of a skeleton's hand. Sometimes I reach the ends of these hard white ridges, and in my determination to press on, I leap over the quicksand to the neighboring fingers. I glance frequently back at my charge, and while we're both stepping into the mire at times, fortunately our forward momentum combined with decent linkages allows us to bridge these hazardous gaps with only a temporary loss of speed.

But then suddenly while looking back, I veer off course and go plodding shin-deep into a pool of muck. Two steps later, I'm knee-deep in the mire and sinking fast. "Umukoro! Turn back!" I cry.

I manage to pivot around and fall crosswise over my big-wave gun. But while the board remains afloat, I cannot forestall my own backward slide into the bog. It's as if a giant octopus has wrapped itself around my legs and is dragging me into the thickening depths. I attempt to roll sideways over my board, but in the rapid pooling of the rainwater, the sandy gruel continues its relentless rise, soon engulfing my breast.

"Xavion!" Umukoro screams, falling to his knees and reaching out for my board as one of my arms gets sucked beneath the wetsand. "Hold fast to your stick!"

As my head begins sinking beneath the mire, I take a final breath, keeping my shouldering grip over my big-wave gun as my last remaining hope. The presence of the prince, I regret, lends little advantage to my exceedingly dire predicament.

But then suddenly, my board begins to pivot! My arm feels as if might break under the strain, but a slight pull upward encourages me to fight through the pain and hold on.

I'm about to black out as the quicksand starts peeling away from my forehead. I force my eyelids open and see Umukoro straining fiercely beneath darkly churning skies. My nostrils break free, and so I discharge a hefty shot of grime, at which I'm instantly rewarded with a precious shot of air back into my lungs. I tilt my chin up, freeing my mouth, and then wrenching my trapped arm from the muck, I regain my gun with both hands.

Umukoro's holding a death grip on the nose of my board and is sliding worrisomely forward into the gruel. "Come on, boy!" I encourage. "Pull back! Pull back!"

He growls, spittle ejecting from his front teeth as he gives his all to reverse-pull me out of the pit.

At last, my knees break free and I'm able to hoist myself further over my board, but my feet are still stuck in the quagmire and Umukoro's slipping in deeper. "Lay back against the ridge!" I command.

He extrudes his chest as if in a surfing layback, his arms fully extended and bulging at the veins as he maintains a death grip on the nose of my board, trying to yank me out. With a final agonizing scream, he falls back against the low ridge, freeing my feet from the mire. He releases my board, his energy spent, while his own legs have become locked fast up to his knees in the muck betwixt us.

With a brief running start over the deck of my board, I leap over him and then turn and lock my arms with his, attempting to drag him back from the sand trap, stretching our bodies to agonizing limits.

Finally, I succeed in freeing the prince, who I deposit onto the coralline berm behind us before retrieving my board from the bog.

With the water table still on the rise, we make a hasty retreat back toward to the leeside, following the coralline ridges as best we

can remember them in our coming—only now, the safe paths are barely visible beneath the water saturating the interior.

At last collapsing onto the leeward beach berm, we both know without saying that we're lucky to be alive. I offer the prince a drink from my plastic vial, but he just opens his mouth to the rain and drinks straight from the sky in a sort of celebratory gesture.

"Thanks for saving my life, Umukoro."

"Just returning the favor, uncle," he replies.

"Fair enow, grom. When we're ready, we'll proceed north along the shoreline. We'll have to risk the village juncture from the central path—we've no other choice."

In time, we gather our battered effects and begin walking north. On the way, we happen upon an intact coconut that's washed ashore. It's filled with milk—a favorable sign and a refreshing drink. I curl the prize beneath my bicep to transport home. The only question now is if we can sneak back into the village unnoticed, sparing pointed inquiries from the king.

Midway along the lee, we turn onto the trail cutting across the center of the island. The skies grow thunderous and violent, with thick bolts of lightning striking down all around us. We hasten our pace.

When we come upon the abode of Jomo, the farmer, we stop.

"We'll likely be pressed about our absence," I warn Umukoro. "When you see your father, you must tell him that early this morning you thought you saw a trespasser north of the village, and so not wishing to disturb your sire, you alerted me to the possibility of an imposter. I instructed you to remain in the village, but out of curiosity, you followed me anyway. I'll corroborate the story, saying that I went up to North Point, and not finding anybody there but you following me, we proceeded down the leeside together—at which point the storm hit, slowing our return. Got it?"

"Aye, we went north searching for a possible trespasser, but got caught in the storm. I'll say that, and I'll tell my dad that on account

of the mist created by the surf, my eyes were probably just playing tricks on me about the trespasser."

"Very well. He's sure to admonish you for following me, but will ultimately appreciate your concern for such matters. As M-11 falls, we must be ever-more vigilant against other-islanders—especially during a storm tide. As for your broken board, I cannot fix it at my place, and so we best stash it here under Jomo's hut. Later, I'll ask his wife, San Jiao, if she'll shape you a duplicate."

"Good plan—it's better that my sire doesn't find out that I busted my stick. He'll kill me for it."

"That's for damned sure, surfer prince. Now let's be squid-like and offload our boards undetected."

Chapter 2
VANISHING WORLD

"Meridian 11 is vanishing," declares Shao Ying, she who augurs the future by deciphering patterns in water and sand. A divining conch dangles from her neck, and her forehead is glittering with crystalline sand. "Erelong, they'll be cast out upon the water."

"She knows," offers Nyoto, a lead warrior affectionately known as "the arrowmaiden" on account of her prowess at the bow. Her cheeks are painted with cobalt hieroglyphics concocted from a mixture of octopus ink and sea cucumber skin, and her biceps are lined with bracelets fashioned from the blue feathers of the plum-headed parakeet. "We should expect a takeover attempt at any moment."

Our king, Tai Yun, stands before us in a coconut fiber (coir) robe, rubbing his graying goatee while fingering the top of his driftwood staff. "We will step up our vigil to an overnight watch between North Point and the village front," he deems. "Nyoto, Yang and Jue shall work in shifts. If Chaka's men attack, they'll likely strike from the northwest. And you, Xavion," he sets a sharp eye on me, the fourth warrior of the tribe and protector of his royal family, "you must remain close to my dynasty until M-11 sinks and its inhabitants are confirmed dead. As for you, my son—don't go sneaking around the Ocean Masters again! Should they confront the enemy, your presence will only be a detriment. Am I perfectly understood?"

"Yes, Father," mutters Umukoro. "I'm sorry. I only wanted to check for trespassers with Xavion."

"No more of that! At the first sign of an other-islander, you must retreat to the residence lest they kidnap you as collateral to barter our landholdings against. Henceforth, you are to remain in the village at all times and are only permitted to fish off the village front. Xavion shall inform me if you go astray again—and if you do, you shall be grounded for a measure of three storms. Now go at once to San Jiao's compound to construct sand pickets!"

The prince meekly takes his leave.

"Your Majesty," Shao continues, "I've dreamt of another way we can help keep our landholdings intact. We must dive for corals and replant them on the windward side. I've seen the toil this will bring, but I see no other way to forestall the erosion."

Respectfully, I interpose, nodding to the seer before addressing the king, "The bull sharks haunting the coral fields to lee are legion, and what of Okonkwo? We haven't numbers enow to guard against him."

"We'll stagger sentinels along the shore," replies the king, drawing a line in the sand with his driftwood staff for effect.

"Aye," puts in Yang, a cocksure young fisherman who often feigns an Ocean Master, "but if the great tiger runs deep, only submerged eyes will see it. Your Majesty," he bows cordially, "I offer my services as diver against the beasties. I deal with them all the time, and they don't frighten me. It's different when you're spear-fishing."

"To not fear Okonkwo," I interject directly to Yang, "is to underestimate his power. I have firsthand experience with the monster, while you do not. If you see him coming in for the kill, you're already dead. You must see him from afar, for he can traverse the depths with birdlike swiftness and arrive within the blink of an eye. But, my lord," I address the king once more, "if we truly have no other option to keep our island intact, then aye—Yang can be a set of eyes below while I and other Ocean Masters dive for corals. But the number of

suns required to extract the requisite amount of material to shore up the windward side will be great and will almost guarantee an encounter with the massive tiger and any number of bulls. It will be essential to develop a plan for evading Okonkwo when he arrives in the vicinity, with the imperative being an immediate retreat."

"Hmm … yes, I see," ruminates the king, curling a brow my way while avoiding eye contact with Yang. "You see no other option, Shao?" he rejoins the oracle.

She shakes her head in the negative. "I've yet to dream a viable alternative, my lord. In a cloudburst such as this morning's, the sand pickets are pushed up with the water table."

"I shall join the extraction team," offers Ocean Master Soko Yun. "I worked on the original site many suns agone, and in my estimation it would've worked had we only applied ourselves with the same urgency that we now face. The first transplant site, being an attempt to enhance our village front with better fishing and surfing opportunities, was done at leisure and took too much time. We didn't do enow to forestall the algae growth and we overfished the site too soon. But the areas in which we planted polyps showed great promise, had we only planted more and tended to them better. The cool northerly current nourished the reef, and I'm certain the colony would've succeeded had we only done more to protect it."

"I see, I see," maunders the king, rubbing his goatee pensively. He saunters before his great golden compass, places a hand atop it and then closes his eyes in deep meditation. The contraption, a talisman of magic begot from a shipwreck in bygone times, had been fashioned by the beings from beyond and intended for great leaders, for its finger always points toward the sure direction of the world regardless of outward shifts in circumstances. This indication is given the marking "North."

At length, the wizened old king reopens his eyes and says, "We must heed the fate of M-11 while we still have time and landholdings, which they're quickly losing, or we'll erelong be in their same predicament. We'll begin the coral transplantation effort at once. The first pods shall be planted as soon as the swell subsides. As for San Jiao, she'll continue fabricating sand pickets, but longer ones, and these shall be planted in a concentric phalanx around the village, with another row encircling the royal residence at the center. I've seen how well they maintain sand coagulation, the recent cloudbursts notwithstanding. We just need longer ones."

At that, the king invites us around his summer table, situated within a semi-covered veranda and affording a view of the waves breaking off our windward front. On a clear day, one can glimpse lowly M-11 from this perch. We hem out the details of the sentry duty and coral extraction operations here in His Majesty's grand meeting room. The goals discussed sound workable enow, but we all know they'll only be won with consistent, untiring effort. The several factors that are certain to assault our ambitious campaign are large sharks, heavy currents (attacking our endurance), incursions from M-11, and the very swiftness with which our island is slipping away.

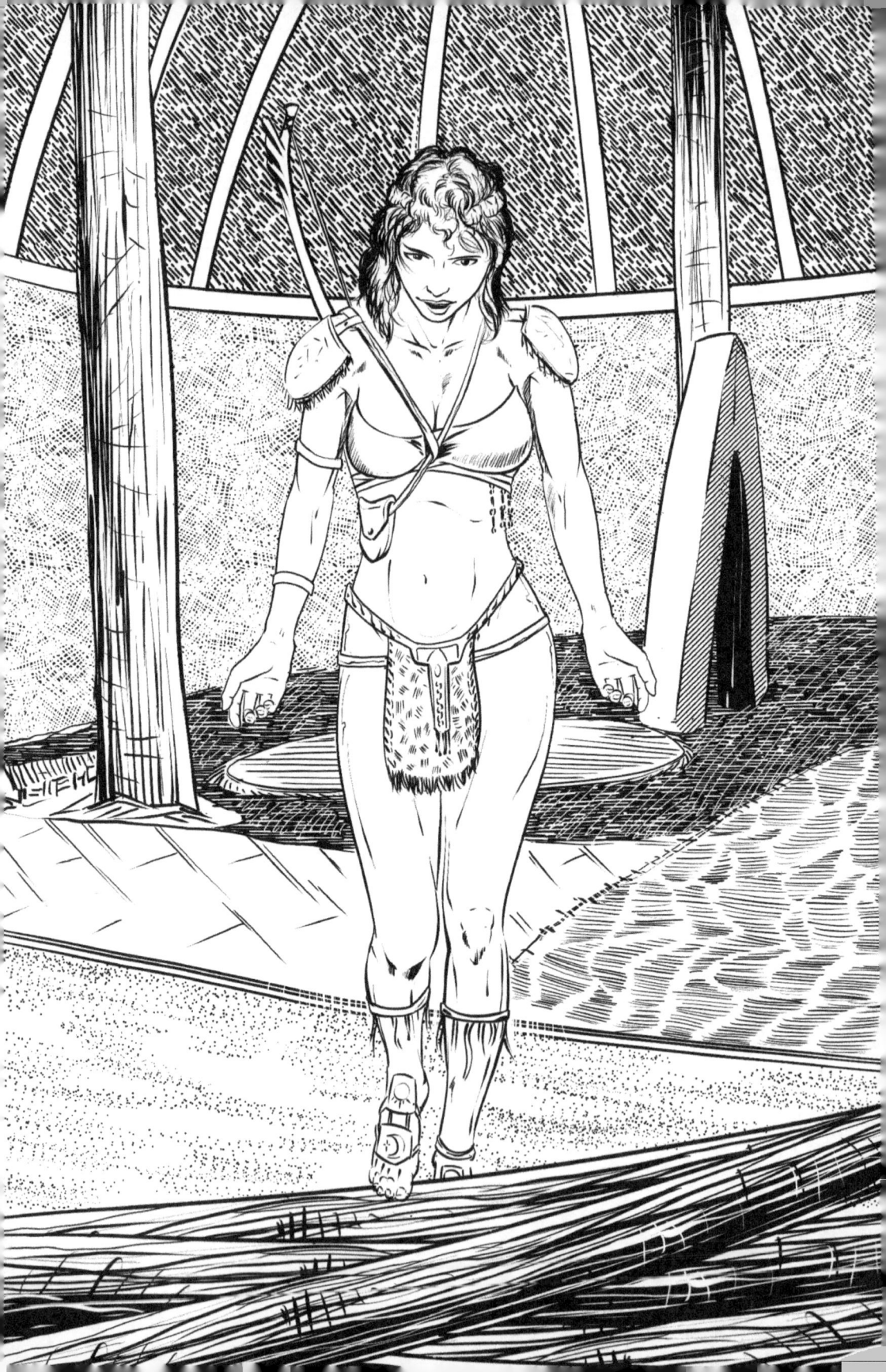

Chapter 3
HEARTWOOD

Nyoto and I pay a royally sanctioned visit to the compound of San Jiao, shaper of surfboards, weapons and staves. When we arrive at her sprawling complex, we find Umukoro there, laboring alongside his sister, Princess Nsia, in the construction of sand pickets.

"*Haa*!" I greet the boardshaper. "By order of His Majesty, we've come to requisition materials for the coral project, as you're well aware."

"Enter," replies the ever-gracious master engineer, opening her arms while effecting a slight bow.

Nyoto bows in return.

San Jiao's husband Jomo is chiseling away at a ponderous wooden beam lying on the floor, and he soon cleaves from it a rough-hewn stave. He sets the splintered stick on a workbench before the prince and princess, who begin refining it further into a proper sand picket. The sand pickets they've shaped thus far are longer than overground fence pickets, but, in usual fashion, will be placed in a line entirely underground to help shore up the sand beneath our village, which becomes porous when wet.

In addition to the burgeoning stack of sand pickets, an abundance of iron tools hang from the driftwood walls. These virtually unbreakable implements were obtained during our former trading proclivities with neighboring tribes and from salvaging wrecks in bygone times.

"I hope the replant works better this time," Jomo remarks.

"It must," say I.

"And it shall," reinforces Nyoto, "with access to your stores. We need iron wedges, anti-shark spikes, hammers, ropes, floats, and your largest slotted boards."

Thankfully for us and Meridian 12, San Jiao's hoard of *matériel* contains all of this and more. In addition to the iron tools and the sea-beast tooth and bone implements, she keeps great beams of wood salvaged from sunken galleons many moons agone. Her compound furthermore houses surfboards that she and other past master engineers have shaped, as well as a collection of boards from other Meridian Island tribes not of M-12—or other-islanders. This hallowed quiver, endorsed by the king as official property of M-12, includes numerous relics still displaying the insignias of legendary Meridian watermen upon their heartwood decks.

"Here in this workshop," I remark in general reflection, "resides the end bounty of all the Meridians, whose ultimate purpose has now emerged."

"Their *matériel* is in good hands," Nyoto adds solemnly.

"*Ya, ya,*" mutters Umukoro, "but we only want their stuff and not them."

His quip doesn't go unnoticed by Nyoto, who rejoins, "In that you are correct, and as future king, you should be able to explain why."

The grommet looks down and continues sharpening his stave.

"Umukoro!" I reproach. "The arrowmaiden has put a direct question to you."

"Okay then!" he ripostes, cutting at his stave more adamantly. "I'll tell you how I see it! Maybe we could use their help just as much as we need their belongings. Ever thought about that?"

San Jiao now replies, "If it were only so simple, gracious one, but the Royal Code of Defense and Preservation has been implemented out of our own dire necessity. I, too, once longed for

archipelago-wide unification, and when the Meridians began to sink, my desire for that only intensified. Even as the other-islanders came spilling down the chain, bringing with them a crunch on the fish stocks, resources and ever-dwindling landholdings of their next host, I still believed that, in working together, we could yet find a way to band together for our collective survival. But then when the famine on M-10 brought war to M-11, my hope for the future drastically changed and aligned instead with the alarming visions that Shao Ying had been alerting us to. She continues her warning to stay the course of isolation, of defense and preservation, for she's seen the alternative, just as we're now witnessing on Meridian 11. These heirlooms you see about us—the legendary surfboards with their sundry coats of arms worked upon their decks representing illustrious royal families now deceased and our expanded cache of tools, woods and *matériel*—all of this is ours only because we're the last island standing now that M-11 is sinking. As for the swarm of refugees, they come embedded with militias intent on displacing their hosts. This is why M-11 has resisted the diaspora to their shore. With their terra firma diminishing by degrees, they refuse to relinquish their vanishing landholdings to a myriad of refugees who come with imposters hungry to depose them, just as we're doing here with our territorial safeguards."

"And so the refugees were slaughtered!" Umukoro counters angrily, swinging around with a sharpened sand picket. "M-11 slaughtered them in cold blood, just as our Royal Code demands of us! Why? Why must we kill the other-islanders? They are no different than us!"

"You've not been listening to San Jiao," Jomo comes to the defense of his wife. "The exodus is too great for the remaining islands to support, while the refugees come with armed imposters intent on displacing their hosts."

"They're right, Brother," adds Nsia, the sixth-born princess and Umukoro's only remaining sibling. "Why do you think Daddy makes people go on sentry duty at night? I heard that M-11 shall erelong attack us. That sand picket you're holding, you should use it to fight!"

"What do you know?!" Umukoro snaps back. "You've only eight summers!"

I wrench the sand picket from his hands and toss it onto the pile of completed staves. "It's high time you get back to constructing dikes," I reprimand, "so that the rest of us can gather *matériel* for the replant project! Later, I shall teach you how to hold a *real* spear. You'll do well to train in our Royal Code of Defense and Preservation. As your protector, I'm responsible for crafting you into your own warrior."

Umukoro lowers his head and laments, "I just want to go surfing," and then resumes working sullenly alongside his sister.

"Eh!" Jomo says. "Here's a pile of staves to sharpen. I'm going crabbing!"

"And I'm going to check with Yang," Nyoto adds. "Make sure he's got his schedule straight." As she dashes out behind the farmer, her arrows rattle audibly in her quiver.

At their departure, I furtively retrieve Umukoro's board fragments from beneath San Jiao's abode and bring them to her, inquiring if she can shape a duplicate, but with wood that is harder than balsa.

"Ah, from this morning," she remarks as if knowingly. "Please come with me."

I follow her into an adjoining structure that houses a deep, brackish water catchment. Submerged in this saline pool are ponderous hardwood beams used for making surfboards, sand pickets and other woodworks needed by the villagers. She wades into the water and reaches under the surface, untying a coir cable from around one of the sunken beams, and soon the spar comes floating up beside her. She grabs a hoist cable from overhead and hooks it on to the beam.

"This is a very old one," she says as we haul it out of the water and set it upon the hardwood floor adjacent. "See how it's turned dark green from many hundred summers of water staining, but the heartwood within will sufficiently resemble the browning balsa of Umukoro's broken board, once it's been carved out. I've plenty of balsa blanks, as well, but I keep those in dry storage."

"Right," I reflect, "balsa in dry storage, hardwood kept submerged to deter rot."

"Precisely. To preserve the woods for many generations, we refrain from alternating them between air and water, sunlight and darkness, but keep them stable in their element each according to their type until they're needed for fashioning something from. Jomo's the one who scrubs the lichens off—he's a farmer, you know." She smiles banteringly.

I chuckle, offering her a kindly twinkle.

She runs her fingers over the slimy, smooth surface of the beam betwixt us, adding, "The sunbed wrecks left from the demon beings beyond have provided us with this rarest type of floating wood, solid through and through without being porous and coated with a water-proof veneer."

I nod in understanding.

Using the davit hoist, we transfer the beam to a shaping gantry, at which point the boardshaper takes her leave, returning moments later with the prince and princess. "We've some important things to discuss," she tells them.

Initially, Umukoro is broody and reluctant to stay, but when he learns that his new board will be carved from the heartwood block, his eyes light up like the sun breaking through a leaden fog.

San Jiao expounds upon the deep significance that goes into crafting a surfboard for Meridian Islanders when they come of age, and for royal progeny especially. She relays how board dimensions are carved to match each grom's height, girth, gait, the manner in which they walk and swim, and even the way in which they behave.

"The core assemblage point," she explains, "is that precise location on the deck which aligns with the surfer's natural stroking mechanism so that the surfer and board act as one, each growing stronger in the symbiotic connection instead of being panged with stress points caused by misalignment, which is the end result of a poorly matched craft and which can especially strain the rocker, as well as the surfer's back."

She is offering insights that nobody taught me as a young'un, perhaps owing to the fact that my first surfboard was a hand-me-down given to me by my father instead of by a master shaper such as she. My dad was first and foremost a spear-fisherman, after all, and he feared no beast of the Mothersea. He would often drag home large sharks with their jaws and fins hewn off and heaved over his back in a loop of coir. The bulk of the meat we would barbeque and share in a great feast, and the remainder we would dry in the sun and eat for many moons thereafter. The jaws we would fashion into weapons and jewelries, and the fins we would boil into a special kind of soup that imbued us with uncommon strength. So in many ways I am by inheritance a waterman, with surfboard design being something I learned later.

"What about balsa?" inquires Umukoro, stirring me from my reverie. "It's good for a shortboard, right? I'm really bummed I snapped my balsawood thruster. I guess I should've ridden a ship-wood board this morning—it was seriously macking out there! But I just need another shortboard."

"You shouldn't even have attempted the waves off the village front today," San Jiao admonishes as she ties her hair up into a voluminous chignon bun, locking the bulbous black arrangement into place with a single hair stick inlayed with mother-of-pearl. She's as comely as she is skilled, and I can't help but smile and shake my head in agreement of her upbraiding the prince's folly thus.

"As for balsa," she continues, "it's a very rare and valuable wood, and because it's highly buoyant, you're correct that it's the best wood

for shortboards that don't require the planing surface and weight of big-wave guns, which are constructed from heavier heartwoods. As you discovered in your shortsighted foray into big surf this morning, balsawood shortboards lack the paddling power and strength of their heartwood superiors. That being said, they perform much better in smaller, snappy surf than do big-wave guns. Balsawood boards are the classic display of high caste and political dynasty in the Meridians, as opposed to the hardwood boards used by fishermen, warriors, and workers in their constant physical toiling. The shorter, high-performance designs of balsa boards are entirely suggestive of, and used for, small-wave free-surfing and competition and are not expected to last unless carefully preserved, such as the showpieces within the palace. This is in sharp contrast to the hardwood boards used by workers, and especially departs from the big-wave guns crafted from pure heartwood and ridden by the great Ocean Masters—a different breed of watermen than the small-wave surf dabblers more common to the political elite, such as yourself."

"*Pfft!*" I scoff, not at her excellent analysis, but at the veracity of her description. "You want to surf big waves, grommet?" I mock the feather-bed prince. "It's time to hang your high cast board pieces up on the palace wall for good and get a *real* big-wave gun shaped from this solid heartwood here!" I glide my fingertips over the slick surface of the sebaceous beam.

The prince glances from me to San Jiao, apparently not knowing what to think. "I *do* want to surf big waves," he says at length, "but I've never ridden a gun."

"Well then," replies the master shaper, "after we firm up our landholdings, I'll gladly shape you one—and then I think it'll be high time for Xavion here to train you out in the big stuff."

"*Tallyho to that!*" the prince excitedly replies, turning to slap my hand, which I oblige.

"*Tallyho!*"

"But for now," continues San Jiao, "we're going to shape a board to the likeness of the balsa stick you snapped, is that correct?"

"Aye," I answer for the grom.

"But why not just shape another balsa board, then?" he inquires. "Why bother with shipwood for a shortboard thruster?"

"Because it'll last longer," answers the shaper. "I'll make it the exact same dimensions of your balsa board and paint it likewise so that your dad doesn't notice the difference." She casts the grom a wink. "Using this timber salvaged from the galleon that shipwrecked off M-6."

"What kind of demons were sailing those galleons, anyway?" he probes. "I've heard tales of ghostly white men who ate something called bean curd and who punctured their skin with bodkins."

"All that we know for certain is that the ships were demon-sent," I interpose gravely. "Their passengers were exceedingly sick and rotting, and their decaying bodies erelong infected our ancients, causing them to die harrowing, long-suffering deaths."

"'Diseased,' the ghosts called themselves," the shaper adds. "But the silver lining is we harvested an abundance of heartwood from their shipwrecks. Their timber has a natural longevity, for they've treated it with some kind of water-resistant stain that's also rot resistant if kept submerged. We only have to check for shipworms. Surfboards became our main watercraft because they're the best object to carve from out of these hardy shipwood beams."

After San Jiao sends the siblings back to their workstations, I help her gather the materials for the coral project and convey them to her loading dock.

———

Upon taking take my leave from the shaper's compound, I stop at the sacrificial rotunda to observe a hen sacrifice being performed by Queen Itoro, and then I stop once more near the royal residence to check up on the work of some fellow Twelves (Meridian 12 islanders) who are hammering dike staves deep into the wetsand. The hardwood retrofits will last approximately two hundred moons in the moist undersand before their decay renders them obsolete, but in that time, they'll hold terra firma together like the stitching in a seal-gut garment, providing an evenly spaced, undersurface fence that greatly slows the ground shifting and filtration decay caused by overly saturated sand. The ultimate rescue of our sinking island, however, will depend upon the success of our coral transplantation effort and will furthermore be subject to the efficacy of our defense against enemy incursions from M-11. Our continued sacrifice of guinea hens to the Mothersea, meanwhile, provides us with the hope that she may yet be appeased by our blood offerings and relent in her rising water level and ever-more frequent storm surges.

Chapter 4
TIGERS AND BULLS

The central juncture trail is wet, but holding firm in the wake of the downpour. I reminisce how, ever since I was a young'un, we've been reinforcing the path with dead coral fragments, maintaining its solidity so that our farmers and fishermen can traverse it in any weather and tide without having to worry about sinking into quicksand. I reflect upon the great fishing to be had at the trail's terminus at the center of the lee, where a cornucopia of fish school around the reef, feeding and nesting. Our undersea garden—the reef—is rare to the Meridian Islands, even to M-12, the largest landholding in the once-expansive archipelago, for even the great length of our windward seabed is naught but sand. While good fishing can still be had in the breakers there, it's nothing like the current-rich supply of sea bounty that can be bagged off the leeward reef. But along with the schools of fish, bull sharks frequent the coral shallows, rendering it a dangerous place for surfing and an especially bold challenge for spear-fishing.

While walking in reminisce, I recall, in a magnificent panoply, sharks' teeth necklaces, earrings and weapons; oversized jaws erected proudly over fishermen's hearths; the billowing smoke of shark meat sizzling upon sunset barbeques hosted by stalwart spearmen. And there, too, over our long history of men eating sharks and sharks eating men, is smeared a great red stroke of blood. My reverie ends

with a sigh of relief, for today our quarry shall be coral, and not saber-toothed monsters.

Arriving at the beach with a heavy load of equipment, I soon find Yang reposing beneath the cover of a fisherman's shack that he's converted into a forward operations center.

"Welcome to my *praetorium*," he says, grinning wryly as he helps relieve me of my equipage. Not only has he accommodated the shelter with chairs and a table, but he's also hung numerous seal bladder gourds from the driftwood walls and rafters, constructed a surf rack, and lined it thick with balsawood thrusters.

I shake my head, chuckling in disbelief. The cocksure young spear-fisherman never ceases to amaze me with his shortboard antics. "How's the surf?" I joke, observing the brisk northbound current and utter lack of swell.

"Just waiting for the tide to drop," he says with a shit-eating grin.

"All right then, Yang, well, the Mothersea won't wait for us, so let's prepare the guns and get to it."

We emplace wooden spikes into their attachment slots around the rails of our shipwood boards to ward against sharks, but we don't insert them where our arms will be paddling.

Nyoto and Soko Yun arrive and also start preparing equipage, and then San Jiao, Jomo, and Jue Yin come with a hearty supply of victuals, which they set in the *praetorium* before giving the shack a good tidying over. Once our boards are weaponized, Yang starts preparing his spears.

At length, Shao Ying and the king come sauntering in. As is common before the start of any significant undertaking, they shall conduct a prevision session to determine if any final operational adjustments are in order. As the king takes a seat in the shade of the makeshift *praetorium*, the oracle continues down to the waterline, fills her large divination conch with seawater and then returns to the modified shack. Today she wears two baby shark jaws worn like goggles, with their tiny, razor-sharp teeth surrounding her eyes like ravenous white lashes. Her face is all aglitter with mother-of-pearl makeup, while her hair, sun-bleached blond, is done up into a tall coiffure resembling an immense golden conch. It is said she can form it that way with the help of an assiduous familiar, who aids in plaiting, wrapping, and tying it off at the top, and then an admixture of carrageen seaweed and octopus sucker mucilage is applied to the surface, imbuing the coif with its holding power and uniformly hard sheen. She proceeds to glide her bare foot across the sand before her, flattening out a swath, and then while closing her eyes, she utters an incantation to the Mothersea while pouring the seawater forth from her outsized conch.

When the great shell is spent, she opens her eyes and studies the patterns the water has created in the sand. There appears to be a pair of narrow ditches between three ridges.

"The endeavor holds promise," she says while gazing out at the sunrise horizon, as if in a trance, "but the transplanted reef should be placed closer to shore."

"Thank you, Shao Ying," offers the king.

Still facing the Mothersea, she affects a slight bow and then takes her leave.

"Looks like we're good to go," I say, pulling on my sharkskin boots.

Soko and I paddle out with our iron wedges sandwiched betwixt our guns and our chests, while our anchors are set atop our boards beneath our shins.

Yang, donning plastic goggles fabricated from plastics that have washed ashore, paddles his shark-encountering board just south of the reef and casts anchor, while Nyoto proceeds to the north side and casts anchor there. Soko and I drop anchor centrally between them, over the reef.

As we dive for corals several breast strokes below, we use our sharkskin booties to protect our feet from the jagged quarry, and then while driving our iron bars into the base of the corals we *heave*

to! The smaller- to medium-sized crowns take three or more soundings before, like pulling out a tooth, their hard roots release from the seafloor, enabling us to convey them in whole to the surface. We stow our coral bounty over our decks in seal bladder bags, and when these become full, we paddle the haul to the shore, handing if off to San Jiao, Jomo, or Jue Yin, who in turn transport the sacks on wooden carry sleds back to the pools in San Jiao's compound. There she will care for the corals until the surf on the windward side drops enow for us to transplant them offshore there.

The first afternoon is productive, with Soko and I successfully removing a steady bounty of corals, coral fragments, sections of branching staghorn and elkhorn corals, and a few massive brain corals, which we extract and haul to the surface in tandem using coir rope. Yang and Nyoto remain over their shark-repellent boards, frequently dipping their heads beneath the surface in the lookout for beasties. The breaks in the sequence of skewers lining their rails where they paddle enable them to easily scan the depths on both sides.

As the tide drops, the sentries move in closer to where we're working, and as the tide bottoms out, they stand in waist-deep water over the reef, eyeballing our surround from there. That we haven't seen any sharks is a blessing, which I can only assume is owing to their likely riding the morning's flood tide up to North Point, where they like to feed on larger fish that cruise in from the open ocean.

Although the northbound current is strong today, there's no swell breaking over the reef. The current, however, sometimes pushes a surge of water into our backs as we sit on the reef extracting corals, for the reef is now almost dry or exposed.

"I'm going in to replenish my water," Nyoto alerts. "Here, I'll take in your bag," she offers Soko.

He heaves his seal bladder sack chock-full o' corals o'er the nose of the arrowmaiden's board, whence she goes paddling in while lying slightly off the tail and keeping her feet raised out of the water.

"Let's get some polyps and call it a day," I tell Soko. "Help me fill my sack."

He agrees to the plan, and so as we stand erect with my bag between us, we begin plucking seedlings from the colony using our wedge irons.

As with the larger corals, the polyps shall be delivered into San Jiao's care, but ironically enough, these seedlings will be conveyed to the transplant site last. They're perhaps the most significant piece to the puzzle of a successful transplantation. After the larger brain corals have been firmly planted, the polyps will be strategically emplaced within the folds of the brains, and there they will multiply quickly, bonding together into a hydra-shaped mesh.

My sack now full and my muscles aching from the day's labor, I traipse over the reef with the haul of polyps, securing the bounty to my gun's foredeck. Soko helps me carry the heavy-laden board into the shallows before doubling back to fetch his own craft from the dry reef. Finally, we push off toward M-12 proper.

"Bull!" cries Yang from nearby.

Soko swings around to retreat to the shelf, but I cannot so easily come about with the heavy haul of coral fragments lashed to my fore-deck, imbuing my ponderous board with additional forward momentum, and so I stroke forth more adamantly toward the greater island.

"Shark!" screams Queen Itoro from the shore.

"X, look out behind you!" Yang alerts as he starts splashing the water, trying to draw the beastie away from me.

A large fin breaks the surface alongside me.

I stand up and brandish my iron wedge. As I continue ghosting forth upon my craft, the bull circles around me two times. On its second pass, it cuts close enough to permit me to jab my bar hard into its side, but in doing so, it thrashes its tail, knocking me off my board.

I grab the rope that fastens my sack of polyps to my deck and try to hoist myself up, but the bull comes back at me in a head-on bearing.

I kick my feet violently and am able to clamber back onto my board just as the creature comes in for the kill. I aim my wedge iron lamely toward its snout, and right before the bull collides with the instrument, it dodges it, submerging beneath me, its dorsal fin just grazing the underside of my craft, rocking me beam to beam in the slipstream. I struggle not to capsize.

Yang continues splashing and cursing in a bid to draw the bull away from me, and then, opening a compartment in his board, he procures a large vial and quickly spills its contents into the water. The blood of a guinea hen starts fanning out all around him, into which he resumes his splashing. Nyoto has meanwhile entered the water from M-12 and is stroking hard in my direction.

Yang succeeds in attracting the bull toward him. His goggles have become so bloodied from the splashing of chum that he's forced to remove them. As the beastie closes in, he hunches over his feet, raises his mighty projectile and begins sparring with the creature, jabbing it as it passes.

Soko reenters the water behind me and starts paddling fervently toward M-12 proper, and I, too, don't wait around to see the result of Yang's epic showdown, for his daring purpose in distracting the shark was to allow us this chance to escape. Furthermore, with blood in the water, more bulls will surely come.

While Nyoto has angled off in Yang's direction, those watching from the shore are shouting for Soko and me to keep paddling. In our transporting corals back and forth to M-12, in the apparent absence of threats we'd long since removed the projecting spikes from the rails of our boards in order to make the crossings easier, but this proved a risky bargain, for now, when we finally *do* reach the shore of M-12 as survivors of a close encounter with a toothy monster, we look back to behold the ravenous beastie impaling itself upon the skewers fronting Yang's board instead. The more the great bull thrashes its tail while lunging, the more the cocksure young hero thrusts the nose of his board—spikes and all—further into the

creature's mouth, until the skewers are breaching out though the shark's gills in a gory display of swallowed thorns.

The arrowmaiden reaches the site of the fray, and standing upon her board, she plucks a bow and arrow from her back quiver and shoots the beastie at close range, the shaft penetrating deep into its head. The bull rolls over dead, to which a robust *tallyho!* sounds out from the shore.

The bowwoman helps Yang collect his personal effects that have scattered over the water in his epic clash, and then they hitch the vanquished creature's tail to the tails of their boards and begin hauling it shoreward. As they draw upon the beach, a pair of bulls emerge and bite into their quarry, yanking their crafts back.

"Shall we spear them?" Yang asks his partner nonchalantly.

"No," she replies. "Too much of a hassle. More sharks could be coming, so it's best we just release the deadweight."

And so they sacrifice their prize to the cannibal sharks.

Arriving onshore in unison, they drag their boards up the sand and then brusquely slap each other's shoulders, pushing each around in the manner of celebrating warriors. And then all of us surrounding them—including the reclusive warrior Ren Mai, who's come out of hiding—also slap their shoulders in approbation. I thank them energetically for interceding in the attack, as does Soko Yun.

"Look!" Yang alerts. "Two more bulls have come to feed on the carcass. Hopefully they'll be finished by tomorrow so we can keep working."

Whatever the case about tomorrow, today is far from over for the Ocean Masters among us, who are slated to work overnight sentry duty on the windward side, which we shall be manning in shifts.

———

The sunrise casts a reddish pallor o'er the eastern Meridians, revealing the black storm peeling away over the southern horizon. Night

watch was as uneventful for me as it was for the sentries preceding me, with only a moonlit surf to be observed rolling the length of the windward beach. Now, as I sit in the shade of my patio sipping seaweed tea, I feel more confident about how our mandates have been progressing.

Erelong, I quit my driftwood abode for the leeward *praetorium*, when suddenly I'm summoned by the crier's conch, diverting me to the royal palace instead.

Tai Yun and a few of the Ocean Masters are gathered in his sunset veranda, spying a pair of sailboarders arriving from the west. The windsurfer in front is transporting a small cage atop his board, set upon a pile of wooden spikes, and inside the cage, there appears to be a fowl.

"Shall we repel them, my lord?" I ask the king.

Suddenly, as if on cue, the windsurfers each raise a hand over their head and start circling it around, indicating they come in peace.

The king sets a sharp eye on them. "They may need help negotiating the shorebreak," he says. "Retrieve them, but keep an eye on their spikes. I'll receive them here, but only if they're unarmed. They can only be from M-11, and so I'll use the opportunity to glean more information."

I proceed down to the beachfront with Jue Yin and Nyoto, from where we hail the voyagers ashore.

A tall set of windswell waves approaches. The sailboarders let slack their sails and let it roll beneath them. Once the set has passed, they pull at their booms and run for the shore, successfully navigating through the impact zone until their skegs come skimming into the sand. They hop off their boards.

"Ojore," I offer with a nod to the voyager out in front, as he draws down his mammal skin sail. I recognize him from previous encounters.

"Xavion, *haa*! *Haa*!" he replies, returning my nod of acknowledgment. "I come with a message from King Chaka."

The other sailor, who Jue and Nyoto are helping, does not look familiar to me. His skin tone isn't dark like that of the M-11 islanders, but he carries their manner of shark-gill tattoo, running down his abdomen.

"King Tai Yun invites you to his summer table," I announce. "Come, let us deposit your boards well above the high tide line—there are still some rogue breakers coming through."

"Indeed," agrees Ojore, "we encountered some out on the water."

As we carry forth their cumbersome heartwood sailboards with their decks piled high with sheets and spikes, I inquire of the second voyager, "Who are you?"

"I am Cadiz, shadower of Ojore on this diplomatic mission."

His name is more common to the now submerged Meridians 2 and 3. Obviously he's transmigrated down the chain.

"I'm Xavion," I continue, keeping a natural appearance about things. "Come, Ojore shall bring his message to my king, who's awaiting you at table."

My team and I flank them on their either side, keeping a close watch that their caged hen is all they're transporting into the royal palace.

———

"I bid you, please be seated," offers King Tai Yun from the far end of the table. "We've prepared shredded crab and brown booby egg omelets. It's the least I can offer King Chaka's delegates for bringing me his gift of hen."

The envoys seat themselves at the foot of the table, opposite Tai Yun.

"Thank you, Your Majesty," Ojore replies, "but we shan't be eating. We've come to deliver a message from King Chaka, along with his goodwill offering, and then we shall be taking our leave."

"Ah, I see," King Tai Yun replies with a wry smile. "Very well then—you've sailed a long sea length and have a strong paddle yet ahead of you, but I respect your training not to partake of food from an old foe."

"Recent foe," Ojore hastens a reply, "but onetime ally, ere the swelling of the Mothersea. We used to be partners in trade and were considered fellow Meridians before these calamities drove us to mutual isolation, which, as we're daily witnessing, is irrelevant to the Mothersea's voracious intent. She does not separate island from island nor king from king, but reclaims all in her stride, and so we've come with an urgent message from King Chaka: he wishes to put the bad blood between our kingdoms aside and work together toward our mutual survival. To this end, he seeks to negotiate a relocation effort so that our combined manpower and *matériel* can be employed to reinforce Meridian 12 faster. We've amassed a large cache of tools and goods in the wake of the outer island closures, the hoard having increased in ever greater measure as the Meridians sank in sequence. We believe we can help to more than double the size and speed of your current coral transplantation project, and in return, we only ask to share a small parcel of your island for our own habitation until we can help grow your landholding further. We've no coral around M-11 in which to mimic your operations, but know that, in working together, we can use our collective tools, strategies, and manpower to help grow your terra firma here, creating more space for all of us to coexist in peace while overcoming the looming threat of our mutual extinction, for, as you know, if Meridian 11 sinks, without the natural breakwater we provide, Meridian 12 shall erelong follow. While sailing in just now, we observed how the waves have reduced your North Point and how the rain has made a flooded tideland of your interior. Our only hope, then—yours and ours—is to join forces in constructing an impervious fortress against the Mothersea's ever-rising threat."

"Quite," replies Tai Yun cryptically, "quite. And what makes you think we're conducting a coral replant project?"

Ojore prevaricates, clearing his throat. "Well, we don't. All that we know is your last attempt at replanting corals failed, but under the present circumstances, we assume you shall be trying again."

"Assume," Tai Yun replies in soliloquy while stroking his goatee, undoubtedly as convinced as I that the Elevens have been spying. "And you, Cadiz," he probes further, "am I to *assume* that you hail from Meridian 11? You do not look familiar to me; your skin is sandy in color and you are without facial scarification and fish bone labrets."

To which the reticent voyager with the hardened countenance replies, "Aye, my sire's from M-11, but my mother was from M-8, and that's why my skin is much fairer."

"Who's your sire?"

"He was Kwame, retainer to King Chaka."

"He is deceased?"

"Aye, Your Majesty. When I was but a suckling, he accompanied my mother back to M-8 to receive the remainder of his dowry, but they were lost at sea."

"Kwame? *Hmm* ... I don't recall the name. At any rate, I'm sorry for your loss. I prithee, tell me, what is the population of M-11 after these recent calamities?"

Cadiz turns silent.

Ojore intercedes, "I'll have to think about that, to furnish a precise number."

"But you've grown your population," my king replies matter-of-factly. "About how many refugees have you taken in?"

Ojore equivocates, "Many refugees have passed us, heading in this direction. Since yours is the largest island left, it makes sense they would seek shelter here, especially since you benefit from our storm shadow. But I see no refugees here. What has become of them?"

"We've had none arrive here," Tai Yun rejoins with a curt tone, "except those that've washed up dead. But it makes no sense that in such a desperate predicament they wouldn't just make landfall on M-11 and instead risk the onward journey here. It has long been known that the channel separating our islands is the worst in all the

Meridians, and so if you did in fact see anyone voyaging here, they did not make it alive."

"They did not make it alive?" remarks Ojore. "Is that part of your Royal Code of Defense and Preservation? I see quite a few artifacts here from the greater archipelago, while territorialism is nothing new to the Meridians, and to M-12 most especially."

There's a slight, almost imperceptible twitch in the king's earlobe. I know from this that he is peeved. But he keeps his calm and replies, "As you know, one of the benefits of our location is that we've always been the end recipient of all sunrise-moving trade, but it's safe to assume that most of the refugees didn't make it this far because they perished at sea or in the interisland wars of the diaspora. Ah, but let us focus instead on the future in which your king bids we forge together. If he wishes to join forces in a coral replant effort, how many workers is he willing to provide? We must consider requirements of food and lodging, as it were."

"We can commit sixty workers," Ojore answers, and thus the king has tricked him into revealing their numbers and the fact that they've been taking in refugees or joining forces with outlying islanders, because the last known census of M-11, prior to the diaspora, counted just sixteen members.

"Quite generous," my king replies, masking his surprise. "I will concede that both our islands are being cleaved away at the same rate, but while M-12 is twice the size of M-11, our actual habitable space is actually rather small, encompassing only this village, because the rest of our island contains a high water table owing to the rising tides and ever-more frequent storms, rendering it a wasteland of quicksand—as you've so perspicaciously observed. As such, our actual habitable landholding cannot support sixty additional workers, let alone sixteen. Therefore, I shall only consider taking in more people if my islanders first launch a coral transplantation effort that succeeds, thereby ensuring we've a breakwater sufficient enow to grow our habitable area further. But the success of this shan't be

known for several full moon cycles, and as you've pointed out from our previous attempt, it is liable to failure."

"Respectfully, Your Majesty," implores Ojore, his forehead corrugating with stress, "to reject our help is to commit suicide. You've even less time than before to construct a viable coral colony, but only now, failure is not an option: there's no other way to stop the Mothersea. You *must* accept King Chaka's offer, or we shall *all* perish."

Tai Yun raises a hand and then closes his eyes and lowers his head, essentially rejecting the emissary's pleas. "Well then," he says at length, looking up again, "I shall give you each a bagful of polyps and staghorns. Take them back to your king as my goodwill gesture. You can attempt to grow a colony off M-11, just as we shall be attempting here. But as of now, we can in no way support even one new settler—our actual landholdings won't support it, nor will our dwindling fish stocks."

"Dwindling fish stocks. *Pfft!*" Ojore bares his frustration. "Very well, then—we shall deliver your bags of polyps to Chaka, along with your message of no direct cooperation. I cannot speak for him, but as a fellow Meridian Islander, I implore you to reconsider while there's still time. We shall keep our seacoast open to your emissaries, since you will inevitably come to our same conclusion. Our islands are doomed, Your Majesty—we must work together without further ado."

"Nyoto! Jue Yin!" Tai Yun calls out to his retainers, completely ignoring the messenger's plea. "Furnish the voyagers with two bags of polyps. Soko will attend them to their sailboards, where they shall await the peace offering before shoving off."

As the former leave for San Jiao's corals nursery to gather the bogus peace offering—bogus because it isn't nearly enough to grow a coral colony with—Ojore and Cadiz proffer a feigned bow and then depart with Soko down to the beach.

"Chaka's a crafty one," Tai Yun remarks to me, as we watch the envoys returning to their watercrafts, "but also very stupid if he thinks I would fall for his trap. It was not long ago, at the onset of this crisis, that he killed our voyagers as they sought safe passage over his island."

"I remember well, my lord," I reply, but keep it at that. The voyagers he's referring to were three emissaries he'd sent to M-10 and beyond for political purposes—enterprises that did not include M-11. On their return trip, it was discovered by Chaka that the delegates had sought an entente with some of his enemies, and so to send a "message" back to Tai Yun, he had them killed. What I wish not to reveal to Tai Yun is my displeasure regarding the planning of that ill-fated mission, in which it should've been made abundantly clear for our emissaries to steer well around M-11. In any event, his mentioning the incident does add credence to the likelihood that other-islanders arriving at M-11 during the present exodus have been executed outright, or forced into Chaka's royal guardsmen, such as Cadiz could only have been. The suppressive King Chaka wouldn't risk an insurgency at the hands of his former enemies, just as Tai Yun isn't risking an insurrection at the hands of other-islanders, especially those from M-11. This is why he established the Royal Code of Defense and Preservation at the outset, the general thrust of which he outlines in extemporaneous argument:

"And now he wants to send sixty of his men into our village of fourteen, with at least three-fourths of that sixty likely being his slaves, or warriors he converted from other tribes by threat of death. But even if I gave him the benefit of the doubt that he's become a changed king in the face of his island's diminishing, where would that leave us? Let us suppose his sixty workers are refugees he's taken in peacefully as allies, and now he wishes to join our numbers to forge a viable future together, as his envoys have said. We will then become a precarious minority on our own island, for we've seen how the sinking of the other islands led to pillaging, deceit, takeovers and massacres, invariably by the outnumbering forces. Should

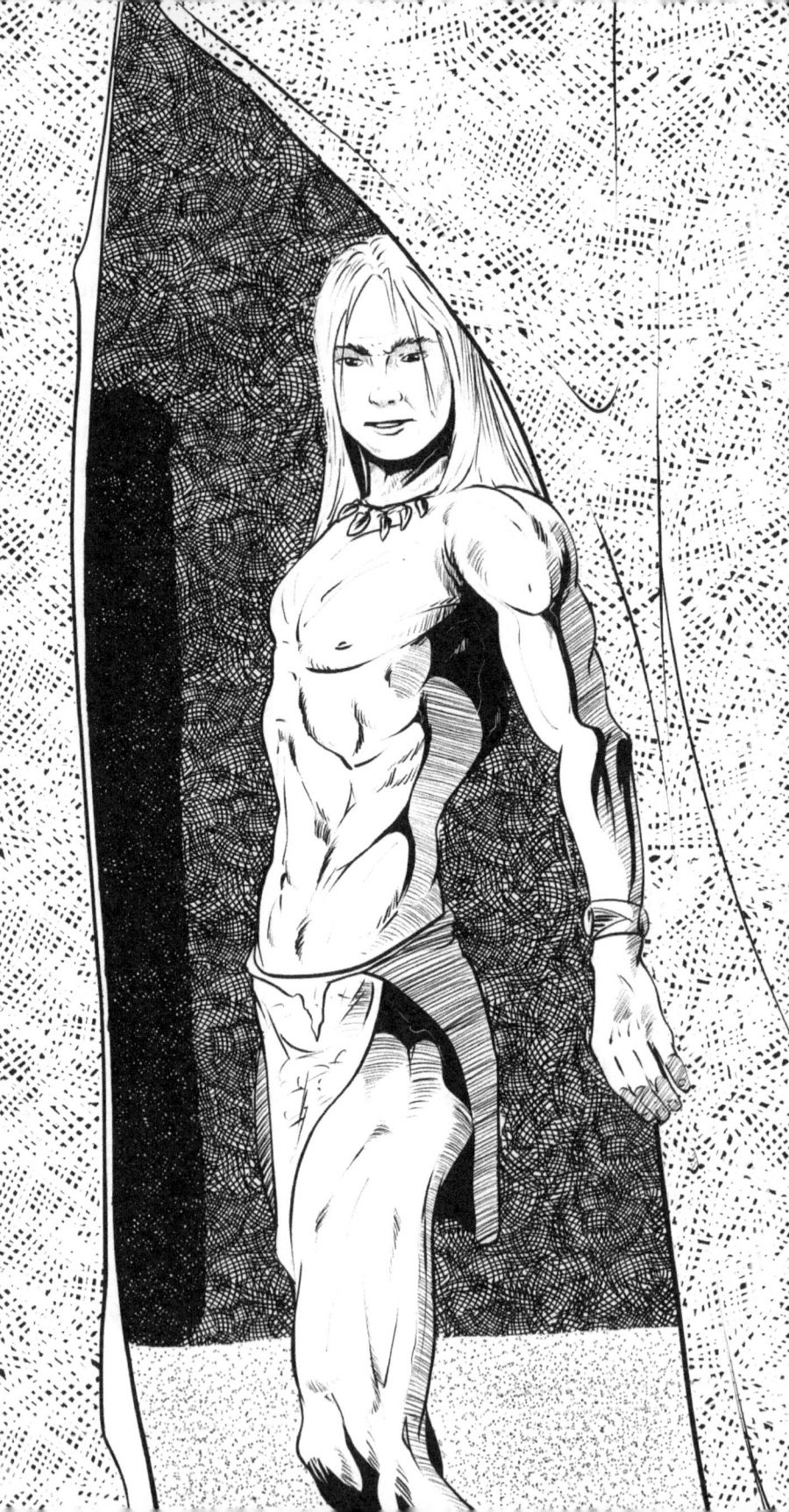

M-11 relocate here and share our limited habitable landholding, our predicament will become far more hazardous if the Mothersea keeps reclaiming our island. Our best and only chance lies in upholding the Royal Code of Defense and Preservation by maintaining our territorialism, outlawing all newcomers, and in successfully growing a new coral colony here on the windward side to help offset the foremost affront of the Mothersea."

Umukoro suddenly enters from behind a coir partition, waging an informed and impassioned rebuttal that evinces he's been eavesdropping, "Father, you're the king and hold the power to save our island. Then why would you reject Chaka's offer? You just said the new reef is our only hope, yet you won't let his workers help to build it. I beg of you, sire, join ranks with the Elevens to maximize the effort."

A twitch in one of Tai Yun's earlobes again signals his displeasure, but I know from experience that it also indicates he is processing the argument in order to formulate a logical response instead of lashing out emotionally. Thus, he erelong replies in a calm and collected manner, "My son, as future king, your fretting over such matters is a great and necessary thing. But as longtime king of this island, and one who's lived nigh four of your lifetimes, I can tell you from hard-earned experience that once the Elevens are permitted here in numbers, they can never be trusted, and so there will always be this greater risk of insurrection, of their making us slaves or burying us outright in the undersand. It's a difficult thing for a grommet to understand, I know: Why can't everyone just get along and trust each other as friends? The reason, Umukoro, lies in the passing of time itself, when trust can be eroded and when one's faith in their fellow man can be supplanted with a desire to protect oneself from further harm by them. If I truly believed that Chaka wished to work together, not as a fellow king, but as a friend, then I would accept his offer in a heartbeat. But as it now stands, no two kings can occupy the same island for long. I urge you to remember that, my son."

"I just think it's a mistake, Dad."

"This is because you have not been listening to what I've been saying, but rather have been following your youthful aspirations, which more than naught come with a heavy dose of naivety and ignorance."

"You must listen to your sire," I put in. "And the way you question him in private—never do that in public lest you seek to embolden our enemies."

Umukoro regards me with a black look.

"There's our offering to King Chaka," Tai Yun continues as he points toward the beach, where Nyoto and Jue are each shouldering a seal-gut sack, chock-full of coral fragments. "If he wants a breakwater, let it be known for all of eternity that we've given him the opportunity to build his own."

The prince shakes his head in disappointment and goes storming out of the room, in all likelihood well aware of his father's duplicity: a reef simply cannot be forged in time with only two carry bags of seedlings, no matter how bulging the said bags may be.

Tai Yun turns to me and says, "I regret my son must one day learn the hard way, just as we have."

"Aye, my lord. His is the folly of youth, but worry not: as your diligent royal protector, I shall help craft him into a great and wise warrior king, not unlike his sire."

The king's sharp eye twinkles in reply.

The M-11 delegates, meanwhile, have erected their sails and then struck them again on account of bad winds and high seas. They proceed to lash the seed bags to their afterdecks, and soon, with their sails neatly stored over their foredecks and anti-shark spikes strategically emplaced along the rails, they shove off into the Mothersea, resisting any further help from Soko Yun and the others. As is the procedure for paddling a board outfitted with anti-shark skewers, they've left gaps in the order of spikes along the rails where their arms can make contact with the water.

In watching them punch headlong out through the breakers, I envy their position even less, for theirs is a long, hard paddle against the Mothersea through Okonkwo's domain—the king of tigers.

Chapter 5
THE ARROWMAIDEN

Yang goes streaking across the shallows to my right.

"Are you sure you want to be doing that?" I shout.

"Ask her!" he bellows in reply, pointing to my other side, where Nyoto is ripping across a wave to my left.

Grrr! I growl under my breath. *Shortboarders, at it again!* I'm sitting in the center of the dry reef, working to extract corals as they surf around me.

"*WOO-HOO!*" the arrowmaiden cries in glee as she free-falls from a snap off the top, digging her rail into a bottom turn and ultimately making the drop.

"There's some southerly groundswell running!" Yang screams out.

"Are you watching out for sharks, at least?!" I quip in all seriousness.

"No worries, X! We got this! The water's crystal clear and the bull carcass is long gone."

"It's going off out here!" Nyoto exclaims while paddling back out. "And yeah, we can see everything while surfing. Look there!" She points at the shallows just beside me, scaring me half to death. "A nice, dark green crown! You should extract that one next, Xavion!"

"Thanks," I mutter, forever growling under my breath.

Soko, who's been working further along the exposed reef, trudges over to his board with his seal bladder sack bulging at the tendon seams. He lashes the bounty of coral pickings over his foredeck as the two whippersnappers go tearing by us once again. "I see that our shark sentries have swapped their shipwood guns for balsa shortboards," he observes. "I guess that means they haven't spotted any bulls."

"Not yet," I remark unenthusiastically.

We watch Nyoto pull into a consummate little curl.

"Well," I concede, "I guess I can't blame them for having a bit of fun. After all, it *is* lining up pretty nicely out here on the dropping tide—rights and lefts."

"Are you worried?"

"Nah, not really, Soko—we're sitting up here on dry reef, while they've a pretty good vantage point while surfing."

"Eh, Ming!" Soko shouts out to the swaggering shortboard maniac, who's just ended his ride with a botched 360 aerial attempt. "Shadow me while I take my load ashore!"

"Sure thing! I'll take point!"

"Well then, Yang," Soko retorts, "you'd better paddle your ass off on that measly little thing! I'm on pure heartwood here, front-loaded with corals, spikes and all. Once I gain momentum, nothing's stopping me until I crash into the beach!"

"No worries, mate! Let's do this!"

I help Soko carry his heavy-laden gun into the shallows, where he waits for the set to pass before pushing off prone toward M-12 proper. After gliding clear of the reef, he reaches down betwixt his spiked rails and starts stroking shoreward, his forward vision completely blocked by his bulging bag of corals.

"*Deg-deg*, Yang!" I shout, "*move it!*" as Soko closes in on him.

Yang slightly alters his direction, slipping off to Soko's side, but then starts stroking like crazy to keep up with the latter's breakneck forward momentum.

That's when Nyoto screams out, *"AIYEEE-HAA!"*

She's caught a good-sized roller, this time going left, only now she's surfing on her backhand, with her back to the wave as it breaks.

"TALLYHO!" she hollers while bottom turning, and then she cuts vertically up the face and throws a vicious snap off the top. As the crest goes over-vertical, she angles her board sharply back down while shifting her weight over her tail in order to keep from pearling nose-first into the trough. Successfully pulling herself out of the impossible maneuver, she shoots back up again into another wicked backside snap, the arrows in her quiver rattling madly as she surfs with reckless abandon.

"Yea-hooooo, arrowmaiden!" I cry, raising my fists high in plain recognition of her glorious ride.

As she passes by, she sets up for an incredible-looking barrel forming down the line, and then, as she ducks into the cylinder, her quiver goes silent ...

Way down the line, she emerges from the tube and raises her arms like mine, emitting an ecstatic scream, and then the arrows in her quiver start rattling once more as she goes to work on the inside section.

Chapter 6
BREAKWATER

Three suns into our momentous project, the north windswell drops off considerably, and so we seize the opportunity to transplant corals on the windward side in the relatively calm conditions.

Grabbing a section of iron bar from atop my board, I dive four body lengths to the seafloor and bury the tie beneath the substrate. The bar is affixed with a cable that remains dangling above the seabed, and this is where the corals will be moored. These iron bars, i.e., coral ties, requisitioned from San Jiao's stores, are now the most precious *matériel* on the island. Tai Yun has likewise requisitioned all of the villagers' steel plates to be used in a like manner—buried into the seabed as coral ties with a projecting cable from which the trunks of the corals can be secured.

Some of the larger brain corals require three workers to properly plant and several ties. While these brain corals, and other outsized varieties such as boulder and massive starlet corals, are stronger than branch corals, they grow much too slowly and so are used primarily as undersea nurseries from which to sow the polyps, for even if the heavy corals don't survive the transplantation, the seedlings likely will.

Once the giant corals are anchored, we wedge the much quicker growing polyp fragments directly into the pucks and folds of their brains. As each polyp grows, it will stretch its tentacle-like members out over the brain coral to a size larger than my outstretched hand, imbuing the polyp with a formidable staying power as it fuses with neighboring polyps, creating a unified mesh over their brain coral host (again, even if the host should die). Neighboring brain colonies will likewise fuse together, the end result being the growth of an expansive coral colony, locked to the ocean floor via the iron ties and the corals' natural grip over the brains and the seafloor.

Once each brain is seeded, we surround it with a cage made of whalebones and coir netting to ward against parrotfish, who like to eat the polyps. Since many undersea predators regard florescent-colored objects as a good source of food, we've also been careful to transplant only the darker brain corals. As for the elk and staghorn variety, we transplant any color available because these corals can grow as freestanding branches and therefore need not serve as polyp nurseries.

Not all fish are a threat to the operation, however. In fact, some of the smaller fish that can fit through the netted cages are a boon to the transplant site, and so in the days that follow, Yang, Nyoto, Umukoro and I work to corral these friendly fish varieties into the colony. However, this requires a lot of swimming, and so unsurprisingly, Umukoro often complains of being tired.

"Keep up your strength, boy!" I encourage. "We only must chase the smaller fish in over the reef! Coral likes a lot of sunlight, but since algae growth reduces sun exposure, we must force in the schools that eat the algae and other substrates off the reef. It will greatly improve the colony's chance at survival. You know, grommet, this reef is liable to create a great new surf spot! Even on a straight west swell, when the beach is closing out, there might be a two-way peak here, reeling offshore."

"So what?" he responds broodingly while continuing back to the shore. "Surfing is banned on the island."

"It's only banned in your father's presence," I entreat, following him in, "but once this war is over, we're going to be surfing this reef, and I'll train you in the big stuff with a heartwood gun."

"Do you really mean that, Xavion?"

"Sure I do."

"That would be epic, man! But why do you keep calling this a war? I know the outer islands have been warring, but we haven't. Do you *really* expect a war here?"

"I prithee not, grommet, but as warriors, we must expect the Elevens to come. But what I was really referring to is our greater war with the Mothersea. We cannot stop our creator from reclaiming us, if that is what she desires—but we can put up a damn good fight and keep offering her sacrifices in hopes she has a change of heart. This reef is our final battlefront: if we win, we can surf it every day—you and me. But if we lose, there'll be no halt in the Mothersea licking at our seacoast until there's nothing left for us to stand on save for our surfboards."

"I see," he replies in soliloquy, momentarily treading water amid his shoreward retreat, and then he turns, facing the budding reef. "Then I guess I'll just have to keep chasing in the little fish, because you know what, man? I'm just really hoping that one day everything works out and we can go surfing again—you and me."

"As do I, Umukoro—as do I. But we must continue working hard for that day."

———

The ban on surfing in the presence of the king remains the rule of the day, while fishing off the village front becomes highly regulated. Only fish that are a nuisance to coral growth, such as parrotfish, are permitted to be caught, while all algae-eating fish are off-limits. Fishing on the leeside, however, remains unregulated, for fish are bountiful there and crucial to our survival. While we often trap birds such as the brown booby for their eggs and meat, and while we consume the eggs and flesh of our domestic hens, and while sea turtles sometimes provide a hearty delicacy of meat to roast, eggs to

fry and shells to forge into armor and ceremonial dishes, and while we eat an abundance of worms, grubs, algae, seaweeds, crabs, sea snakes, jellyfish, sea cucumbers, squids, etceteras, *fish* has always been our greatest source of food, and their stocks have remained in abundance on the leeside even when these other victuals have fallen into short supply.

As for our new reef, it's fortuitous that we're planting it during the time of the cool northerly currents when the corals fare much better. Otherwise, there's something about the warmer, southerly current that places undue stress upon the polyps. This we learned not only through past trial and error, but from oral lessons passed down from our ancestors, for our leeward reef was not a happenstance occurrence, but the result of a dedicated transplant effort long ago. Only M-12 has a coral colony because we gained a separate block of knowledge from the alien settlers than did the other-islanders, and coral transplantation is believed to be one of the things we learned from the demon beings. The demon beings who settled our archipelago did so piecemeal and never relinquished their hostilities against each other until long after their arrival. As such, even our closest neighbors, the Elevens, acquired vastly different traits than we did here across the channel. The M-11 colonizers were dark-skinned aliens who promulgated a strange language and rituals of evil from an insidious black thing they called a book.

That we did not hail directly from the demon beings from beyond is readily understood by everyone except for the Twelves. The ways of the Mothersea and her creatures are readily familiar to us and are our everyday utility for the simple reason that we initially evolved from the depths and *not* from the alien beings, who only influenced our ways but did not create us. What further proof of this is the Mothersea's seeking to reclaim us now? It is owing to her jealousy, a love for her children so strong, that she now seeks to draw us back into her watery bosom. And so, in a bid to remain in the sky

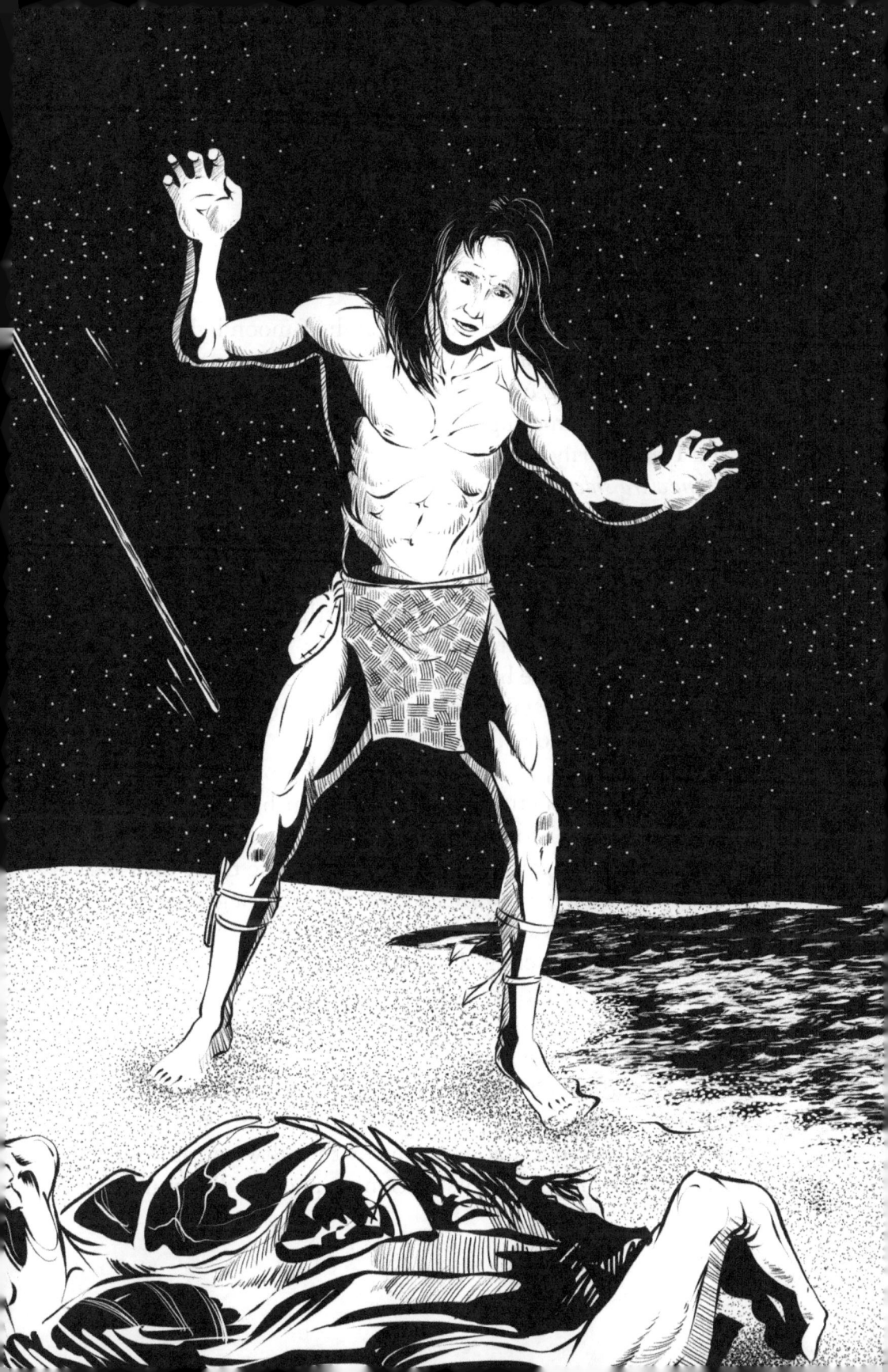

realm, we construct our new reef and make continual hen sacrifices in hopes to offset her swelling fever.

———

As I stroll up the beach in the crepuscular, half-moon light, a hint of north swell is gently lapping the shore, its tiny rollers so quiet that I can hear the chirping of shorebirds as they forage for sand crabs along the faintly shimmering waterline. Suddenly, my toes sink into a bog, and I summarily retreat, fearing quicksand. *But how could this be? The windward side holds good ground clear up to North Point!* I peer ahead into the semi-void, and I am shocked at what I see ...

A vast floodplain is splaying out before me where the Mothersea has saturated North Point on the medium tide. I can only imagine what a king tide coupled with a strong north swell might do—it's liable to wash away the entire point!

Sidestepping along the breach, attempting to gauge the extent to which the saturation has taken hold of terra firma, I trip over something clumpy and fall down.

What the—? I gasp, trying to focus on the object in question. There's a ghastly silhouette of a man lying on his back, or half a man, for his legs appear to be missing. His rib cage is extruding out so pronouncedly that I can distinguish each rib like those on a skeleton's chest. His head, meanwhile, is cocked back in a gaping, toothy yawn. His skin is so black that those are the only features that I can fairly discern in his starveling silhouette.

I rise to my feet and kick the body warily, checking for any sign of life. The corpse rocks lifelessly to and fro, and now, from above, I can discern that its legs have been ripped off by sharks—or perhaps it was the one giant Okonkwo who severed him at the waist. Furthermore, there appears to be spear holes in his stomach and chest—wounds grotesquely accentuated by the saltwater, as if a giant octopus had attacked him with its suctioning puckers. But as my eyes

adjust further to his tenebrous skin, I see that he only looked skeletal to me at first, but in fact I can now discern flesh traits that help to solve the mystery of his identity. His surface is as black as the night, far darker than any M-11 islander. Only M-2s have a skin tone so inky, while his blue facial tattoos not only prove me correct but their design also reveal his true colors as Babacar the Daring—one of the most illustrious warriors of my time. And then I make out, within a pucker hole in his stomach, the faint glint of something preternatural lodged under his rib cage.

Casting my eyes aside, I reach into the putrid carcass and extract the object in question. By its weight and shape, I know straightaway that it's a spearhead. I douse it in the water breaching across the island and then study it further in the half-light, finding an engraving. I rub my thumbs over the marking to reconfirm, and indeed the spearhead holds the insignia of King Chaka's guardsmen. I pocket the instrument of death in my waist pouch and march determinedly southward.

Babacar's carcass bespeaks horrors committed both at sea and on another island, but leaves no evidence of the present intruders on M-12. The most pertinent threat that I discovered in his vicinity was the Mothersea overtaking a vast swath of our island in her unmitigated coveting. Her wholesale affront to our North Point almost negates the value of an empty plastic bottle that I find, with lid attached, as I march down the beach. Hitherto a treasured commodity to own, gift, or trade, the intact container now seems immaterial in light of our being dragged undersea at the end of the vanishing chain.

———

King Tai Yun sits at his summer table, viewing the spearhead through a gold-rimmed magnifying glass begot from a shipwrecked galleon many moons agone. *"Hmmm ..."* he ruminates aloud, *"yes, yes, I see ..."*

He looks up and says, "Indeed you are correct: this spearhead contains the inscription of the M-11 guardsmen. You must take me to the body and show me the North Point calamity at once."

———

"Babacar the Daring," confirms the king as he points his staff down at the swirly blue tattoos covering the corpse's face. "You know his markings as well as I. This is a bad sign, Xavion, and a damn shame. He would never have surrendered to the rule of a despotic king, and so they killed him, most likely. I would've readily allowed him into our tribe, no questions asked. He was that great, and this is a terrible waste. Remember when, at the age of sixteen, he toured the chain alone on a heartwood paddleboard in order to gain a better under-standing of his fellow Meridian Islanders?"

"Aye, my lord, I know well of the feat, and many other legendary acts performed by Babacar the Daring."

The king grips his chest and keels over his staff.

"My lord!" I gasp, coming to his assistance.

"I'm okay." He waves me back. "It's just my heart, panged by such malfeasance. Chaka has taken the soul of this great Meridian hero to further demonstrate his power. Come," he says, taking my arm, "we must find a place in the wetsand and give him a proper burial. I can-not stand to see the carrion critters pull him apart like this."

I assist the king inland along to the breach until we stop near a fresh sand trap. "Please retrieve the body, Xavion."

I double back and try to drag the fallen warrior by his swol-len hands, but alas! His body continues to fall apart in ever-more unsightly degrees, and so while holding my breath against the sour tang of putrefaction, I cradle him in my arms and carry him back.

"Thank you, Xavion," Tai Yun remarks. "Now please, toss him into that bog forming over there."

I honor his request, at which he pushes Babacar further into the quicksand by the end of his staff while uttering an incantation

reserved for the greatest of warriors: "May this hero be received into the undersand by the joint powers of terra firma and the Mothersea."

But Babacar's head won't submerge, and his eye not eaten out by seabirds remains open and staring, as if watching us.

"May I?" I offer.

Tai Yun hands me his staff, with which I force Babacar's head under. "What now?" I ask, as I return His Majesty's driftwood walker.

The old monarch's brows furrow with sadness. He slowly turns while uttering solemnly, "We must prepare for the war ahead."

———

I remark from within the summer veranda, "That's a massive storm drawing upon the Elevens."

"They'll probably get hammered," Umukoro mutters as he chews on a strand of dried seaweed.

"What about us, Daddy?" inquires the princess. "Shall we be hammered, as well?"

The king places an aged yet agile hand over his daughter's shoulder, answering sweetly, "We'll get hit, my love, but spared the full brunt of the tempest thanks to M-11's storm shadow."

"What's a storm shadow, Daddy?"

"M-11 serves like a wall before us, taking the full brunt of the Mothersea and sparing us the worst of her power."

"But our new reef?" inquires the queen, her comely visage half-draped behind a shawl of coir. "Shall it hold?"

"Aye, my lady," I interpose, "I do believe it shall: we've anchored it well, while His Majesty is wise to point out the shadowing effect provided by M-11 against a sunrise-moving tempest such as this."

"Until it falls," Umukoro checks me in provocation.

"What's that you say?" his mother probes concernedly, removing her shawl. A mother-of-pearl diadem coruscates brilliantly upon her forehead.

"M-11 is getting hammered," continues the grom. "What if it sinks? What of our storm shadow then?"

"Then we still have our reef," I check him in return, "while the sand from their vanquished island will collect upon our shore and augment our landholdings even more."

"Until the next storm hits," he quips.

"That's enough, Umukoro!" his father snaps in a rare moment of open exasperation.

"But what then, my king?" his wife anxiously reproaches. "Perhaps Umukoro is right: M-11 is the last storm shadow, and so what then if it founders?"

"Then we shall act as our own storm front," the king replies with a phlegmatic growl. "We have our reef, we have our size and we've reinforced our village with dikes. I welcome the destruction of M-11 and the venomous King Chaka, for Xavion is on the mark here: when M-11 sinks, all that sand will wash over here and build up our seacoast, layer upon layer with each turn of the tide until we've been restored and then some, and then, finally, the Mothersea might relinquish her essay against us, finding our shining example of resilience worthy of keeping intact, like a rare pearl kept safely within its shell."

The queen, appearing lost in thought, rubs the surface of a black pearl ring she wears, at length responding, "I shall take my leave and perform a sacrifice ahead of the cloudburst."

"My lady," I oblige with a bow and outstretched hand, vouchsafing her to pass. The comely matron glides out of the summer room, her sweet coconut scent remaining fresh in the air.

With a distant, rolling thunder, all eyes settle back again upon the sunbed horizon. Strobes of lightning flash through the gloam, some striking M-11 dead center, while in the foreground a windswell—rutted, shoddy, and lacking in depth—sweeps unhindered over our submerged reef and laps at our shorefront in sickly yellow undulations.

———

After having passed most of the night on sentry duty, I remain splayed out across my seal-gut matting in the comfort of my hut, in no particular hurry to get up. My seal bladder pillow, which I hold snugly around my head, contains a stuffing of dried moss and coconut husks, muffling out the roaring gale.

After an interval, I stretch my legs, arch my back and extend my arms high over my head like a sand crab. When I go to fix some seaweed tea, I open my door to retrieve some rainwater from a catchment there, and I am shocked to see Umukoro surfing the windswept waves off the village front.

Wearing only my loincloth, I make haste out into the cool, driving rain unto the edge of the Mothersea, from where I call out through my half-cupped hands, *"Umukoro! Halloo Umukoro!"*

Either ignoring me or unable to hear me over the all-pervasive echo of surf and rain, the prince paddles into another wind-hacked swell and vaults to his feet, plunging leftward down the face of the overhead wave (overhead for him, anyway). I don't know what he's doing out in such terrible conditions, as he tries to make something of the surf by racing up into an adjoining peak and snapping off the top, transitioning off-the-lip into a roundhouse cutback to keep with the quickly folding section, and then, cutting leftward again, he regains speed enow to effect a pair of brief, low floaters off the crumbling remnants. After kicking off his board with an affected snap, he grabs his stick and turns back toward the Mothersea, eager to nab another crappy crumbler.

"Umukoro!" I holler again.

He turns around in the waist-deep water and shouts, barely audible through the sousing wind, "Eh, Xavion! Howzit?"

"What you doin' out here, grom?!"

"Surfing out of view of the king! That's the rule, ain't it?"

I glance up the beach, and indeed, in the driving rain the summer house is just out of sight. "But the waves are crap!"

"Not for me! It's so shitty out here, it's good! Hey, what do I care? I'm just a grom, right?"

I'm nonplussed, not sure how to react. "Is that your new board?" I hasten a reply.

"Yeah! San Jiao just finished it! Pure heartwood! She told me to break it in!"

Regardless of the veracity of his instruction, I'm intrigued by the concept of a shipwood shortboard. "Can I see it?" I try to hail him in.

Initially he's reluctant to turn his back on the waves that beckon his fanciful mind, but he soon comes to his senses, hopping in through the shallows while calling ahead, "Yeah, Xavion—check it out!"

But something strikes his legs, taking him down.

I rush to his assistance, when all at once the object surfaces between us. I gasp. *Another dead body!*

Umukoro stumbles back in fright, falling again into the pee-yellow whitewater.

I seize the corpse's arm and pull it ashore. Umukoro follows from a fair distance away, utterly rattled.

We stop above the waterline to observe the dead weight. Umukoro shudders, for the lifeless corpse looks not unlike himself. The victim is perhaps thirteen summers of age, with Umukoro's build, but the deceased's skin tone is dark and his right leg and hand have been bitten off. Even his visage carries the prince's same manner of benign smile, but the former's countenance has been falsely altered as such by the effect of saltwater upon his inert facial muscles. It is his incipient scarification and necklace that give him away as an M-11 grommet.

"The whiskers," I explain to the trembling prince, entreating him to study the corpse objectively and without fear, "those scars are a rite of passage on Meridian 11, while the crossed bone necklace is worn only by the Elevens."

"And his chest markings," Umukoro remarks with a shiver.

Indeed, there are shark-gill tattoos across his lower ribs. These markings are another rite of passage for some M-11 males, who receive the first bar of the tattoo at an early age—an inking that is only completed once they become full-blown guardsmen. Additionally, a bird bone is pierced through his forehead and another through the septum of his nose, and he wears a hen claw earring: all the decorum of our perfervid neighbors. But there *is* something more— something that helps solve the question as to if he drowned first or was initially killed by a shark. Peculiar markings on his neck suggest he was strangled. Looking closer, I point out the bluish bruise encircling his neck.

Umukoro spins around and vomits. "He was murdered!" he gasps, stabilizing himself over his knees. "Wasn't he?"

"Aye, it appears so."

"But—but who would do such a thing?"

"The world is not as you think, my boy—at least not on M-11. Do you see now, why we must protect ourselves? Why I must protect you?"

"But how do you know the Elevens did this? Maybe he was killed by invaders."

I regard the benign smile of the warrior-to-be set in sanguinary death by the Mothersea and shake my head. "I don't think so, Umukoro, for the Elevens would tell us as much, if only to gain our sympathy. It's more likely he was insubordinate to the king, as grommets can sometimes be. King Chaka is nothing like your sire. He's a ruthless, cold-blooded killer."

"What a shitty way to end a surf session," Umukoro mutters despairingly. "I'm going home."

———

When word gets out about what has transpired, it sends a chilling sentiment directly into the heart of the royal residence: a boy, not unlike Umukoro, has been brutally murdered and fed to the sharks. I'm tasked by Tai Yun to bury the corpse in the quicksand away from the village and to step up my guard over the prince and the royal family, with Qi Dong being assigned my nighttime sentry duty so that I can stay close to the palace. Surfing, moreover, is placed on an indefinite moratorium until the upheaval of the Meridians finds its conclusion, whenever that may be.

As I carry the corpse along the shore through the hard-driving rain, villagers spy me from their sodden balconies and cracked-open doors. I turn toward the sandpits and am blasted in the back by the tempest, sending me stumbling forth like a zombie. The cyclone roars ever louder over the island, like a voracious monster coming to devour us all.

———

A full day has passed in the cover of San Jiao's compound, where I've joined many of the villagers in the construction of dike staves and weapons and engaged in archery and spear-throwing exercises. We had little choice but to hold the exercises indoors, for the relentless downpour would've made it too difficult to find and retrieve our discharged projectiles in the giant puddles.

———

Today I awake to a morning unlike any other, for an event has occurred that has never happened before in all the history of the Meridian Islands—an event made all the more significant in light of the chain's sinking. Today, a new island has formed.

In hearing the cheerful cries of Jomo, Soko Yun, Jue Yin and others, I stagger out onto the beach to behold our new creation. There beneath a clearing sky, across a tranquil channel, a great mass of sand has heaped up over our transplanted reef, forming a significant islet that stretches approximately one-third the length of Meridian 12 along our windward front. Nyoto and Yang are already

paddling over to it, and surfing ban be damned, this has nothing to do with that pastime, for the island—or cay, more exactly—has created our own nearshore storm shadow: an exposed barrier that blocks *all* westward sea action, rendering our oceanfront idle and protected.

"*Wooo-hooo!*" and "*Tallyho!*" the warriors cry as they mount the cay, while from all around me on M-12 cheers sally forth, for we have at last succeeded in forestalling the Mothersea.

"Congratulations, Xavion," offers Queen Itoro, approaching me from behind. "Your labors have borne fruit."

"As have your sacrifices, my lady," I offer with a deferential bow.

Nyoto and Yang start hallooing again while pointing toward the sunbed horizon. "*M-11 has sunk!*" they scream.

The king comes by my other side and confirms, "Meridian 11 has been destroyed by the Mothersea. You can see it from my balcony."

"Destroyed completely, my lord?" inquires Shao Ying, as she gravitates into our group. "Is that what you have seen?"

"Come, see for yourselves."

We follow Tai Yun back into the royal palace, mount the shipwood stairs and enter the summer veranda, and there, looking toward the sunbed horizon, we ascertain bombora surf breaking around the carnage and oddments of a decimated island.

"As predicted," offers His Majesty, "their downfall has been our gain."

"How so?" inquires Umukoro, who was in the room with his sister when we arrived.

"The westward moving torrent has gifted us with their sand, creating this barrier island, while our own landholdings are brimming fat with fresh deposits, buffering our every shore."

"But will it hold, Xavion?" Umukoro probes further, putting the question to me.

Everyone stares at me unflinchingly, silent as the grave as they await my response to his incredibly significant question. As chief

engineer of the transplantation project, I weigh my answer carefully, "That's a very good question, Umukoro. It may be that the sand has suffocated the coral colony, killing it, but only time will tell if the cay holds. You can see the wind is already shifting south, and with it comes a warm current, so come what may of the underlying reef, the cay hoisted upon it is a great blessing, because the warm current would likely have stunted the reef's growth anyway, increasing its chance of failure."

"Was this the objective of the replant project all along?" inquires the queen. "To create a new island over the reef?"

"No, not exactly, my lady. The objective was for the corals to bind to the seafloor and grow into a living undersea breakwater, much like its parent reef on our leeward side. It was not intended to harbor terra firma in and of itself, but to act more as a shoal, and this in turn would halt the wave action from further eroding our windward coast. However, the cay that has formed may serve the same purpose, if not better."

"But you do not expect the buried reef to survive?" she checks me by her inquiry, and once again all eyes target me for a response.

"No, I do not, my lady—but the new island it has formed has bought us more time."

"Time to do what?" inquires Shao Ying, who, while a visionary, cannot see all parts of the future clearly.

"Time to build more dikes and increase our shoreward defenses. As the warm season nears its end, we'll transplant a new colony directly in this sheltered lagoon. It will be so much easier."

The king adds to my estimation, "Worry not, my good Twelves— our island has grown overnight, and Xavion is right: whatever the health of the transplanted reef, it has gained us valuable time. Perhaps this new barrier island will solidify further in the warm season, becoming a permanent fixture. I suggest we start planting dikes on it, and perhaps connect it to the village front via a walkway."

"But, Father," protests his daft and recalcitrant son, "wouldn't that kill the surf in the channel?"

"There's no more surf there, my son," answers his sire, "precisely because the reef has succeeded in forming a protective cay."

"But maybe on a sharp north or south swell—"

"That," I interpose, "remains to be seen. The reef may have been good for surfing once it grew into maturity, but that's no longer relevant. We may, however," I pause to cast the prince a kindly twinkle, "find some breakers off the cay's sunbed side, that is, when the moratorium on surfing is eventually lifted."

"And it shall be lifted, in due time," trumpets his father. "But presently, we must reconnoiter M-11. If the Mothersea has indeed drowned those murderous savages it would be a great blessing, but the full extent of their fate remains difficult to ascertain from here, and so we must go and investigate. One can still discern *something* there, be it only wave activity around the sunken remains or a partial landholding still intact. The only way to know for certain is to send a reconnaissance party. Now that the wind is shifting south, it presents the perfect opportunity. Xavion, you are to arrange a team of three sailors: yourself, Yang, and Nyoto, or possibly Qi Dong if any of the aforementioned exhibit reluctance, which I don't believe they shall."

"Qi Dong, my lord? Ren Mai would be better."

"Provided one can ever find him when he's needed," Tai Yun quips. "Let's just hope that Yang and Nyoto are ready. As it were, you are to salvage or raid anything of value that you can safely carry back, that is, if there's still anything left to be found out there. In these winds, it's a morning's crossing by sail. But you'll need to paddle back, which is perhaps a partial sun crossing."

"I wish to go," Umukoro bids.

"Out of the question, Son."

"But I can be of use, Father! I shall carry the water and victuals."

"Your request is honorable, good prince—and I would let you go on the expedition to develop your experience further, provided you knew how to surf sail."

"But I *do* know how to surf sail!"

"Not well enow, my son—I witnessed your last practice. This is not a journey of discovery in that sense, but a trip for seasoned watermen over a moderate distance. Furthermore, we cannot know exactly what awaits on the storm-ravaged island, and so I must decline your volunteering, however valiant."

Umukoro hangs his head in dismay.

"I shall teach you how to sailboard in the warm season," I offer the befuddled grom, "right here in this channel we've created, and your sire can observe your progress from this very veranda—if he shall allow it."

"Yes, X, I would like that," the boy replies. "I would like that very much."

"As would I," adds his sire.

"But how I desire to see those bombora waves up close," continues the ocean-obsessed grommet as he gazes out at the unusually high surf activity surrounding the oddments of M-11.

"I don't imagine that anybody would wish to behold such a dangerous shoal up close, if that's what it is," I warn, and then address the king, "but you are right, my lord—the wind has shifted, and so it's high time to make the crossing with the rising tide. I shall assemble the expedition party posthaste."

"You may take your leave, Xavion. I'll meet you on the beach prior to your shoving off."

I offer the aging monarch a slight bow, and then while hastening out, I cast the prince and princess a kindly wink.

———

Yang, Nyoto and I prepare our sailboards in a beachfront shack that serves as a staging area for oceanic activities. We insert specially designed spikes into the emplacement slots along the rails of our boards. The spikes are shorter than shipboard skewers and tilted

slightly upward, enabling us to traverse swiftly over the sea chop whilst under sail, for the longer, straighter spikes designed for standard prone paddling would plow too swiftly into the whitecaps common to the open ocean, slowing forward progress and making steering difficult. The actual purpose of these spikes is something we refrain from speaking, embarking as we are over the lair of the great tiger.

For sails, rolled triangular sheets of sea mammal intestine are affixed to our detached masts with seal sinew twine until we're ready to launch our crafts, at which point we'll raise the masts, unfurl the sails and tie their bottom edges to slots along our booms.

The final matter in sailboard preparation is to load our compartments with equipage such as food, water, knives and twine. For items found at sea or in salvaging, almost any object no higher than our thighs can be quickly lashed to both our fore and afterdecks by means of sturdy coir twine. The twine is wrapped around the anti-shark skewers lining our rails and crisscrossed over the spoils for a quick and secure tie-down.

As we assist each other in carrying our fully laden crafts down to the water, Queen Itoro slashes open the neck of a hen before us and then drains its blood upon our path, uttering orisons to the Mothersea all the while.

Tai Yun meets us at the point of embarkation to summarize the expedition: we are to conduct a physical investigation of M-11 and raid or salvage anything of value. If an Elevener is encountered at sea or otherwise, we are only to inquire about the fate of King Chaka and his royal lineage, but are not to provide any information of our own, nor any assistance unless we happen upon a helpless young'un *not* of royal lineage. Our total trip time shall likely see us back before the daystar dips to sunbed. Upon our return, we are to repair to our abodes and prepare ourselves for a special dinner briefing with the king.

Our mission well defined, we wade into the shallows and screw our masts into their threaded emplacement receptacles atop our sailboards. Several villagers enter the water, but merely watch us from a distance and do not assist in launching our crafts.

Umukoro, his longing to join us yet unrequited, wades too close to our spiked boards, and so both his father and I admonish him to stand back.

At last, we wave farewell to the king, who remains standing above the waterline, and then grabbing our hardy boom bars, we begin gliding north into the channel.

Cruising the greater length of the cay, I take the opportunity to study it further. A copious mound of sand has accumulated over our transplanted reef, rising gradually out of the water and slanting up to the islet's center to about the height of my chest. If I didn't know the cay was underpinned by a firmly anchored coral colony, I'd probably just assume it was an ephemeral sandbar. While the islet splays out in a near prefect line just a short paddle offshore of our hamlet, it stretches well beyond our village boundaries in both directions, blocking perhaps a third of our total windward front from the blunt force of the Mothersea.

In rounding the tip and cutting west to sunbed, I'm able to better ascertain its breadth, and this is where it's found to be lacking. To put it in waterman's terms, a large breaker, perhaps triple the height of my mast, given the proper run-up and wave period could in one fell swoop wash over the cay from its windward side to its leeward shore in a fairly quotidian manner.

Chapter 7
DESPERATE MESSAGE

Angling seaward, we extend our arms and lean back, plain sailing with the wind nearly at our backs. I take the glide in anxious stride, knowing full well that every interval we pass swiftly over the depths is a blessing from the Mothersea. The spikes surrounding our boards just scrape the sea surface to aft, while afore they're completely risen out of the water as we pick up speed toward the mysterious shoal enwreathing the oddments of Meridian 11.

Fortunately, the going remains easy, and it's only when we draw upon the shoal that we face our first real obstacle. Meridian 11 hasn't been washed away completely, for its two-story palace appears intact, however precariously, upon a plot of terra firma, and some wrecked dwellings can be seen here and there on the devastated island. From our distance, however, we can't yet ascertain any sign of life on the blighted landholding, but we do observe that the island's extremities have been taken wholesale by the Mothersea, causing great maelstroms and tidal waves over the sunken detritus.

"Yang! Nyoto!" I cry back. "It looks like there's a channel into the lee! I'll take point! Beware of obstacles afore and breakers astern!"

I pull at my boom, catching the wind as my team falls in line, when suddenly to port, a heavy tidal wave goes lopping into the shoal, creating multifarious whirlpools that go ghosting out into depths all around us.

"We're too close!" I warn, the perilous teetering of our boards manifesting in our sharply listing mastheads. We're saved only by our anti-shark spikes, which push down against the water with each radical list, preventing us from capsizing.

Alas, a truly monster set appears amid the mayhem, swinging wide around the shoal.

"*Deg-deg!*" I goad my team to *hurry!* as we go racing for the channel, where, from starboard to port, great shipwood beams, whalebones and other detritus start jutting up out of the water.

The first wave of the set is gaining on us fast, lifting us backward along its ever-steepening face. Our only hope lies in surfing the roller as it advances, sparing us from colliding with the many hazards beneath, for in riding upon the peak we're well above sea level where the obstacles are everywhere appearing, most of which appear to be anchored to the bottom.

Suddenly, a half-smashed house emerges afore, just as the roller we're riding begins cresting over our heads. Caught betwixt the obstacle afore and the avalanche astern, we cut sharply off in different directions, navigating around the giant obstruction as best as we can. Yang pulls a massive floater in the plunging whitewater, just skirting the jagged roof of the bobbing superstructure. "*Woo-hooo!*" he screams, stoked beyond belief as he goes racing down betwixt Nyoto and me, the lot of us having successfully rounded the harrowing obstacle.

As Nyoto's arrows rattle loudly in her quiver, we bellow a hearty *tallyho!* and outrace the whitewater together. At long last, our seagoing crafts come settling into the wetsand, whereupon we strike sail and unscrew our masts. After dragging our sailboards further up the beach, we stop to slap each other's shoulders and push each other around in celebration.

Suddenly, Yang raises his spear and Nyoto whips an arrow into her bow, for a dark man is striding adamantly forth from the gutted palace. I unclasp my spear from my mast and point it likewise

toward the mysterious other-islander. As he draws closer, he falls to his knees and circles a hand over his head while panting heavily.

"Lower your weapons," I instruct my team. "I recognize this man. It is Bobo the farmer." I return the husbandman's comity gesture and offer, "Bobo, I am Xavion from M-12. We've met twice before. What has happened here?"

"A great cloudburst!" he gasps. "Lightning, thunder, *the waves!* A tremendous army of breakers overtaking us from every direction! The throne is ravaged!"

"And what of your king?"

"Crestfallen! To be so aggressed by the Mothersea! But he lives, along with the royal family, thanks to our concentric dikes. He awaits you in court to discuss this calamity peaceably. As you can see, there's nothing left for us here. Please, you must come."

I glance over to my team. They carry wary expressions.

"And the royal guardsmen?" I inquire of the lowly famer. "How many remain?"

He returns to his feet and circles a hand over his head once more, saying only, "We're downtrodden and receive you in peace."

No sooner than he finishes this prevarication does a swarm of warriors come spilling out from the royal residence armed with spears, bows, arrows and *tawi-manus*—large, paddle-like clubs ringed with shark teeth and sharpened bone fragments.

We raise our weapons in defense, but I quickly realize we won't be able to parry ourselves out of this one so easily, for we're vastly outnumbered and our sailboards are hauled clear out of the water, sails furled. "Lower your weapons!" I alert my team. Their countenances are rife with skepticism, and they're hesitant to follow my command.

At the onrush of warriors, I circle a hand over my head while proclaiming loudly, "*Haa! Haa!* We come in peace with an important message from king to king!"

The army encircles us with their jagged weapons drawn, at which Bobo pleads with them, *"Haa! Haa, I prithee! The delegates of Tai Yun bring good tidings. Haa! Haa!"*

An infamous she-warrior named Fela saunters forth from the pack, commanding, "Everyone! Stow your weapons, and that includes you, Xavion, Nyoto, and Yang Ming! We've been expecting you. The great King Chaka is pleased that you've risked the passage to take table with him. Come, His Majesty is waiting."

Undone by the sudden arrival of the dozen-plus guardspersons, we've little choice but to comply. What began as a mission to salvage the spoils of M-11's downfall has now become a test of wits of how we can leave with our necks intact. But I've already formulated a plan, and that is to play along with whatever ideas Chaka has about emigrating to M-12 and joining ranks in a coralworks project. I must only inform Bobo, or some other underling as we're pushing off again toward M-12, which we have not, in fact, come by authority of King Tai Yun, but of our own volition in a salvaging mission, thereby rendering our uncorroborated meeting with King Chaka null and void. In an attempt to communicate this contrivance to my cadre, as we're being marched over the inundated island toward the decimated palace, I frequently cast them a smirk and a nod, indicating we'll be shamming and little more. It seems they understand, or at least trust in my scheming.

As we transition from the wetsand to higher terra firma, Fela points at several deep cracks in the ground, explaining, "That's where we planted concentric dikes. The undersand is pulling away from the pickets, causing terra firma to list."

In one particularly deep cleave, the tops of the sand pickets can be seen angling sharply over the surface as they lose the battle to terminal erosion.

"Our landholdings beyond these dikes have been lost," she concedes. "We were so inundated from the cloudburst and high seas that the only thing holding the palace together was this ring of

concentric dikes. We tried to fabricate a reef from the polyps you'd given us, but it was too little to grow anything from in time. In light of all these calamities, my lord is extremely pleased that you've come to reconsider negotiations."

We march onward between Fela and Ojore, another well-known guardsman, while Chaka's detachment of rough-hewn grunts follows in our footsteps in gruff and guttural muckrake.

As we draw upon the despot's once-imposing palace, I observe how, in the wake of the Mothersea's greater tyranny, it now resembles something closer to a shipwreck. Torn, seal-gut sheets hang fluttering from splintered stanchions; shipwood beams, snapped from their second floor braces, angle down, half-sinking into the wet-sand; whalebone and driftwood rafters are fractured; great swaths of moss have become dislodged from the ceiling, causing direct sunlight to penetrate into the tousled chambers of a garish nobility; and there, from the sunrise veranda above, an imperial guard donning an elaborate red headdress—or perhaps the bloodthirsty king himself—spies us from over a badly cracked, shipwood railing.

I tell my team, openly but curtly, "So as not to complicate things, remember that only I have been tasked to deliver our lord's message." They respond with a nod, trusting in my skullduggery.

After being conveyed up a sturdy flight of shipwood stairs that survived the devastating tempest, we're guided into the half-gutted sunrise veranda, where Chaka's company of grunts fall back. Significantly, we've been permitted to carry our weapons into the heart of the battered penetralium.

King Chaka, donning a lofty crown of wood, bone and bright red feathers, is seated at the end of a lengthy shipwood table. His face resembles that of the deadly stargazer fish, with bulging eyes and a broad mouth lined with an overabundance of pointy teeth. Queen Sassandra, his termagant second wife, is standing behind his right shoulder, her face mostly veiled beneath a wrap of rare red silk, while His Majesty's royal protector, Temitope, stands guard over his other

shoulder, donning a similarly elaborate headdress as his despicable master.

"*Haa*!" the dreaded king welcomes, circling his dark hand before him. "The delegates of King Tai Yun! You've sailed a long, untamed sea. I bid you, take a seat and partake of fish and hen salmagundi."

"*Haa*!" I follow along. "It's an honor, Your Majesty."

We sit down, but know from our warrior's training not to consume the food or drink, especially when offered by the Elevens. Fela and Ojore meanwhile remain at arms behind us, guarding the threshold.

"I know who you three are," the chilling chief begins, his copious whisker scarification curling as he speaks. "How could I not? You number so few, yet have such a broad reputation. You are Yang Ming-Hua, the great spear-fisherman and hunter of beasties; you are Xavion, guardian of His Majesty's royal family; and you are Nyoto, bow-woman extraordinaire who can fell tiny birds mid-flight. Please, make yourself at home in my sunrise keep. The stew is good, I can assure you—you must try it. And lest I be rude, I don't believe you've met my lovely Queen Sassandra or my royal keeper, Temitope Mukondi."

His consorts offer a subtle bow, and so do we, over our plates and coconut shells filled with the steaming, strange-smelling stew.

"It seems you've had a testy ride in," the tyrant continues, adjusting a bone cross necklace (whose bones look like human finger bones) over his chest. "My apologies. The recent cloudburst has significantly altered our seafront, as you've just experienced. But a toast to great surf-sailing, nonetheless!" He raises a tarnished gold goblet high and then quaffs of whatever is inside.

We likewise lift our cut-out plastic bottle cups, and I silently pray that my team merely feigns at drinking the contents.

"Thank you, Your Highness," I offer. "You are correct: it was a rough ride in through the whirlpools of your sunken landholdings. We deeply regret this relentless scourge of the Mothersea in all her jealousy of us above-water beings."

He chuckles knowingly, or mockingly, answering, "Yet your king believes that the fate of the Meridians is still in our hands, nay? I see that his artificial reef has succeeded in buffering your windward front with an impressively long cay. I can only imagine how much of our sand has contributed to such a barrier, and therefore out of the beneficence befitting a great king such as he, he has sent his highest emissaries to reconsider my offer, aye?"

"We've come with news from our lord, aye," I counter, all the while looking past him and his ravaged balcony to the beach below, where several of his operatives are dragging our sailboards into his compound. "News that should greatly please you, King Chaka: Babacar the Daring is dead—killed by a shark, we have confirmed. My lord knows that Babacar was an enemy of yours, so thought you might like to hear it. I prithee, Your Majesty, why are our boards being stowed? We seek but an update regarding the status of your island, a message from king to king, and then we shall respectfully be taking our leave."

"The tide is yet rising," Temitope gruffly interposes. "We must secure your boards from danger."

"Clear into the palace?" I counter pointedly. "Is that really necessary?"

"Our landholdings are not what they seem," Queen Sassandra puts in mellifluously, removing the silk wrap from around her face. "As His Highness has stated, half our landholdings have been swept away by the Mothersea and gifted to you instead, and so we can never be certain what the tide shall do next, what new section of beach might be cleaved away or where the next sand trap might emerge to swallow your boards into the undersand—and we certainly shan't allow that."

"Thank you, my lady," her heavyset husband replies, while we remain silent and wary. "So Babacar the Daring is dead—a tremendous loss to M-12 no doubt, but your artful king is right: what good was he to us? When that blowfish came here on his interisland

journey we treated him well, that is, until he tried to force himself onto one of our maidens. She fought him off like the urchin he was, biting his face and ejecting him from her hut, whence he deserted our island shamed and derided. Then, as he completed his puffed-up journey from your island back to M-1, he spread false imaginations about us, claiming we kept sex slaves and practiced a dark witch-craft—cannibalism, preposterous things like that. Anyone here will tell you that our one and only god is the Mothersea, even as she turns on us—owing to lovesickness, as you say—but we don't blame her for our calamities. Nay, our problems started long ere her swelling fever began, when our fellow other-islanders, in the wake of Babacar's callous rumors, disinvited us from the games and sum-mits, refusing to hold counsel with us and ostracizing us as a brand of man-eating sharks. And then the Federation levied higher tariffs against us and bypassed our trade in favor of yours: the largest land-holding in all the Meridians and the only one with a coral reef and all its bounty, not to mention your abundant shipwood and other treasures wrought from the wrecks on the sunbed horizon, which, I might add, we were prohibited from salvaging. If the shipwrecked galleons truly harbored diseases, then why were some Meridian Islanders, such as you, allowed to salvage them, but others, such as us, were not? Or so we were told not to salvage them lest we be exposed to the bad omens they were rumored to carry."

"But clearly, this cannot be all that the great and venerable King Tai Yun in all his wisdom has sent you a perilous sea length to tell me, seeing that we are presently sinking? Babacar the Daring is dead. Good riddance, and so what? We all shall share his fate ere-long, unless we raise an abundance of corals up from the deep to encircle our island with a breakwater, just as you have done. Surely you've come to reconsider my coral replant unity offer? You see that only my concentric dikes have prevented M-11 from sinking in its totality, and so what good and benevolent king would deny his long-suffering neighbor a chance at survival?"

Chaka's fiery eyes smart on us and his brows curl sharply, causing the bird bone pierced through his forehead to push up against the bottom rim of his unruly crown.

I've all the while been stealing glances at the cache of interisland goods piled up in his sunroom, and his wife's *rivière* of rare pink pearls. The implacable despot has earned an abominable reputation for killing those Meridian Islanders who came leapfrogging down the chain in a desperate search for terra firma. It is rumored their bodies were roasted and eaten, their treasures—these treasures— kept as his trophies.

"Why, of course, my hale host and most illustrious king," I play along nonchalantly, noticing that, aside from the dozen odd grunts who've stayed out of the sunrise veranda, his general population appears either very low in numbers or occupied elsewhere, advantaging our chance at escape. In all likelihood, his commoners, whose huts were situated further toward the peripheries and likely undiked, perished in the overnight catastrophe, while his slaves—or those such as Cadiz, who is being paraded as a warrior recruit—are likely being used for food and as human sacrifices in his reputed blood offerings to his ancestors buried beneath this palace. Contrary to his lies about believing in only the Mothersea, of the twelve Meridian Island kings, only he still subscribes to the old shipwreck heritage theory—that is, only King Chaka seeks his place in the hierarchy of things as a *direct descendant* of the demon beings from beyond who came in the great galleons. The vast majority of Meridian Islanders and especially our kings (or what is left of us) ultimately rejected that notion in favor of the Mothersea-as-creator belief, proclaiming that we issued forth from the Mothersea when she created our landholdings so that she, through us, could gain a foothold in the sky realm. We, along with sea turtles, crabs, lungfish, and other dual-realm creatures, were sent above water as her proud new offspring and *did not* issue forth from the demon beings' ships and their alien world beyond. Those imposters came later, it is a near certainty. This is

why we still make sacrifices to the Mothersea and not to terra firma, nor to the alien icons, because we haven't forgotten who sent us and who now seeks to reclaim us into her watery bosom.

Our practices, like those of the greater Meridians, stand in opposition to the ways of the Elevens. Here, they smear themselves with wet undersand and then go dancing around a small black book marked with gold crossed skewers—a dark sorcerers' manual thought to be a human cookbook that they've placed upon a pedestal in the center of their shipwood rotunda. Aye, there's a reason that King Chaka was long shunned by the Meridian Confederacy, and it goes far beyond the gossip started by Babacar. Chaka holds vastly different beliefs from normal people and practices ways that remain alien to the rest of us, worshipping a black book the inscriptions in which nobody understands—but again, is believed to be a cookbook for cooking humans, its crossed skewers resembling the kind we use when roasting sharks and other large sea creatures over a pyre. The black recipe manual is the surest sign of dark witchcraft, left by the demon kings of yore who came in their shipwood galleons, their lips swollen blue and cracking open as they fed upon their own deceased crewmembers before inflicting horrible diseases upon our outlying islanders. These are not the kinds of invaders we wish to embrace as our ancestors. But Chaka does.

Meridian 12 shall *never* be shared with such a defiled tribe as the Elevens, lest we one day wake up to find ourselves skewered and turning over King Chaka's long-burning pyre, his minions prancing around us with their demons' cookbook clutched tightly against their chests all smeared over with funerary quicksand.

"We've much to do yet with the coralworks," I continue evasively, "and have indeed come with a special offer, and not just with news about the passing of your old enemy Babacar, who by the sound of him appears a grand storyteller who'd been deservedly given the cold shoulder by one of your virtuous young'uns."

"I regret the maiden you speak of," remarks Queen Sassandra, "has recently perished in the Mothersea, along with many more commoners who resided along our seacoasts. But what really did become of Babacar the Daring? This is indeed a good question, given the strict 'no-trespassing' rule you have on Meridian 12. You see we have received you freely here, but tell me, what has become of all the other-islanders who passed us by for your greater landholding?"

"Our habitable landholding is not so large, my lady," I reply. "But what are you suggesting otherwise?"

"Where have you come upon your hoard of treasure," she persists, lacing into us over her necklace of rare pinks, "and why have so many seafarers who bypassed us never returned? Has your population grown so large?"

"As the last landholding in the chain," Yang interjects, "long ere the present crisis, we've always been the largest recipient of trade simply because merchants preferred to offload whatever they carried to M-12 in order to make room for fresh cargo to return home with. Such is the way of imports and exports, Your Highness."

"Who is it with the reputation of a no-go island, anyway?" Nyoto adds sharply, none too pleased by the queen's insinuations. "And how is it that your island has swelled with so many warriors not of your race? Is Royal Guardsmen service mandatory for refugees?"

"*Haa, haa,*" supplicates the despotic king, signaling by a circular motion of his hands for everyone to calm down, at which the queen replaces her silk sash over her scurrilous mouth.

"I prithee," I comment, "forgive what sounds like pointed inquiries, and no pun intended, but an M-11 spearhead was found in Babacar's chest. And so, while we come in peace, we've a few questions of our own to clear up before a fresh accord can be struck between our respective kingdoms. It is true that M-12 does not feign to be an open house: we have our Royal Code of Defense and Preservation, and as such, trespassers are dealt with swiftly and severely—but that doesn't mean we aren't open to formal interisland negotiations."

While my team regards me nonplussed, the queen's breath grows visibly stronger beneath her veil. "Babacar is disapproved here!" she counters impatiently. "He hasn't touched foot here since his rumor-spreading mission a grom's generation ere."

"Aye, my lady," Temitope adds, "and anyway, we would never waste a good spear on a blowfish such as he. More likely, he continued around us to M-12, his onetime ally, but was dealt with *swiftly and severely* there."

"Perhaps it was merely a setup," King Chaka offers in a bid at mediation, "to induce these hostilities between us. Observe the conflict it brings to our table even now."

"But we're the only tribes left," Yang reminds. "Who would stand to benefit from our division? M-2 has long since sunk."

"Perforce they're still holding out on a flotilla somewhere," Chaka suggests incredulously, "or have found a new cay to occupy, such as yours. You know they always hated us, while Babacar made quite a few enemies among his own people. His confederate islands tour may've been grand and daring, but unfortunately, rumor has it that he couldn't stop bragging about it upon his return to M-2. You know, some Ocean Masters there had placed high in the interisland games, while others had paddled big-wave guns as far as M-10. And here comes Babacar, never accepting the challenges of the games, but only bragging about his paddleboard journey to M-12. Did he deserve the title of Ocean Master? A lot of watermen on M-2 didn't think so. In the end, maybe he was put to spear out of spite in an internecine killing, and by making it look like we killed him, well, that would certainly alarm you—perhaps to the point of launching a preemptive strike against us."

"But why would the Twos care so much about that," Yang checks the crafty king's theory, "when they, if they're indeed still alive, are likely facing their own imminent demise in the ever-rising tides?"

"Perhaps he dispatched himself to revenge us," Temitope posits in a low, stolid voice. "He hated us that much, and if he was to die anyway, this would be his way to get back at us from beyond the grave."

"Planting a broken spearhead into one's own chest?" Yang snorts disparagingly. "Babacar may've been daring, but few people I've met are so brave—especially the scoundrel you are describing."

"Falling upon a spear," returns the king's keeper, "or rushing into one planted on a beach before one's island succumbs to the sea would be easy and, as painful as it sounds, would be preferable to drowning or facing the beasties. What would you prefer, Yang? The shark or the spear?"

"*Eh! Wot you say*?!" the cocksure young spearman retorts heatedly, while the rest of us are put on edge.

"*Haa! Haa*!" Chaka renews his conciliatory gestures. "Babacar's death is irrelevant to the challenges we now jointly face, while you, my fair guests, could only have braved such a dangerous journey here in order to transmit a message from your benevolent king. I prithee, sup a moment on my salmagundi, and then we shall get down to the business at hand."

I pretend to take a sip of the strong-smelling stew with its odd-looking meat, replying afterward, "We *do* bear tidings in which you'll want to hear, provided I can first take my relief. My innard is bulging, and I fear it shall forthwith burst lest I be conveyed to an outflow chamber posthaste. Upon my return, I will present an emigration offer that I'm sure you'll find agreeable."

As the enemy king responds with a wily grin, Nyoto and Yang eye me coolly. I deflect their latent concern with a subtle hand gesture, and then ask Chaka once more, as I motion to get up, "I prithee, Your Majesty, will this be possible?"

"Aye," he replies with a toothy smile, leaning comfortably back in his chair. "Let bygones be bygones. Fela here can convey you to the outflow chamber. Our island may be sinking, but we're not without this basic necessity."

I leave my spear at the table to further the guise of a genuine entente before following Fela back into the wreck of the greater palace. The tempest has blown large swaths of the roof away, while the floor beneath us is rickety and prone to collapse. I do my best to follow gingerly in Fela's footsteps, who leads me down a different flight of stairs than the ones we first mounted before turning at the bottom and proceeding past a cage-like room made of whalebones and shipwood beams. As she strides ahead, I pause to observe a band of warriors inside the holding area, preparing their weapons, painting their faces in battle mien and rubbing moist undersand in a cross formation over their shark-gill tattooed chests. They're so preoccupied with their activities that they pay little, if any, attention to me in the adjacent hallway.

But Fela is quick to double back, and when she sees me gazing at the armaments propped up in the cell, she makes haste to close the whalebone gate. Some of the warriors take happenstance notice of our interaction, but the bulk of them remain unconcerned by our presence.

Continuing on, I put to my well-built hostess, "They appear to be preparing for battle."

"*Naaay*," she replies with a casual lilt, "they're just preparing for battle games. Come, the outflow chamber is right this way."

"Battle games? Why would Chaka hold battle games at a time like this?"

She replies over her shoulder, "My lord is a perceptive king who knows the best time to test a warrior's mettle is under the most extreme pressure." She steps aside and points toward a door just ahead. "The outflow chamber, Xavion. Please flush the vessel when you're finished. I shall await you here."

With everything else going on, I find it odd and indecorous she should be so concerned about my flushing my pee down, but she's a woman and I her guest, and so I thank her kindly before proceeding into the chamber. In truth, I'm not swelling at the innard one bit,

but am succeeding in my investigation of the greater palace and its present occupants.

My feigned duty done, I return to my hostess, who guides me back in the direction of the stairway. As we pass by the warriors' cage once again, its lodgers still paying no mind to us, I stealthily slide the whalebone lever over the gate's latch, locking them in. Even if I were to trust Fela that they aren't preparing for an actual attack, I nonetheless seize the opportunity to vex the grunts any way I can.

Back in Chaka's veranda, I find my seat at the foot of the table while Fela remains guarding the door alongside Ojore. Two more characters have since arrived in the blown-out sunroom.

"Xavion," Chaka announces, "it is my pleasure to introduce to you my firstborn son and heir to the throne, Prince Kendi. Kendi, this is Xavion, retainer to King Tai Yun."

The boy, dressed in a coir sash and red feather headdress, appears younger than Umukoro and rather timid. As he stands near the table regarding me witlessly, I offer him an economical bow.

"It serves well for my successor to be present at such a significant meeting," Chaka remarks, "so that he may carry on the history of our ascension."

I eye my team. We're all concerned. Kendi meanwhile gravitates behind us, essentially blocking the threshold betwixt Fela and Ojore.

"And Adisa, our oracle," Chaka continues, signaling to a tall, dark and slender figure donning a crossbones necklace and white band of silk wrapped tightly around her neck. Her hair is clumped apart in umpteen knots like a nest of black sea snakes, her yellowing eyes point in slightly different directions and her purplish lips are ringed with browning bird bone labrets. She carries beneath her arm a bright red pouch of median coverts plumage.

"Adisa is completely blind," continues Chaka, "but she can see things that nobody else can. The book, Adisa."

The blind seer reaches into her pouch and procures the black book with the gold crossed skewers.

My team and I push our chairs obstreperously back, gripping our weapons as we stand.

"At ease, my friends," implores the conniving king. "It is our custom to share of our convictions before an official covenant. Observe how we take communion with the Absolute."

We remain tense, leery of the black book and whatever the despot is saying.

Another minion enters wearing a black feather robe, but is otherwise matched to the same eerie habits of Adisa, with a crown of knotted locks, bird bone labrets, a bone cross necklace hanging at his chest and a thin ribbon of white silk encircling his neck. He places a strange dried, sponge-like substance on the table before the rummy king, and then he sets down upon a cross-shaped stand a pure white conch that is filled with what appears to be blood. Hen blood? *Human blood?*

"We've prepared a special kind of cracker," Chaka continues in all his guile. "First Adisa shall tell us what the holy book portends, of *he* who dies on the cross and is risen again, and then we shall break and consume his flesh before drinking his blood."

Convinced we shall shortly be eaten or forced into cannibalism, my team and I vault toward the door.

Fela and Ojore converge on us, and so Yang, out in front, knocks aside Ojore's *tawi-manu*, causing its serrated end to fall over Prince Kendi's neck. As blood comes spurting out from the boy's slashed throat, Ojore and I stop to assist him, but with Fela trying to assault me with her spear (which I narrowly deflect), and with the king, the queen, and Temitope rushing at me, screaming bloody vengeance, I make haste out the door behind my team.

As we're rumbling down the stairs, Chaka roars out, "Release the sea lions of war!"

The whalebone cell I've encaged his warriors in on a ruse is now proving crucial in giving us a running start to our sailboards, but I don't know how much longer the snare will hold. We follow the sand

trails to where our boards have been stashed beneath the royal palace, and then, dumping their masts and sails, we grab the spikes afore and begin dragging our crafts toward the waterline. I'm startled by a piercing cry of grief from Sassandra, and then Chaka appears at the veranda railing with a bow and starts launching arrows down at us, screaming, "You shall die for this! Every last one of you! I shall avenge my son with the blood of Prince Umukoro!"

Suddenly, a whole host of warriors comes gushing out of the compound brandishing spears and *tawi-manus*.

"Prepare the boards for fast paddling!" Nyoto cries and then falls to a knee and reaches for her back quiver. Whipping around with a bow and arrow, she flings a reed directly into the heart of an onrushing guardsman, killing him instantly. "I'll hold them off!" she commands. "*Deg-deg!*"

And *hurry* we do, with return projectiles whizzing over our heads. Yanking the spikes away from the rails of our boards where we will be paddling, we launch the crafts into the water.

"Let's move!" I call back to the arrowmaiden as the swarm closes in.

She fires off another arrow at the foremost combatant, striking him in the neck, and then she turns and jumps prone over her board betwixt us, and we all start paddling like crazy.

Spears and arrows narrowly miss us in a return volley, and then a crier sounds forth through a conch, *"Fast-attack crafts!"*

A set is approaching, drawing the water in the channel back out to sea and causing wayward roofing material and beams to come jutting unpredictably above the surface. I alternatively eye the massive waves wrapping around the shoal to starboard and a group of warriors launching swift boards into the water behind us.

"*Paddle! Paddle! Paddle!*" Nyoto screams as the first wave swings wide, standing up across the channel and threatening to close it out. We stroke ever harder up the rapidly steepening face.

I glance back to behold in horror a whale bone thrusting up from the shallows and skewering the foremost pursuer through his gut. As he remains impaled through his intestines, the other attackers don't stop to assist him, but continue swiftly forth in the sea-bound current.

My team and I are meanwhile whipped completely airborne over the crest of the first breaker, splashing down upon its back in a tremendous triple volley.

"*Ha! Ha!*" Yang laughs derisively while glancing over his shoulder. "They got caught inside!"

Nyoto and I look back to see an open market of dislodged boards, balsawood pieces, weapons, and royal guardsmen attempting to recover from the blast, while several of their crafts have been taken in wholesale with the flood of whitewater following the wave's detonation.

But then suddenly, three pursuers, firmly holding on to their boards, pop up from the maelstrom and resume paddling.

As we rise upon the face of the next rock and roller, it squeezes vertically up into the channel, launching us skyward. We splash down heavily upon the receding back slope, our protruding spikes helping to cushion and stabilize what otherwise would've been a disastrous impact.

Another glance behind reveals the three pursuers emerging from gainful duck-dives through the second wave no different from the first. It's now abundantly clear they're paddling shortboards—but these shall prove neither so agile nor advantageous o'er the interisland main, and so we hasten our advance.

Having maintained enough forward momentum to surmount the next towering swell, we rise and fall o'er it in a great oscillation that pendulates our every nerve and sinew. The triple-tidal-wave set is followed by a smaller, swiftly moving comber that passes white and frothing beneath our juddering rails. At last free of the breakers, we stroke at full flanking speed, south by southwest toward the motherland.

A final glance behind shows Chaka's shortboard sea lions getting swept askew in an undertow begot by the expiring set, the greater riptide scudding them toward the shoal to starboard.

We take a moment to dislodge more spikes from our rails in order to increase our paddling power, and these we tuck beneath our foredeck netting in the event their utility as spears becomes necessary.

"I didn't mean to kill the boy," Yang laments.

"I know you didn't," I allay, as I regain our forward bearing. "Nonetheless, we're now at war and so must gain as much leeway as possible in order to warn M-12 of a pending attack."

"Things got ugly on us back there real fast, X," he sobs. "Slithering sea lions! Why'd we ever hold table with King Chaka?"

"We had little choice, mate. Once they surrounded us on the beach, the game changed for us, big time. I was only trying to negotiate our escape, but I regret it didn't go exactly as planned."

"I'm all good with it," Nyoto interjects between strenuous paddling breaths. "Away with those stonefish! I feel bad about Prince Kendi and all, but they were going to eat us for Christ's sake!"

"Damn straight!" I exclaim. "They were going to eat us in the name of their god! You know this war was coming no matter what happened back there, so it's best we just get on with it."

"At least we have the lead out here," Yang says, still pouting. "How many of them do you think are coming?"

"About a dozen I reckon, but they'll be winded from the journey, while our warriors will not only be fresh, but will have the benefit of our new breakwater from which to launch a preemptive attack."

"And we're flush with projectiles," adds the arrowmaiden, "giving us a major advantage."

"Aye," say I. "Truce with the Elevens is now impossible, if it was ever viable to begin with. It's better we get this frivolous war over with quickly so that we can fortify our seacoast against our much more formidable opponent, the Mothersea."

"She's not our opponent," Yang hastens a reply. "Please take care not to speak such things upon her back."

"Aye, matey—I misspoke. If she no longer wishes to support our landholdings, so be it—we can do little to stay her advance. But I still have faith that she may yet relent, if only we can hold out until the dry season."

"Aye," agrees Nyoto, still breathing heavily, for the return trip against the south wind and seas is already proving a major test of endurance, especially since we've become so garrulous.

"We should belay and drink some water," I suggest.

"Let's wait until our advantage is better," urges Nyoto.

The M-11 shortboarders, thwarted by the rough water encircling their island, have since come about and are trailing us again, albeit from a moderate distance. Of greater concern is a fresh flotilla of guardsmen paddling heartwood boards not far behind them. While our hardwood sailboards paddle much swifter than balsawood shortboards, they cannot be conveyed forward by arm as quickly as dedicated heartwood paddleboards, which the *derrière garde* appear to be using. As they overtake their forward flotilla, we endeavor to increase our pace.

Erelong, the detachment out in front redoubles their effort, and then while gliding forth, they stand upon their paddleboards and begin launching spears at us. The projectiles, lobbed into the wind, strike the water several board lengths behind us, which slows our pursuers somewhat as they go to retrieve their floating shafts.

Thus, our bowwoman seizes the opportunity to stand upon the deck of her sailboard and return their favor with a quick 1-2-3 volley, the third arrow finding home in the body of Cadiz, the mercenary, who in all likelihood was press-ganged into joining the royal guard after arriving to M-11 as a desperado from his tanked M-8.

The pitched battle of paddling and then volleying from varying distances continues for quite some time, until the paddleboarders finally fall back, apparently to give their shortboarders a chance to catch up—or it may be that, with M-12 a committed sprint ahead, they are seeking to regroup before launching an organized assault on our beachhead.

After finally gaining a comfortable distance ahead of the enemy, we sit upon our crafts and open the compartments within our decks that contain our water vessels. My plastic vial remains almost full, as does Yang's seal-gut sack, but Nyoto's plastic container is nearly empty because it's sprung a leak around its lid. (All Meridian plastics are scavenged from beaches and the Mothersea, and as such, they're often weathered and prone to ruptures.)

I paddle abeam and offer Nyoto my vial. "Drink, my lady. I've had my fill."

In truth, I stopped drinking when I saw that her vial was spent, saving several deep gulps in my container for her—enow to clear the salt from her throat.

"*My lady*," she bandies with my formality. "Why, thank you, *my Ocean Master*." She hands me my now emptied vile, adding, "I needed tha—"

Midsentence, she's exploded skyward by a great leviathan launching from beneath her, blocking out the sun and causing me to list radically back in the wake of the massive blast. The titan, with the arrowmaiden's craft in its jaws, wriggles madly in the air before coming down again with a cataclysmic splash, submerging swiftly with the sailboard in its mouth.

The arrowmaiden splashes down shortly thereafter. She's able to keep her head above the surface, and while there's no sign of blood anywhere, she's severely rattled by the surprise attack.

"*Arrowmaiden!*" Yang screams, paddling toward her, when suddenly her sailboard comes shooting up betwixt them, its spikes broken jaggedly off.

Nyoto eyes her board warily, perhaps looking for a place to climb on betwixt the outsized splinters.

"It was Okonkwo!" I warn as I struggle to regain my bearings. "*Deg-deg*, Nyoto! Hurry!"

She reaches out for her board.

Ku-BLAM! The colossus torpedoes her again, this time taking her body in its maw and splattering her blood sunward as she is halved.

"*Nyoto!*" I cry as her body parts come raining down with her blood, bow and arrows.

"*Arrowmaiden!*" Yang peals, racing to her upper half, which has been savagely severed at her breast. He grabs her arm and attempts to pull her torso onto the deck of his board.

"No, Yang! Let her go!" I warn. "Okonkwo is here!"

He regards me with wasted eyes, and then, staring into the frozen open deadlights of his rent heroine, he begins to whimper, "*Nyoto … Nyoto …*" before reluctantly setting her adrift.

"Yang! We must get away from the blood! *Deg-deg*, Yang! And do not splash!"

We hasten away from the site of the attack. A short interval later, I spy the leviathan from the side of my eye, and while it's still a fair distance away, it's swimming toward us at full flanking speed, its dorsal fin rising from the water taller than a full-grown man, wakes throwing mightily off its massive, tiger-striped back.

Learning from the fate of Nyoto that my board will have little effect against a broadside, I come about, righting my craft to face the behemoth dead-on, and then I begin paddling full speed ahead. I obliquely spot Yang stroking hard abeam in conjunction with my forward charge. He rises to his feet and brandishes an anti-shark spike.

The monster, its breadth greater than the length of my board, its length at least four times that of my craft, pushes a tidal wave of water off its rubbery bow as it closes in, its speed approaching that of a flying fish.

"*Aaarrgh!*" I grunt in the final affront as the colossus extrudes its massive jaws, revealing several rows of serrated teeth, each tooth bigger than my hand. It effects a final lunge …

I hop on to the tail of my board and shoot the entirety of my craft into Okonkwo's maw. The skewers fronting my board slam into

the giant's rugged gullet, and then the beast dives with my board sticking halfway out of its mouth. Meanwhile, Yang has aimed his anti-shark spike with laudable success, his strong arm ejecting the projectile with force enow to penetrate the tiger's resilient back, at which his armament is likewise dragged down into the depths.

"Yang!" I shout, struggling in the undertow begot by the submerging behemoth.

He paddles toward me, and then my board comes shooting out of the water betwixt us with its skewers nigh gone—but the board is fundamentally intact. I can't help to think of what happened to the arrowmaiden at this juncture.

I grab on to a spike floating at arm's length and dip my head underwater, scanning the depths for the leviathan. Bubbles come filtering up from the darkness. They grow in intensity until I'm engulfed in a void of turbulence and can't see a thing. With my heart racing, I extrude my spike before me, expecting to forthwith be devoured by the beastie. But then the bubbles stop ...

I come up for a breath. *"Where's the bastard ... ?"*

"Just get on your damn board!" Yang exhorts while brandishing another spike. "I'll keep watch!"

I begin swimming toward my watercraft, realizing the incredible buffer of defense it can still provide. San Jiao shapes our sailboards with the sturdiest of hardwoods, using beams so solid that they couldn't be cleaved by Okonkwo unless he sawed through them first with his jaws to weaken their indomitable strength of rocker.

"Deg-deg!" Yang alerts.

I glance around in panic, and while I'm almost to my board, Yang is standing upon his and cocking back his improvised weapon.

"There!" he points, but he doesn't need to signal the gargantua's heading, for even while I'm floundering about in the water, I can see its towering dorsal fin zooming back in the direction of Nyoto's killing. Once there, the beast splashes fiercely about in the bloodied water, finishing off the remnants of our beloved bowwoman.

"*Deg-deg*, Xavion! This is our chance!"

I wrest myself over my board, and we start stroking hard prone toward M-12's new sandbar, now within striking distance of an adamant paddle—a sprint we have no want of mustering. Frequently looking back to take stock of Okonkwo's position, we notice the enemy flotilla, either in an incredible act of folly or a supreme feat of bravery, pursuing us through the bloodied kill site. Or perhaps it's just that they, like us, are making haste toward the nearest landholding: our windward cay.

With a thunderous *boom!* from behind and a brouhaha of commotion, we glance back to see that Okonkwo has torpedoed one of the M-11 paddleboarders. As the victim and his weighty craft come crashing down upon the water, the great sea tiger torques around and swallows him whole.

The pandemonium astern continues, for more sharks have come to attack the shortboarders further back. While their screams are horrific, for us it is a benison to witness the reduction of their navy, if only we can make it safely ashore ourselves.

Spurred on by the Mothersea's unrelenting terrors, we propel ourselves forward with superhuman speed, henceforth ceasing to look back. The swells and currents that've been plaguing us with a sideswipe to full frontal contest no longer appear relevant as we plow our ponderous shipwood sailboards forth through the incessant wavelets, our eyes steeled to the shoreline ahead.

With our shoulder, back and calf muscles bulging and glistening with sweat, we at last drive our crafts headlong into the sand. But the M-11 navy remains in hot pursuit, likewise licked on by the horrors of the deep, and so we waste no time in dragging our windsurfers over the cay and into the channel opposite, from where with all due celerity we attain the motherland, hallooing the alert of the coming flotilla as best as we can, given our shortness of breath.

Our desperate message registers quickly among the islanders, who organize a hasty counterattack. Alas, as fresh boards, weapons and combatants are assembled on our beachfront proper, the time to act has come to an end, for the M-11 warriors can already be seen mounting the breakwater.

Yang takes an archer's position at the waterline, while I refresh myself with drinking water before returning to the channel on a battleboard beside my fellow warriors. Our adversaries appear winded and struggling to regroup in the wake of their brutal interisland paddle, and so we hasten our blitz against them.

A lame volley of arrows and spears eject from their beleaguered bivouac, but the projectiles are nonetheless hazardous, and so as soon as we gain the cay's leeward shore, we thrust the sharpened tails of our battleboards into the sand, erecting our crafts as heartwood stanchions from where we shield behind and return fire, peering through narrow slits in our decks to better establish enemy positions.

Our counterattack goes well, as we slowly advance while keeping the enemy pinned down on the windward edge of the bar. Sporadic return fire sometimes strikes the undersides of our boards with a hefty *thump!*—but neither spearhead nor arrowhead breaches our movable barriers, while we score several flesh hits against our opponents.

Alas, as we're advancing, a virtual deluge of reinforcements arrive from the sea, and using their shortboards as shields in conjunction with turtle shells, they wage a vicious counterattack.

A close-range combat ensues, with hefty *tawi-manu* clubs slamming into our resilient barriers as we strike back with spears, primarily. Several warriors on both sides get rudely scathed, and Ren Mai delivers a casualty strike into the gut of an assailant. Ultimately outnumbered, we're forced to retreat back across the channel in a methodical, well-practiced amphibious withdrawal, aided by Yang Ming and a phalanx of friendly archers on M-12 proper providing steady air cover.

Several guardsmen from M-11 make the mistake of trying to follow us across, but with the tide now at its apex, they're easy targets

upon the high water and are picked off by our archers and spearmen before they can reach the shore. The remainder of the invading force gets the message and so decamps to their beachhead on the opposite side of the cay, while we set to reinforcing our village-front garrison.

Word of Nyoto's death circulates with immense sorrow around M-12, adding to the anxiety of having the M-11 navy suddenly at our doorstep. She was a master archer and first-class warrior, her unsurpassed aptitude as protectress of M-12 matched only by her good nature.

As for the garrison, we're constructing it from San Jiao's cache of shipwood beams, for we know already that it must be impenetrable to projectiles and the swings of *tawi-manus*, and furthermore, it needs to serve as the forward *praetorium* from which we can conduct expeditionary operations while guarding the royal palace behind.

The M-11 battalion, for its part, has posted sentries along the cay as their navy establishes an encampment of sorts on the far beach-head, where their reinforcements continue arriving in small flotillas.

While constructing our garrison, we take frequent breaks at the serving of fresh victuals, and those who've incurred flesh wounds from our scuffle on the bar are given nourishment and coir bandages lined with seaweed poultice.

King Tai Yun arrives in glimmering, turtle shell armor. "I didn't expect you to return so soon," he says, "and thus was not watching for you. But I see you've encountered some serious trouble, which has followed you back. My condolences about the arrowmaiden. I trust you did what you could to save her."

"Okonkwo," I answer plainly.

"So I've heard. He takes whom he pleases, and there's only so much one can do."

"If it wasn't for the anti-shark skewers, he would've swallowed our sailboards whole."

"He's really that massive?"

"Aye."

"And what of Chaka's navy? Did he mobilize them as you approached his territory? What are his present landholdings?"

"His landholdings have been decimated and his palace ravaged. His concentric dikes are succumbing to the wetsand and shan't last. As such, we must prepare for a total assault by the entirety of his guardsmen, who are continually arriving. Our breakwater will not sustain them: erelong they'll attempt to take us here."

"And what of King Chaka?"

"A heavy surf overtook us as we approached the shoal, depositing us on what is left of his island. His guardsmen quickly outnumbered us, and so we feigned a diplomatic mission in order to escape his landholding alive. At his table, I affected light negotiations with the intention of canceling them as soon as we were released back into the water, but then suddenly, he procured his black book and said he intended to eat us, or that we were to take part in some manner of cannibal witchcraft. While attempting to flee his veranda, Yang knocked the *tawi-manu* out of guardsman Ojore's hands, and it came down across the neck of Prince Kendi, mortally wounding him."

Yang regards me with a serious expression that harbors a black look, for I know he's irked by the outcome of my improvised plan.

"Kendi, the firstborn son," Tai Yun remarks gravely.

"Aye, my lord. You must know that, as we were fleeing, Chaka vowed to avenge him with the blood of Umukoro."

"That shall never happen! We will vouchsafe my son the highest level of security and keep him in hiding."

"Aye, my lord."

"And so the three of you escaped, only to be ambushed by Okonkwo?"

"Aye, and let it be known that it is owing to the arrowmaiden that we escaped M-11 alive, for she singlehandedly held off Chaka's guardsmen long enow for us to launch our watercrafts."

"With bow and arrow, I presume."

"Aye, my lord—she shot a perfect fight."

"Damn that Okonkwo!" the king execrates in a rare display of anger.

"The tiger took a number of Chaka's men, as well."

"Good, but can you relay their present numbers? We've counted about twenty on the bar. Are there more?"

"I don't believe so, excepting for the king himself, his family and royal entourage."

"Temitope Mukondi?"

"Aye, and a few others. My lord, they're arriving here enervated and weak from the passage, just as we have—I know from combating them hand-to-hand—a battle you saliently missed. We must launch another attack before they can recoup further."

"But shouldn't we finish the *praetorium* first?" Qi Dong interjects while working nearby, erecting the structure. "We at least need a viable fortress from which to protect the hamlet should we need to fall back again."

"*Hmm* ..." Tai Yun ruminates aloud, stroking his graying goatee.

"Our able-bodied combatants are what, but ten?" I counter in contempt of Qi Dong, our least adept warrior. "And we've lost our best archer. I suggest we attack now while we still have the advantage of freshness, for we certainly don't have their numbers."

"Now is too soon," the old monarch relents. "Dong has a point. Since we are, in fact, less their numbers by half, it's more expedient to finish the garrison before launching a fully coordinated attack. Or better yet, let them try to come over the channel again, with our easy landward advantage."

"And if they attack by night?" I probe his logic.

"We'll post sentries," he replies unconvincingly.

———

In a gust of warm air, a newly placed tent flap blows back, and Shao Ying glides in wearing a large conch necklace. Her forehead is pasted with crystallized sand fragments still glittering from their exposure to the sun, while dozens of white puka shell bracelets engirdle her arms from her wrists clear up to her biceps. She removes her hood of coir, revealing a crown of golden locks fixed hither and thither with sea stars and other Asteroidea, some of which appear to be alive. "These questions you speak," she begins, which is odd, since she has just arrived, "I shall consult the Mothersea."

"Aye, my lady," replies the king. "We welcome your counsel."

"It is by the design of our maker, my lord—not mine."

"As you were," offers Tai Yun, opening his hands to the sandy floor, which has been raked clean and flat by his dutiful operatives—such is his obsession with domestic tidiness.

The seer removes her divining conch and hands it to San Jiao, asking her to fill it. The craftswoman obliges, returning moments later with the giant mollusk brimming with seawater. The oracle has meanwhile tousled the sand with her feet and tossed some tiny shells over the permuted patch. She removes an animate blue starfish from her hair, causing her blond locks to come spilling down over her shoulder at one side, and then, taking the conch in one hand while holding the Asteroidea in the other, she pours the saltwater over the sea star. The water cascades over the starfish's five radiating arms, expiring into the sandworks beneath. Small hills and valleys are reordered, pebbles shift and the tiny shells sink into fissures.

After carefully studying the outcome, she addresses the king, "My lord, I advise not to pursue the enemy on the sandbar at this time."

The king's brows scrunch in critical thought as he stares down at the sandworks while stroking his graying goatee.

"What have you seen?" Qi Dong inquires of Shao Ying.

"I prithee, take this for a moment." She hands him the sea star with its five members slowly undulating, and now with both hands free, she returns her conch to her carcanet of multicolored interwoven plastic strips, at length answering: "It is better we reinforce our

landholdings with longer dikes and finish this *praetorium* without delay."

I shake my head. "But why, my lady? Will not waging a counter-attack *now* augur a better outcome than delaying further?"

She resculpts her coiffure back into the likeness of an immense golden conch, and then retrieving the starfish from Qi Dong, she coaxes the Asteroidea's sticky members into gripping around her locks until the arrangement is fixed firmly into place. Finally, as if we had all the time in the Meridians, she answers, "Waste neither the time nor the effort, for the Mothersea shall erelong overtake the storm barrier, and then thine enemies shall arrive here in weakness and disarray."

"When?" inquires the king.

"Look." She points at the tent flap fluttering in a warm gust of air. "Your counsel is everywhere evident, if only you had the eyes for it." She replaces her coir hood over her ornate crown and takes her leave.

"Queer one, she is," I mutter.

"*Xavion!*" Tai Yun scolds under his breath, and then he draws nigh and whispers scathingly, "You know it only seems as such, for she sees that which we do not!"

"Aye, my lord," I reply in strained undertones, for those working around us are plainly eavesdropping, "but in this instance, I see things differently: I see a beleaguered force just arriving, and so I strongly urge, once more, that we strike while they're still winded from the journey."

I perceive a slight twitch in his earlobe, at which he responds, "While your sense of urgency is appreciated, your suspicion of the seer here is unsound, for it does appear by a gradual change in climate that a storm is indeed brewing again on the northern horizon."

Now even he tries my patience, but with the king and everyone beneath him save for me seemingly more interested in building the garrison than fighting forthwith, I cannot so summarily rile the

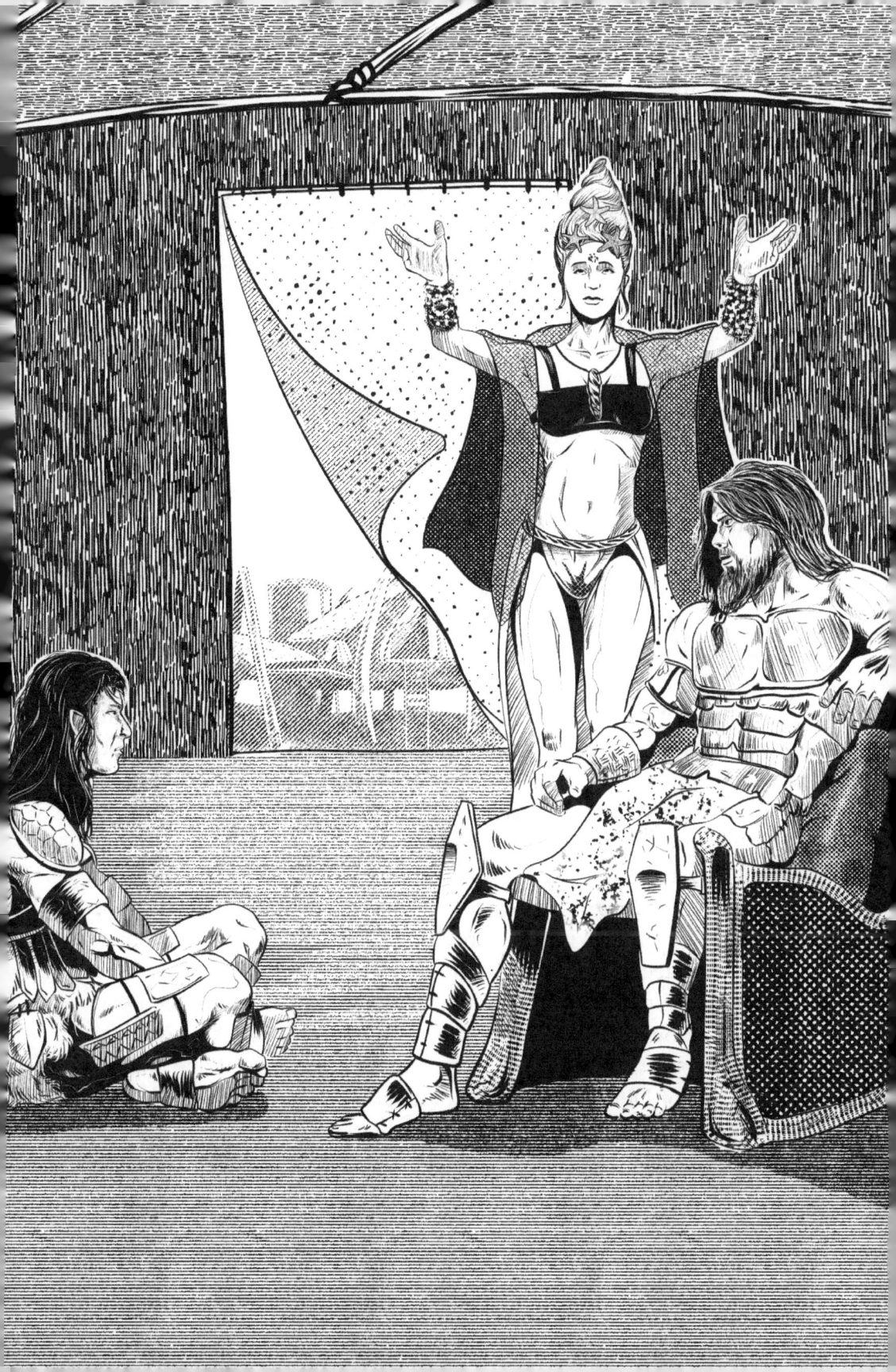

troops into both war and mutiny. Thus, I grab a shovel and quit the confines of the half-constructed garrison in a temper, where I shall vent my energy in the digging of another hole along the exterior. A stack of shipwood stanchions lies nearby, awaiting emplacement to further the walls. If this is what the king requires to get back on the warpath, then let him repose inside while *I* see to its swift execution.

———

A long interval later, I'm sitting in the summer veranda, sipping seaweed tea with the queen while staying in close proximity to Umukoro, who's been scanning the cay intensely. I've asked him to keep watch on the islet because I've grown tired of seeing it freely occupied by the enemy. Suddenly he blurts out, "See there! The arrival of their king!"

A fleet is drawing forth with King Chaka commanding it from a throne erected upon a raft of paddleboards, while beneath him a band of warriors convey the floating monstrosity forward with stand-up paddles.

"Damn sweepers," I mutter.

Other minions stand around him on SUPs, driving their sharpened blades into the water to ward against sharks. As for the tyrant, he's wearing his bright red feather headdress, tall and teetering over his fat head, which with each rocking of his craft over the rough water rudely accentuates his pompous swagger.

"*Pfft!*" I spittle through my teeth. "He ought to be toppled over forthwith. How I would've loved to see him arrive to his troops royally routed, but now we're the ones being jested. So much for our Royal Code of Defense and Preservation!"

"Wasn't that invented ere the breakwater was formed?" Umukoro inquires.

"What difference does it make!?" I judder in exasperation.

The grom and his mother regard me uneasily, and so I temper my frustration, explaining in mottled syllables, "The Code was intended to protect our landholding against foreign incursions. This is a foreign incursion, and we're sitting here doing nothing!"

"Respectfully, Xavion," counters the queen, "Shao Ying has had a vision, and His Majesty has certified it."

"And so we are guided by the happenstance play of water upon sand and a puff of wind? My lady, I'm neither a magician nor an old thinker. I'm a warrior, and a warrior is a man of action. We've waited long enow."

The queen winces at my insolence, which for my part is not without sufficient justification. I've a mind to go marching out, when suddenly she squeezes my shoulder and quietly supplicates, "I know how you must feel, my dutiful protector, but I prithee, for the sake of my son and I, the king has asked you to stay and watch over us, as you've always done. What's more, we've a better view here from which to monitor their movements. Should a blitz transpire from the cay, I concede by return: I would not wish a counsel of runes and retiring thinkers to stay our virile bulls of war."

I squeeze her hand as it rests upon my shoulder, offering her a kindly twinkle. Her son may not understand the bearing of her sentiment, but for me her desire is clear: I shall safeguard her until a closer tumble eventuates, her featherbed something I could utterly destroy with my present virulence.

Restraining my aversion to that parasite Chaka, however, becomes a significant inner test as he delivers two shipwood beams to the shore opposite and orders his minions to erect them into a mighty cross. *"Aargh!"* I growl, and I'm not the only one outraged by the diabolical symbol, for several other Twelves can be heard screaming out in protest. "My lady!" I plead. "We could probably shoot them with arrows from here!"

The queen, gazing alongside her son in wide-eyed horror at the icon of cannibalism being erected, appears visibly shaken, but offers

only, "I shall sacrifice three hens against this abomination!" and then she goeth swiftly from the veranda.

I remain with Umukoro, painfully watching as Chaka strides before his monstrous cross. He stops, turns and looks in our direction. Raising a hand high over his head, he starts whipping it around in a histrionic peace gesture.

"*Pfft! Pu-lease!*" My contempt is unshaken. "To think we'd fall for that a second time!" I begin sharpening my longspear rudely with my iron knife, hoping for some sudden hostility that might trigger the final conflict.

———

"That's a solid-looking turtle shell breastplate you're wearing," remarks Jue Yin. "That's not the same one you use in training, is it?"

I tap a wooden stave I'm holding against my chest piece. "Nay, this is my real battle armor. And yours?"

"Same—real battle armor. While Tai Yun is intent on a siege, we're all taking the M-11 contention seriously. Our garrison is fully armed, our troops at the ready."

"Good—Chaka's navy didn't come here to be starved out. We must count on a putsch at any moment. Where's Tai Yun gone, anyway?"

"He went to seek counsel with Shao Ying."

"Again? So, who's in charge of the forward command post?"

"I think Soko's commanding it now. Should war break out, he'll sound the battle conch. In the meantime, let's get stitching this new dike line according to Shao's vision."

"Very well, Jue," I sigh. "But I think you should sit on my shoulders to get the longer staves started."

"Forward or backward?" She laughs.

"What?"

"Ha, ha, never mind. I'm just glad you're here to help us shorties out, X."

"Nay, it is my duty." I chuckle. "While I've been tasked with protecting the royal palace, I've meanwhile decided to come down to assist you. If war breaks out, I'm closer to the frontline, but nigh enow the prince to guard him."

As we set to work, prepping a new dike line in full body armor proves arduous, but it gives us the opportunity to acclimate to our combat gear, which most of us haven't worn since the interisland games many moons agone. Jue is wearing a coir loincloth beneath her turtle shell kilt—I know this by the way she squiggles around on my shoulders as she attempts to hammer an oversized stave into a moist crack that we've dilated open by hand. We eventually lose our balance and tumble down together.

We switch places, and I start pounding the thick shaft deeper into the undersand, my partner grunting ever harder as she tries to hold my powerful thrusts steady in her sweaty hands.

"Hold it right there, Jue, just like that!" I urge.

"Aye, aye, X-X-Xavion!" she stutters and groans with my every thrust. "*Harder! Harder!*"

"That's it! That's it!" I moan as I hammer.

At the climax of our intercourse, a call sounds forth from the *praetorium.*

We stop and look around. "*Shit!*" I curse, for it's not the battle horn, but a call of lesser importance. I reaffix my weapons to my belt and Jue readjusts her loincloth before we proceed down to the garrison together.

All eyes are steeled on the breakwater, where M-11 guardsmen are launching a raft stacked high with fish, plastic bottles, giant cowries, coconuts and other valuable commodities into the channel. Bobo yells from the cay that it's a peace offering from King Chaka, who "regrets the current state of affairs and doesn't want any more bloodshed."

The giant cowries are of particular significance, being an age-old sign of reconciliation, while the food offering, and especially the coconuts, is a notable accommodation in light of our opponent's limited supplies. Yet, our warrior training and our past history with the Elevens force us to assume that Chaka is merely sending a trick of poison or some other contrivance, and so Soko sounds a follow-up call to ignore the offering.

The makeshift raft, composed of two shipwood guns lashed together, never makes it to our side regardless, for it gets drawn into the northward current and swept out to sea. That Chaka doesn't send a paddler to recover the offering adds credence to the assumption that there's something truly fishy about it.

———

As the daystar dips to sunbed, turning the sky to gold, the southerly breeze abates, at which Chaka sends several of his warriors armed with shortboards to a wave breaking off the cay's southern tip. It's a symbol of dominance on his part, for pioneering a new spot is a way to claim localism—or territorial rights—over it. It's also a clear act of taunting, for the surfriders hoot and whistle each other on and frequently hail us over to join in the merrymaking.

"Can't we just shoot them with arrows?" I growl under my breath.

"As when Chaka erected his cross," Jue says, "Tai Yun believes the enemy is out of firing range, and therefore, it is better we deprive them of our fallen shafts, lest they try to retrieve them from the water and use them as their own."

"But what about our rule of no surfing in view of the king? This is a disgrace!"

I quit the garrison, marching determinedly back to the summer veranda in search of Tai Yun, but instead I find only Umukoro, mesmerized by the exhibition and not a little jealous that it was not he who cracked our newest surf break. We march back down to the beach together in search of the king and to get a closer look at the new surf break. It really is going off.

As we watch another Elevener rip apart a beautiful right-hander, the little monarch trumpets, "I don't care if they surfed it first—I'm naming that spot Umukoro's!"

I cannot deny his aggravation. I'd promised him the wave when we were constructing the reef upon which the sandbar has formed. The taunting being exhibited by the Elevens really gets under my skin. Here we are on the brink of war while they play up their charade of good times and reconciliation. It's as if they really think we'll fall for it—that war can be averted—even as we've killed their beloved prince and they've chased us back to our cay, made battle upon our breakwater and erected their hideous cross directly across from our hamlet in a perpetual mockery of our safety and convictions.

"Aye, lad," I assuage the rankled grom, "Umo's it is, then. Once we get rid of these imposter scum, I want you to paddle your short-board over there and rip it up."

"I wish I could paddle out right now, man! It's right there! Why can't we just accept their peace offering?"

"*Pfft!* With cannibals? Never!"

"Do you really believe they're cannibals, Xavion? Or was that just a rumor started by Babacar? Has anyone actually seen them eating people?"

"Grommet! We were seated at Chaka's table just this morning when they procured their black book and said they were going to cleave and eat human flesh. They told us there are people on M-11 who rise from the dead."

"Zombies?"

"Aye—it's part of their demonic rite. Whatever these people are doing over there is a black art that must never reach our shore. They're not like us, Umukoro—not in any way, and believe me, their peace offering is just a ruse. We must be extremely careful. King Chaka will do everything he can to get at you. But don't worry—I shall always protect you, even as I train you to protect yourself. Have you been doing your sparring exercises?"

"Aye."

"Very good, Umukoro. There's nothing greater than a warrior who becomes king."

He seems oblivious to my statement as he fixates on the enemy surfing off the bar. Suddenly, an M-11 rider launches off a wave in a looping aerial maneuver.

"Wow!" Umukoro ejaculates, verbally.

I shake my head in remorse. *Enough of this talk!* spurts my inner dialogue. "Where *is* your father, anyway?" I grunt. "Is he even seeing this?"

"I don't know, X—I thought you were with him."

"Nay, not anymore."

———

"The crab taco was good," I thank the queen as a retainer collects the seal-gut wrapping upon which it was served.

"I do enjoy the red crabs that live underwater," she says. "I shall inform Soko that we were pleased by his catch."

"Indeed, my lady."

Tai Yun saunters over to his private collection of salvaged treasures, procuring from it five silver spoons, which he carefully places around the table. Jomo enters shortly thereafter, shouldering a hefty wooden chest. His forehead is rippled with stress as he tries to hold the box level. After painstakingly setting it on the table, he announces, "San Jiao and I have prepared coconut pudding."

With the help of the queen and the princess, five coconut bowls filled with the succulent dessert are distributed around the royal plank, with a sixth slated by the king to be delivered to Yang's hut. The porter is given explicit instructions not to wake the spearman if he is found to be sleeping, but instead the delicacy would then be left in Yang's floating food storage tub, where ants and other terrestrial insects wouldn't be able to access the dessert as it bobs in its coconut shell upon the water.

"San Jiao and I are deeply saddened about Nyoto," Jomo remarks softly.

"As are we," says the king.

I recall how gallantly the arrowmaiden performed on the expedition, offering, "It was because of her that we escaped M-11 alive. But for Okonkwo!" I snarl and bang my fist against the table, soon releasing my grip and burying my face in despair.

I look up to see Umukoro staring at me in wide-eyed terror. And why not? The colossal shark could swallow him whole and has long been the subject of storytelling frights among Meridian men and grommets alike.

As the others take token solace in their desserts, their precious eating implements casting a reflective shimmer beneath the whale oil lanterns, I've naught appetite for sweets, for any of this. Jomo, San Jiao, the king and the queen—they all mean well in honoring the arrowmaiden with a taste of dazzle and opulence, but she was a far different creature from all of these, having spent most her life excelling in warrior training, war games and Mothersea operations. Even King Tai Yun, bred to engage in hard political positioning for goods and influence, is more a master of statecraft than an acolyte of the spear. Where was he when we made battle upon the cay? I cannot help but think of all the feather-bed Meridian Island kings who valued their warriors merely as protectors of the monarchy and little more. It seems to me that kings should also be warriors who are able to safeguard their subjects with more than just words and posturing, but with swords and true valor.

"Look there!" the prince exclaims, snapping me out of my somber reverie.

The Elevens have placed King Chaka's throne on its side and set it alight, and as the flames grow in might and bearing, the pyre illuminates the underbelly of an immense shark erected upon a spit. A pair of bare-chested warriors, one standing before the shark's mouth and the other at its tail, put into operation a set of hand levers, giving slow rotation to the vanquished creature. Erelong, the firelight lays bare an expanded scene of a great band of warriors sitting around the skewered beastie, while behind them the shipwood cross flickers red and orange in the light cast off by the demons' roast.

Theirs is an eerie rotisserie to behold, made all the more uncanny by Chaka apparently watching us as plainly as we're watching him. Tai Yun's veranda is lit only by his oil lanterns, making us nigh impossible to see from a distance. It's not long until the freakish king starts flinging a hand loosely 'round over his head, trying to hail us over with an uncouth comity gesture.

"It's a trick," I warn, "and I prithee, that's obvious by now."

"The indignity!" fumes the queen. "To think we'd dine with him upon the landholding in which he's appropriated from us!"

"Aye, my lady," adds the king, "his behavior is indeed disturbing. But worry not, our terra firma is not his to settle."

As we keep the enemy under surveillance, our strange fascination turns to horror as they cut open the shark's belly and remove from it a human arm. While we cannot clearly ascertain what they are doing with the steaming limb, I nevertheless take the opportunity to whisper into the ear of the shivering prince, "There's the proof you seek. For all we know, that may be Nyoto's arm upon which they feast."

"But that's not Okonkwo, is it?" he asks, quavering.

I do not respond, choosing instead to let the spectacle of horrors spur the dark imaginations of those among us who might find anything remotely redeemable about our adversaries, and the demonstration before us does not fail to disappoint. After the tribe feasts upon the beastie, they start dancing around the pyre in a bizarre and perverted manner, shaking around disjointedly while yelling unintelligible things, their blind seer all the while sashaying and jolting about the shallows like a possessed zombie. Meanwhile, their deranged king, stripped down to his loincloth, coir cape and feathered headdress, wades out into the water beyond the witch, and then

while raising his fists high in histrionics, he cries out, "All are forgiven who submit to *he* who hath risen from the dead!"

"Not this again," I mutter, shaking my head.

Tall Temitope enters the scene, also stripped down to his loincloth and headdress, but with the addition of a thin white band encircling his neck. He coaxes forth a warrior from the whorl of dancers, taking him first to Adisa and then further out to King Chaka, who slaps the recruit's forehead hard enow to cause him to fall back into the water in a disgraceful domination ritual. This rite of subjugation to the king and his core group of freaks is repeated ad nauseam to the remainder of the dancers, each in their turn.

Umukoro and Nsia remain glued to the exhibit in terrific fascination, until their mother removes them to an inner chamber, well out of sight of the depraved procession.

"This subversive display of taunting in plain view of our hamlet," I quip to Tai Yun, "makes me wonder if following Shao Ying's advice was truly expedient."

He casts me a black look beneath his scrunched brows. His ear twitches. He farts. His lips remain silent, but his visage and butthole action speak volumes about his antipathy for my challenging his authority, if even offhandedly. A real gust of warm wind courses through the veranda, enticing him to speak, "If foul weather is drawing upon us once again, then the oracle was correct: the enemy has little protection out on the cay and shall only be weakened and humiliated by the Mothersea for the insolent path they've chosen. They're merely trying to test our patience and resolve by performing these provocative and ludicrous acts. But let us not go to them where they have the land advantage—by the will of the Mothersea, let them be forced over the water to us, and then we shall pick them off like sea turtles dragging their haunches ashore to lay their eggs."

"*Tsk-tsk-tsk*," I openly deride his asseveration. "I only hope it is so easy, as you are always talking. Meanwhile, as they captivate us with

this stupid diversion, they're probably sending operatives over in the cover of darkness."

"Aye!" he concedes like a buffoon and then halloos in panic over the beach, gaining the attention of some sentries manning the garrison. He orders them to splay out along our windward shore to guard against a possible amphibious assault.

I offer my services, to which he reluctantly agrees, for while my primary duty has always been as his household protector, tonight the air between us has palpably soured. I'm indeed pleased that a reliable phalanx shall finally be guarding our greater beachhead, because it should've been our stratagem since eventide. Tai Yun simply forgot. One thing's for certain: our feather-bed king has lost the judgment to properly safeguard our island. We've long required the leadership of a capable warrior, not a loafing, flatulent thinker.

———

A queer chorus fills the air as Chaka's navy sings unintelligible dross from the cay—another meretricious display to undoubtedly mask a military strategy, such as to conceal the sounds of their crossing. *Let them come!* I and my fellow warriors are evenly flanked along our windward front in easy earshot of one another, should we be graced with the chance to shout *Invader!* and kill them once and for all.

As the night draws long, puffs of warm wind draw in from the south in fits and starts. I crumple down, cross-legged upon the sand, my eyelids sagging from the day's long trial. In trying to focus on the tenebrous water before me, I suddenly realize the gravity of my present duty and so force myself back to my feet and continue in resolute sentinel duty, far into the wee hours.

Near dawn, the southerly gusts morph into a steady wind, which shifts briskly northwest, auguring a powerful storm approaching from the cool regions.

Soko relieves me of my duty, for in the twilight he can now see past me to the next defender up the beach. He's well aware of my previous day's epic paddle and my dire need for an interval of sleep, which I greatly appreciate. I push his shoulder in the manner of obliging warriors, and when he returns the gesture, I nearly topple over.

Finally, I push open my whalebone door and collapse over my seal-gut mattress. My head hits my seal bladder pillow, and I'm out like out like a whale wax candle blown by a heavy sigh.

Chapter 8
STORM SHADOW DOWN

The blast of the battle conch awakens me. It's morning. I hop out of bed in my turtle shell armor, readjust my shoulder pads, quaff a bottleful of seaweed-infused water, wolf down a handful of dried crabs, grab my spear and then go bolting out the door.

Storm clouds are rolling low over the cay and heavy swells are overcoming the breakwater, reducing it to a miserly sliver of sand. The M-11 navy are struggling to assume battle formation amid the flood of breaching waves.

While Shao Ying has proven correct about the storm, it wasn't the most impressive act of divination considering how they've been arriving in ever greater strength and frequency. Alas, Meridian 12 is also eroding at a disconcerting rate. The northerly current is sweeping along our beachfront in a southerly bearing, and so the sand from the vanishing cay is not accumulating on our landholding like it did during the sinking of M-11, but is being washed clear out to the southern sea. I trudge through the wavelets of our diminishing beach toward my battalion, who are forming a phalanx in front of the garrison.

Across the channel, Chaka has taken a seat atop a makeshift raft at the center of his unstable phalanx, which numbers about twenty fighters on battleboards. His craft is manned on either side

by stand-up paddlers, who presently dig their oars into the sinking shoreline, shoving off.

"Be at the ready and wait for my command!" Tai Yun *yodels* from the middle of our line with his hand raised high. I think he's been eating too much coconut pudding, our dainty excuse for a king.

Meanwhile, Chaka's brawny deckhands are working hard to navigate his craft through the rough current. The surf spilling in over the sinking cay is pushing into the channel, making for choppy, brown water. But the belligerent king remains stoic, going so far as to raise his black book before him, while with his other hand he starts waving the peace gesture over his head. "*Haa! Haa!*" he calls through the driving rain. "Let us put our hostilities aside, and I shall forgive you for the accident that befell my son! *Haa! Haa!* The Mothersea will subsume us all unless we work together! *Haa! Haa! <pause> Haa! Haa!*"

Liar! I growl, while Tai Yun keeps his hand held high, indicating to hold our fire as the despot draws nigh.

And then, to my utter shock and consternation, Tai Yun responds to Chaka, "*Haa! Haa!*" while circling his raised hand!

"*Pfft!*" I ejaculate a sour discharge of rainwater from my lips and then snarl into the ear of Yang, "In memory of Nyoto and all your archers' outings together, I beg of you, depose that wretched curse of a king who precipitated her untimely death. I'd do it myself, but you're a far better shot in these conditions."

He turns his arrow toward Tai Yun. *And why not?* Our flatulent king was the one who ordered us on our ill-fated mission M-11, not to mention he has always denied Yang the status of Ocean Master for no good reason. Nonetheless, I direct his reed back toward King Chaka, prompting, "Right now, *that* is your man. Do it for Nyoto, and to save our island. This is our best chance."

"For the bowwoman," he utters plainly, releasing his shaft. The arrow goes zooming through the rain, impaling Chaka's book dead center.

Tossing his arrowshot book aside, the king of cons brandishes a small iron implement that he'd been concealing behind it. He extends his arm, aiming the object at Tai Yun …

BLAM! sounds the device with a report of smoke from its tip.

Tai Yun clutches his breastplate and falls to his knees, then lies back with blood spurting up from his chest. Pandemonium breaks out on M-12, for all are terror-stricken by the black magician's weapon.

"Charge!" Chaka orders his navy behind. His phalanx goes amphibious, launching their battleboards into the tempestuous waterway.

My warriors volley a hail of projectiles at the enemy king, for his navy is still out of range.

Chaka dives behind some beams stacked upon his raft as his oarsmen protect him with turtle shell shields. Afterward, they fling a seal-gut tarp away from a stockpile of spears and begin lobbing them at us in swift succession.

We protect ourselves from the onslaught and then redouble our assault on the raft—all save for Jue Yin, who's set down her spear to come to the aid of our king.

Chaka's crew lose control of their craft in our return volley, and it goes rotating around in the torrent. As they're trying to recover, we score an arrow hit into one of the paddlers' shoulders. He arches back with a wail and goes splashing into the water. The seaworn float meanwhile continues scudding out of control toward the open ocean.

Jue Yin cries out, "The king is dead!"

All along the frontlines and from abodes overlooking the beach, the generality of M-12 wails out in lament. The panic and confusion begot by the discharge of Chaka's secret weapon has hit home in a very real way, adding a palpable sense of FEAR to those who placed such high stock in our king. I am not one of them, for while I do regret the loss of a onetime friend, his slew of slipups that have

precipitated his untimely death could've been entirely avoided had he been making the right decisions regarding the Chakanian contention—determinations I'd been advising him on, in vain—from the start.

My opportunity to fill the power vacuum now come, I march along the frontlines, rallying the M-12 phalanx like a *true* leader, "Archers at the ready! Spear throwers at the secondary! All await my command! The enemy is paddling prone, so you must aim in an arc to strike their backs!"

A tremendous wave suddenly overtakes the sunken cay, cresting well over it and crashing down on the heels of the oncoming navy, issuing them forth more expeditiously across the channel.

"On your ready … !" I shout as another great comber rolls into the channel unimpeded, its face turning ominously brown as it advances. It sweeps up the assailing navy from behind, lifting them upon its darkening wall, clear up to its lofty crest. They stroke feverishly to keep up with the rogue wave, and in doing so, they draw into the range of our spear throwers.

In aiming ever higher at the amphibians rising upon the monstrous wall of water, my phalanx starts backstepping.

"Hold your line!" I order.

As the crest pitches over, the storming squids rise to their feet and begin surfing down the breaker while brandishing all manner of spears and *tawi-manus*.

"Charge!" cries Temitope from the peak as he comes plunging forth betwixt his navy, riding a big-wave gun with an immense spear fixed to its front, and then suddenly his board rises completely out of the water upon an iron blade that appears to be attached to a turtle shell gliding beneath the surface. As this undersea wing glides through the wave's subsurface, its bladelike mast, which is connected to the underside of his board, lifts his craft ever higher into the air. Temitope surfs upon this alien craft in a queer and inexplicable manner, with his shoulders squared off, his arms opened wide and

his weight shifted hard forward. *"Charge!"* he cries out again, thrusting forth a tremendous *tawi-manu* in his bony hand.

"Fire!" I command.

My frontline responds in kind with a swift volley of arrows and spears discharged on high. Our salvo takes out several enemy surfers, but most of our projectiles are deflected by their turtle shell shields or the undersides of their crafts as they surf down upon us. Meanwhile, the wave upon which they're riding is growing evermore menacing to our position, with Temitope flying out in front upon his narwhal-nosed board (a creature we are familiar with from carvings salvaged from the old shipwrecks).

"AAIIIYEEEAAH!" the retainer emits a terrible cry as he rams his narwhal spike into Soko Yun's heart, killing him instantly.

The breaker hits us before we can react further, plowing us asunder. But the rogue wave may've proven our saving grace, because the navy surfing it, when they went to strike us with their spears and *tawi-manus*, could not for the most part get a clean shot at us while we were being swept under the trough. Instead, most went riding clear over us before crash-landing downshore, from where they were dragged further toward the transept—that area of treacherous rip currents at the southern extremity of our island.

As the discombobulated squids in their heavy-laden armor struggle to regain their bearings at the southern beachhead, we, too, grapple with our own Mothersea complication, having been plowed over by the cataclysmic roller. Thankfully, we're able to retrieve our footing and begin wading ashore with our spears raised high in defense.

Alas, our foes, quicker to pull through the devastating crash, start discharging arrows and spears at us from afar. Jue Yin, trudging just beside me, gets speared through an eye and drops onto the waterline, dead.

"Shields!" I cry, then briefly wipe my eyes, for my tears fall freely over Jue Yin's demise.

Quickly calibrating, we raise our turtle shells over our heads, blocking many more projectiles that continue raining down in swift measure. And then, when the enemy runs low on throwing things, they trudge forth on foot, drawing us into close combat with their hefty *tawi-manus*.

Most of us came to the battlefront with three or four spears, while our archers convey back quivers rife with arrows. Some of our weaponry has already been discharged, while yet more has been undone by the rogue breaker, but we collectively retain arms enow to wage a fair counterattack. The challenge is in effecting the requisite distance between ourselves and our opponents to properly unfurl a clean shot. Mostly this is attained by knocking the squids back after their *tawi-manus* have become lodged into our shields, and then a swift follow-up kick is delivered, usually into the opponent's groin, sending them floundering back onto their posterior, from where we can impale them by spear or arrow from the requisite distance.

But enemy reinforcements keep arriving from their reviving southern flank, creating an asymmetrical engagement upon a shoreline increasingly encumbered by incoming waves. As we fight in ankle-deep—and frequently knee-deep—whitewater, the greatest technicality of the battle becomes the prerogative to remain steady over one's feet amid the crashing of waves while concurrently engaging in close combat, the proper ejecting of longspears and effective pulling back of bowstrings amounting to the final and most crucial test in the perilously awkward challenge. It is here, unfortunately, that our adversaries win out in the surf battle, for they only must lift their hefty *tawi-manus* high enow to drop on us again with the inherent force of the clubs' weight, regardless of any imperfections exhibited in the combatant's aim.

Temitope, after having impaled Soko with his bowsprit, leaps off the side of his board and is now coming at me with his *tawi-manu*. As he's gained the advantage of the higher side of the shore, while I'm still struggling to emerge from the intense longshore current, we go

sounding off in close combat, grunting as we strike out at each other with our implements, mine being a second spear that I've fetched from its latch at my armor's back.

"*Hi-YAA!*" *<SMASH!>*

"*AARGH!*" *<CLASH!>*

"You should never have come!" I warn, as I thrust my spearhead toward his chest—a volley he narrowly deflects.

"We've come to make peace!" he ripostes, long-arming his club hard into my shield and nearly succeeding in yanking it from my grasp as he pulls back.

I counter with a hard downward turn to my left, causing his club to release rudely from my shield, at which we go tumbling into the surf.

As we fight to recover, numerous dead bodies rolling around in the shorebreak thump heavily against us, throwing us off balance.

"Does this look like peace to you?!" I growl at the gay but lethal Temitope, whose headdress has listed sideways in the fray. As more waves separate us further, we endeavor to keep our footing in the onslaught of breakers, while all up and down the beach, our opposing armies are similarly engaged in rough shoreline combat, the blood of the wounded and dead turning the water ochre red.

"Gain the offensive!" I encourage my forces as I emerge from the shorebreak with Temitope coming after me, and then I turn my spear on him once more, forcing him back into the roiling water.

"Break their spears with your clubs!" Temitope shouts to his troops as he fumbles with his club in the surf zone.

A fin suddenly emerges, and then just ahead of it, the open jaws of a hefty bull break the surface and devour a man floundering in the water next to Temitope. Alas, the savaged victim was one of our own.

"Elevens, out of the water!" orders Fela as she attempts to command her navy who've been swept offshore, for a frenzy of bulls has come to encircle them.

"*AAAI-YEE!*" and "*GRUUGH!*" the amphibians wail in sequence as they're dragged underwater by the swarming gam—bull sharks with a bad reputation for shallow feeding. How many of those devoured are from my company, I cannot so easily ascertain in the bloody melee and pouring rain. But I do observe several more enemies getting grubbed by massive bulls further down the beach.

While prodding Temitope with my longspear to keep him pinned in the surf zone, I'm drawn downshore to where is Yang battling Ojore on the wetsands. Temitope gets swept into the transept current and taken swiftly offshore, and so I turn my full attention to Yang in action.

Yang, the great warrior emerging, grabs an arrow from his quiver, but instead of arming his bow, he drives the projectile hard up beneath Ojore's breastplate, penetrating the guardsman's gut so forcibly that his arrowhead faintly glimmers within his gawking victim's mouth.

"Behind you!" I warn, tossing my comrade a spear, for another assailant is rushing at his back with a *tawi-manu*.

As the assailant swings at Yang's head, Yang ducks into a spin and thrusts his freshly acquired spear once again into his attacker's belly. And then, while lifting his impaled victim completely off his feet, Yang stares up at his quarry through the hard-driving rain. With blood showering down over Yang's face, he widens his eyes and extrudes his neck until his jugulars are blue and pulsating, and then in a great display of vigor, he emits a terrific roar of conquering strength—a roar that ends only after his prize is released, dead off his shaft.

"*WOOO-HOO!*" I whoop, and then scream inside, *if only Tai Yun could've seen that!*—remembering well how the king regarded Yang as little more than a cocksure young imbecile.

By now, I've seen enough of Chaka's navy close up to know they're not all stalwarts of his royal guard, but include a mixed bunch of grunts from varying Meridian Islands now obliterated, most of

whom don crossed-bones pendants strung to coir chokers. In observing one such necklet on the throat of a dying other-islander, I grab the icon and demand, "Why? Why have you joined Chaka's navy? Why would you sacrifice your life for the vulgarian?"

"We—" the squid strains to reply, gargling on his own blood, "we've found God with him, and life everlasting, while you *<cough>* you shall die *<gasp>* once and forever!"

He tilts his head aside and his breathing stops. I shake my head in disbelief at his sacrifice to the tyrant's black arts beliefs, which he could only have subscribed to by threat of death. Meanwhile, in the movable drama down the beach, I've allowed Temitope to drift further out with the current, where, like his red-crowned master and the rest of his henchmen, he's destined to meet his end in the open ocean swells or the jaws of the beasties.

Alas, Yang's and my celebration is cut short by Fela, who comes sauntering before us with two sharpened staffs dripping with blood from all four ends.

We split up and slowly start circling her in opposite directions. She eyes Yang obliquely over her shoulder. I stomp my foot, momentarily distracting her, whereupon Yang thrusts his spear at her back, but she somehow deflects it.

I follow up with my own spear strike down at her calves, but she leaps over it in a whirl and swats the side of Yang's head, tossing him unconscious onto the wetsand.

The infamous warrioress turns again toward me, gyrating her staffs menacingly while extruding a fang over her lower lip in a darkly sensual way, as if she desires to eat me once I've been culled.

I take a step back, feigning retreat, and then surprise-lunge my spear into her blurring weaponry, whereupon my shaft goes flying out of my hands.

She springs over me.

I duck, raising my turtle shell shield while reaching for my hip knife with my free hand.

As she vaults over me, she beats my shield several times fast with her staffs until I'm eating the sand.

Suddenly, Yang leaps up and hooks his bow around her neck. She struggles to seize the bowstring, but he's relentless in dragging her back.

I aid in the offensive by attempting to jab my knife into her chest, but my assault lacks conviction, for with Yang standing behind her, yanking her to and fro, I'm worried I'll miss her and strike him instead. As he forces her down to the waterline, I notice he's bleeding from an ear.

All at once, a rogue wave comes cresting through the black sheets of rain, smashing o'er their shoulders and plowing into my waist. I'm able to keep my balance and stay on the beach, but they get washed into the channel with the receding whitewater. With Yang still holding Fela fast in his bow, a fin emerges behind him.

"Shark behind you!" I alert.

Fela kicks madly as Yang wrests her around, positioning her betwixt him and the shark. The bull lunges at her, biting off her head and running over Yang as he tries to duck beneath it.

The spearman quickly resurfaces, apparently unharmed, but then a much larger bull strikes from beneath, taking him by his midsection.

"*Yang!*" I cry, but to no avail, for he's dragged rudely under in a flood of blood and never seen again.

Erelong, anguished refugees from M-11 come spilling in over the sunken cay on a flotilla of paddleboards and makeshift rafts, the most prominent craft being a shipwood throne not unlike King Chaka's, but only smaller and more ungainly o'er the rough waters.

I survey the coast, and finding the enemy essentially routed, I focus again on the arriving fleet, searching for possible threats. I discover that it is Queen Sassandra seated upon the bobbing throne, which, just like her husband's indecorous watercraft, is being tossed radically about in the surf as her stand-up paddlers struggle to maintain control. As they rise upon an incoming swell, a grommet can be seen clutching on to the throne's support beams. It appears to be Princess Iniko, next in line to Princess Adeze, who perished many moons agone.

The royal float and several other makeshift flatboats carrying passengers are rolled by the waves over the sunken breakwater, scattering a flotsam of timber, bric-a-brac and floundering persons everywhere into the channel. The casualties flail their hands desperately and cry out for help. I remain unmoved by the spectacle, however, embittered at having lost most of my friends to their invasion.

A massive gray and white striped fin, taller than a full-grown man, suddenly comes careening into the channel from the north. *Okonkwo*, I utter plainly, my indifference turning to terrific fascination as I behold great wakes pushing off the leviathan's preposterous breadth. The gargantua takes aim at a young woman who is flailing helplessly in the water, picks up speed and then submerges.

In an enormous detonation, the giant strikes from beneath, swallowing the maiden whole as it lunges skyward. It torques its massive frame thrice before impacting the surface again, sending forth an explosion that seems to drain the very channel, with great, arcing waterfalls shooting aloft its flanks and sending a floodtide rushing up around the beams of the royal palace, whence a woman screams out in terror.

"*Itoro!*" I gasp.

Chapter 9
THE DEAD GHOST

Dashing up to the summer veranda, I find King Chaka holding a shark-toothed knife to the neck of Princess Nsia, while Queen Itoro cowers down under the spearhead of one of his minions.

"Where's Umukoro?!" Chaka demands of my queen.

I grab a longspear from the wall and drive it into tyrant's left eye before he can react, but as he goes cavorting back, he slices open Princess Nsia's neck.

Itoro shrieks in terror at the sight of her daughter gurgling up blood, while the minion freezes in shock at the sudden killing of his king.

I yank the spear from the minion's hands, break it over my knee and then thrust the jagged ends deep into his ears, giving the sticks a little twist. He gawks back at me in brain-scrambled terror, his eyes roll up into his head and he falls back dead.

Umukoro emerges from a chamber adjacent to behold three bloodied bodies lying on the floor and his mother slumped against a wall in a paroxysm of weeping; then suddenly, Temitope comes vaulting in through the balcony, his shoulders draped with entangled seaweed.

He appears unarmed, and so I take an appraising step forward, at which he throws his hands up in the circular gesture, pleading, "*Haa! Haa!* I beg of you, stay your vengeance! Behold our collective dead! *Haa! Haa!* Let there yet be a peaceful resolution to this madness, lest we seal our mutual demise!"

Umukoro draws closer, returning the knave's reconciliatory hand gestures while asserting, "I, too, have seen enough!"

I hold the prince back, warning, "Don't trust him! They've slaughtered your father and your beloved sister just now! They have *not* come in peace!"

"Please!" Temitope entreats while pointing fervently toward the beach. "I implore you, call off your soldiers!"

Umukoro rushes to the balcony and peers through the squall. I spy over his shoulder. On the beach below, a number of refugees are crawling out of the water, while several M-12 warriors are approaching them with weapons raised.

"Do you really intend to slaughter the innocents?" Temitope continues his diatribe. "Umukoro, you are now rightful ruler of Meridian 12. I beg of you, stay your forces and let us strike an accord this instant!"

"*Pfft!*" I mock, driving Temitope back with my spear.

"Have mercy, I prithee!" a woman screams out below.

We crane our necks over the balcony to see a refugee holding a hand out against Qi Dong, who's standing over her and swinging a *tawi-manu.* "Our island is gone, and we have nowhere else to go!" the woman cries while pressing her other hand over her bloodied thigh, which has been rent by a weapon, a shark, or both.

More noncombatant women and children are similarly cowering down before San Jiao, Jomo and the reclusive warrior Ren Mai, who's finally decided it's time to come out and defend the hamlet.

"Just do it!" I shout. "End this!"

"No! Stop!" Temitope yells down in protest, as does Umukoro, who screams out, "Don't hurt them!"

I manhandle the ignorant prince with my free arm, covering his mouth with my brawny hand. *"You fool!"* I castigate under my breath,

and then I shout down to my operatives again, *"Deg-deg!* Hurry up and execute!"

A warrior donning a coir raincoat and brandishing a silver cutlass suddenly comes rushing through the incessant rain while screaming forth a queer war cry.

"Queen Sassandra," Temitope utters in soliloquy, gaining the attention of the sobbing Queen Itoro, who draws nigh to observe the commotion below. I can't help but notice that Itoro's dress is soaked with the blood of her slain daughter, who she's been cradling in her lap.

Sassandra's zealous charge is short-lived, however, for in rushing through the cloudburst with rain in her eyes, she goes tumbling headlong into the barbs fronting San Jiao's shield.

Temitope gasps in horror as his queen is subsequently driven backward into the wetsand by San Jiao, who doesn't relinquish her downward pressure until the monarch is dead.

And so, too, Umukoro and his mother gasp at the carnage, having been bred under royal protections and unaccustomed to such hard realities.

"Remember, my lady," I remind my queen, "that Sassandra's ruthless consort killed your husband in their attempted overthrow, while Temitope here was sworn protector of King Chaka, your husband's killer!"

"Nay, my lady!" the gay knave objects. "This is a misrepresentation!"

"How dare you call my queen 'your lady'?!" I shoot back, jabbing him with my spear.

"Your Highness!" Temitope implores anew as blood issues from his shoulder. "It was Xavion and his team of sailboarders who first came to my island and killed Prince Kendi. I beg of you, order this brute to lay down his spear and release your son, the king!"

"Haa!" Umukoro cries out. I press my arm much harder over his chest, at which he bites into the web of my hand, forcing me to release him.

"You fools!" I reprimand, shaking out my hand. "Behold the tragic death of Nsia here, her life cut brutally short by King Chaka, and so I summarily dispatched that abominable man, and now his reprehensible protector and the slayer of Soko Yun and how many more of our islanders, now he stands here in the palace of our once great king, begging for reconciliation. You're being duped by the worst of the invaders!"

I go to impale Temitope. He jumps aside, narrowly evading my thrust.

"Look there!" I motion toward the beach while keeping Temitope under my spearhead. "Another M-11 urchin comes to do us injury! Is that Ekon I see, the M-11 boardshaper? How many battleboards did he craft to wage this war against us? How well did he arm the narwhal board of Temitope here, who proceeded to ram his bowsprit into the heart of my good friend, Soko Yun? And now he comes, this builder of our enemies' floating thrones and dark arts crafts, no different than the squids preceding him, to usurp us from our sovereign shore!"

Sure enow, Ekon the Strong is marching up from the south, where he was undoubtedly cast ashore with the bulk of his navy when they first attacked. He strides through the wetsand, swinging a hefty *tawi-manu* over his head, and then he screams forth a warning, "I've come to avenge Fela, my betrothed in whose life you have stolen from *me*!"

As he locks his toothy weapon with that of Ren Mai, I thrust my coup de grâce against Temitope.

Unfortunately, Umukoro intercedes once again, knocking the butt end of my spear and causing me to miss.

"Please, Xavion!" Umukoro peals. "Please just stop!"

I respond by ramming the blunt end of my shaft hard into the grommet's belly. He curls forth, clutching his stomach and wheezing heavily.

"Never surrender!" I advise the wayward grom before impaling Temitope high against a shipwood stanchion.

Taking a step back, I slowly tilt my head from side to side as I study my pinned-up victim. Blood issues from his mouth and pools on the floor with that of King Chaka and Princess Nsia, who lie nearby. Temitope's toes twitch thrice and then fall still, as he remains lifeless on the post.

Umukoro and the queen, unable to fathom the gory glory of my deed, retreat to an inner chamber. Mine is the vengeance of Nyoto, Yang Ming, Soko Yun and the king, and last but not least, Princess Nsia. Mine is the continuing reign of Meridian Twelve!

I glance over the balcony to see Ren whaling down on Ekon with a dual-coconut ball and chain.

Ekon flails his *tawi-manu* about wildly in defense, landing a lucky strike against one of the weighted coconut shells, exploding it in a blast of sand.

Ren responds in kind with his other shark-toothed ball, swinging it hard against Ekon's forehead, where it remains impaled as he falls back dead.

I'm disheartened to watch more enemy combatants come ghosting in through the downpour, threatening to surround my squad of fighters as they guard the refugees by the water.

I detract my longspear from the stanchion. The lifeless Temitope goes splashing down into his own bloodbath.

I leap blindly over the balcony, quitting the sunroom. I eject my spear as I go tumbling to a stop behind the *praetorium*. Quickly retrieving the weapon, I continue furtively around the side of the garrison, from where I intend to launch a surprise attack against the arriving combatants.

Princess Iniko, would-be queen of Meridian 11, had it not just been scuttled by the Mothersea, has come to our stormy beach to make known her rage at the demise of her mother, Queen Sassandra, and her brother, Prince Kendi (while the death of her father, King Chaka, likely remains unknown to her at this time). The lone dynast is approximately sixteen summers of age, but unlike the feckless Umukoro, she's geared for hostilities, donning a headband with

thee-quarter cheek wraps, turtle shell armor, a toothy knife in her hand and brandishing a long *tawi-manu* whose array of sharks' teeth are as profuse as the spines on an urchin's back.

Not far behind her, Kamali, protectress of Chaka's royal family (consisting now only of Princess Iniko, last of the M-11 monarchs), strides forth with bowstring drawn.

The M-12 detail manning the hostages raise their shields in precaution.

In seeing my warriors take a defensive stance, Iniko lunges at them with her *tawi-manu* while screeching out like a frenzied wisp of sandpipers, "*YIEE-YIEE-YIEEEE!*"

Ren appears intrigued by the little snipe, taking a few steps back as she charges him, even permitting her *tawi-manu* to strike against his shield, whereupon he pivots to the side and lets her go tumbling forth into the wetsand (and preventing her from falling directly into his spiked shield, as was the fate of her mother when she charged San Jiao).

Just kill her! I ejaculate mentally, as I watch the encounter from the *praetorium*.

But Ren refrains from finishing off the enemy princess, turning instead to engage her protectress, Kamali, while leaving the fate of the befuddled monarch to his fellow soldiers.

Kamali releases her arrow, but even at close range, she proves a terrible shot, for her reed shoots well over Ren's shoulder and into the waves behind.

Meanwhile, Iniko has gotten back to her feet and procured her bow, firing off an arrow at Ren's back. He spins around, and the reed goes thumping into his shield next to her *tawi-manu* still stuck there. "Restrain her!" he directs Jomo and San Jiao, and then ignoring the witless princess, he turns again to face Kamali, who's taking too long to reload her bow, and so he waltzes right up behind her and nudges his prickly shield into her posterior.

"*Ouch!*" she squeals, holding her reed flat against her rump where she'd been pricked.

Ren summarily confiscates her bow and arrow, tossing it into the surf. "Surrender your quiver," he says, "and get down there with the rest of the prisoners."

But now Princess Iniko renews her attack, launching a war of arrows against San Jiao and Jomo, who easily deflect her piddling shots with their shields—or the few that find their mark, anyway.

Now comes Bobo the farmer. Bereft of weapons and armor, he strolls across the wetsand while waving the comity gesture before him. "*Haa! Haa!*" he declares shamelessly. "I'm surrendering."

The M-12 fighters pussyfooting around with Iniko generally ignore the craven husbandman as he takes a seat beside the captives.

And then Kamali comes again at Ren with a death wish, and so as to neutralize her this time, he strikes the helve of his ball and chain against her head, knocking her unconscious, after which he starts bantering with Jomo and San Jiao as they casually deflect Iniko's cockeyed arrows.

Enough of these pleasantries! I quip and then go marching forth with spear in hand. Iniko is fresh out of arrows when I reach her, and so I cock back my longspear and take aim at her heart, but when I go to release my shaft, someone holds it back.

I spin around to see Umukoro there, once again yanking at my shaft. "You stupid boy!" I blast. "Stop screwing with me!"

"Get over there, Princess Iniko!" he dares to call around me. "Stay with the refugees!" He's taken on tougher airs, aye, but only to rescue the bonny enemy from condign execution.

I turn again to smite my quarry once and for all, but the prince rushes betwixt us, forcing me to retract my instrument of death.

"She surrenders!" he admonishes me and my fellow warriors. "No need to kill her!" He goes to confiscate her bow, at which she expectorates into his face.

I and my cadre share a guffaw, and then they move in to restrain her, seizing her weapon.

I laugh in the prince's slimed-up face. "The return on your charity, Umukoro. Why don't you just give her a knife and remove the armor from your chest?"

Ren binds Iniko's wrists to her ankles and then dumps her off with the other captives.

I promenade over to the prisoners, using my spear as a cane as I affect myself a great, seasoned leader in the manner of Tai Yun. "And what do we have here?" I quip to Bobo, who's cowering down before me, begging for mercy. As the sole male survivor from M-11, he evidently expects to be executed. I share a boorish laugh with Ren, while Umukoro regards our loutish behavior with open disdain.

"Fetch the wench," I instruct Ren while motioning back toward Kamali, who's lying face down in the wetsand.

"She's dead," he announces, when he reaches her, "suffocated in the mire."

San Jiao attempts to revive the protectress by blowing into her mouth and pressing against her chest, but is unsuccessful.

The remaining captives are relieved of any armor and weaponry, and then the adults, along with Princess Iniko, are bound together in a line of coir rope. The prisoners number nine in all: Iniko, Bobo, Adisa, three woman noncombatants and three children.

Iniko's ankle restraints are removed so that she can effectively march, while the young'uns are permitted to walk unfettered behind the chain gang. As we go plodding through the rain toward the rotunda, I observe many failing dikes and sand traps along the way. The water table has risen almost to the surface, creating widespread viscosity seeping up around the dike staves, tilting and ejecting them from terra firma.

We deliver the prisoners to the sacrificial rotunda and then free them of their binds—all save for Princess Iniko, who we tether to the central receptacle. I instruct, with stern warning, for the other captives not to release her.

As Jomo and Qi Dong keep watch, the detainees who've been injured are tended to by San Jiao. Before I go, I instruct my comrades to leave the prisoners with some drinking water and victuals, and then when they quit the rotunda, they are to put a plank before the door.

In repairing with Ren back to the beach to make sure the enemy has been well and truly routed, we pass many new sand traps and fissures created by the collapsing dikes.

"We must upgrade Tai Yun's sequestration cells and transfer the enemy combatants there as soon as possible," I tell Ren Mai.

"Aye," he agrees. "The skookum house is best. The enemy cannot be trusted and are a stain to our rotunda."

Down on the swamped beach, we swing-toss the dead out beyond the shorebreak. From there, they ghost southward with the current to the greater extent of the Mothersea, or otherwise are eaten by sharks while drifting.

Our fallen are dealt with later, when we've additional help to convey them to the quicksands of the interior. There, Shao Ying utters an incantation in honor of the illustrious Twelves who've perished, King Tai Yun foremost among them. She takes special care to direct her invocation to the Mothersea and not to terra firma expressly, because we haven't forgotten who sent us and who now seeks to reclaim us into her aqueous bosom. As she solemnly requests for our deceased to be received back by our creator, we push their bodies under the bog with our longspears.

———

It is twilight. I'm in the *praetorium*, sweeping out the seaweed in the wake of the storm.

———

Darkness falls. My comrades and I construct a bonfire on the beach with the detritus of the battle, including any and all crosses we find, such as the one monstrous cross erected on the cay opposite, before the evil symbol washed upon our shore. Our conflagration burns brightly over our convocation, but in light of all we've lost, our victory is a melancholy one.

Queen Sassandra's silver cutlass, a galleon relic that she could only have acquired via the black market, theft or murder is brought down to the assemblage, and when it is found to carry the bad omen cross worked into its pommel, we attempt to remove the helve in order to save the shimmering blade. Unable to free the silver from the handle, I toss the sword well beyond the breakers.

——

At length, I retire to my seal-gut mattress. The storm surge is receding with the tempest, and coupled with the low crescent moon tide, further concerns about the Mothersea's activity are laid to rest for the night. The island has meanwhile been fully checked for enemy in hiding, and none have been found. The only real danger we all have to sleep on is the ground itself, which has been almost completely saturated by the rain and storm surge. Qi Dong has opted to sleep in San Jiao's compound because a sandpit has formed beneath his hut, swallowing his coir flooring into its swampy maw.

My own family is long deceased, but others, such as Queen Itoro, have just lost loved ones in the bloody engagement, and so from all quarters, a general mewling issues into the night. What's of specific concern to me, as I edge toward sleep, is how M-12 might possibly move forward with Umukoro as king—an ascendency that, for the life of me, I cannot take seriously. Ever since the Meridians began to sink and war broke out, pushing down through the archipelago, I knew that Tai Yun was too retiring to assume the role of last man standing and absolute king—to say nothing of his feckless son. As

for Queen Itoro, she now requires a lord of vigor to reign over the new empire, as her mewling is ever so evident on this victorious but melancholy night.

———

Rising early, I spend the greater part of the morning helping to upgrade our holding cells, which were constructed from whale-bones and shipwood beams at the onset of the war as part of Tai Yun's Royal Code of Defense and Preservation. Once completed, we transfer the principal captives there: Princess Iniko, who technically now bears the title of queen, even though Meridian 11 is obsolete; Adisa, seer of the dark book; and Bobo the farmer, who, while a cowering simpleton, can nevertheless not be trusted due to his hailing us ashore on M-11 just prior to our ambuscade there by Chaka's royal guards.

Umukoro, who comes to the rotunda to assist with the transfer, tells Iniko, "You shall be more comfortable in our custodial apartments for the time being."

Custodial apartments?! Is he alluding to the detention facility or his private apartments?!

Regardless, the vanquished princess remains disconsolate, trudging forth with her head hung low.

While guiding Adisa by the arm behind them, I clarify: "They're cells for prisoners and little more. You shall be separated from one another and kept under close guard until we have time to adjudicate your crimes."

Bobo, who's marching out in front, twists around and bleats, "But I've committed no crime! We had nowhere else to go, but you forbid trespassers and—"

"Just keep walking, Bobo."

Chapter 10
SOVEREIGN OF THE EBB

"Prithee, my lady, forestall the coronation for the time being, at least until he has a better handle on the gravity of his responsibility."

Itoro regards me blankly from across the table, and then she lowers her head and resumes picking at her shredded crabmeat omelet.

Meanwhile, the prince, sitting catercorner betwixt us, rejoins, "I do know it's a big responsibility, Xavion, but at the same time, I don't see what difference it makes if I become king now or later. We're the last kingdom remaining in all the sky realm, and anyway the priority should be in securing our landholding against the Mothersea. While the storm has passed, I'm worried about what I've seen on the peripheries."

The queen suddenly speaks, while keeping her eyes cast down, "There's no reason for an interregnum. As firstborn son, his accession is automatic upon my husband's death. The coronation is merely a formality."

"My lady," I supplicate, "you can hear even now that he contains some of his sire's wisdom, but given the critical state of our island, it would be unbecoming to levy such a responsibility on a grommet his age. I'm only suggesting a temporary regency in which I can train him for the expanded duties of M-12, which are unprecedented in scope. Your consort was a brilliant thinker, a master statesman and a magnificent king—"

At this, the queen begins weeping, her tears flowing unchecked …

"I prithee, my lady, for your husband's sake, if we might imagine him looking upon us now, I do believe he would agree to forestall the coronation, at least until we can improve upon our physical condition."

"Physical condition?" she probes between sobs.

"Aye, my lady, fortifying terra firma against the Mothersea by maintaining our dikes, shifting great tracts of sand around, draining the water table, building new reefs and so on. We've been thrust into a new phase—an era of brawn—where the old ways of interisland diplomacy, dialogue and statecraft have become obsolete: the fate of our island now hinges upon an understanding of its structure and the strength required to modify and amend it. It is my sincere belief that Prince Umukoro shall forthwith understand this, once we apply ourselves to the undertaking, and that this tutelage will do him a great deal of good as he strengthens his body and skills to manage such operations. Then, once we've properly buttressed our landholding against our only and greatest remaining threat—the Mothersea's swelling fever—Umukoro can ascend to the throne in full procession as sovereign ruler of the sky realm."

"I suppose," the queen sighs. "It does make sense to know we have a future before allotting too much importance to the crown."

"Precisely, my lady, and in the meantime, he can assist with these projects until he feels ready to command them officially," I reply with a smile, knowing all this implies a very long time.

Umukoro all the while has been squirming restlessly in his seat, undoubtedly over the rigors I've been estimating.

"And furthermore," I tender his way, "all great kings should be big-wave surfers. Tackling large waves grows their stature, maintains their vigor and strengthens their character, especially in regard to matters requiring critical judgment. As such, I shall take you under my tutelage in Ocean Master training, even as we're transforming our island. In this way, our work will be more interesting to you as we explore the local breaks in an effort to gain a better understanding of the Mothersea's changing dynamics. In fact, surfing is part and parcel to the knowledge we require to mitigate her affront to our landholdings."

Itoro checks me by her answer, "Just mind the sharks, seigneur."

I chuckle disarmingly and cast her a kindly twinkle. "Aye, my lady. I've survived this many summers for good reason."

Only on the rarest of occasions have I been called *seigneur*, usually in jest and never by the queen, and so I'm very pleased that she regards me as something of a palace lord. *In Tai Yun's stead?* It could only be.

"That's all very well and dandy, *seigneur*," Umukoro counters insultingly, "but what exactly is happening to us here? We're the last people in the world—all the other islands have been swallowed up by the Mothersea, and now she's taken our breakwater because the corals didn't have time to bind. These storms that come, they're ever-more powerful and frequent. Our dikes are failing, and just this morning I surveyed the entire island to discover that we are, in fact, sinking. And now you talk of surfing big waves, when the arrival of such a swell may very well do us under? True, I do not feign eagerness for the crown, for I do agree that our priority should be in securing our landholdings, but the happy way in which you chirp about our future, Xavion, frankly I have a hard time believing."

"And this is why, grommet, you're not yet ready for the throne. One thing your sire had, which you have not yet developed, is the quality of surety in the face of great odds. A king must never waver, and especially not publicly, in his conviction that the kingdom shall always conquer, always prevail. But you're right: in the interval of recent summers, the storms have been arriving with greater strength and consistency. But in this I see an opportunity. Before, it used to rain for days on end, but now the rainfall comes more like squalls that hit in a heavy cloudburst and then blow over. We can work in these intervals to see where the problem areas are arising

and adjust our engineering accordingly, unlike before when, after many moons of torrential rain, the entrapment of water in certain places led to terminal erosion before we could rectify the situation. The changing weather patterns are bad, aye, but they afford this blessing of swifter intervals that we can put to our advantage. As for our barrier reef that's run afoul, summer is nigh, and so I think we should construct a new one, but be more proactive in keeping it clean of sediment."

"With what manpower?" the prince hastens a reply. "Qi Dong? Can he even swim? Ren Mai? We don't even know where he is half the time. Jomo the farmer? San Jiao? We had our chance, Xavion, but you chose war, and now instead of a village filled with an army of readymade workers, we hold a sad stockade of despairing children and prisoners. And what of our losses? The blood of my slain sister is still wet at our feet, while down on the beach, the ghost of my dead father moans upon the wind. I've no words, Xavion, except that I warned you, all of you, that we should have accepted peace with Meridian 11 when it was offered."

"With Temitope? As he charged forth upon his narwhal-nosed board, impaling Soko through the heart? Or with Chaka, as he feigned peace while concealing behind his insolent black book the weapon of your sire's death? Or maybe with his multitude of guards-men who chased us off his island, forcing Nyoto into the jaws of Okonkwo as she held her hand out to me for a sip of fresh water? Or maybe the argosy that followed, with its scores of readymade warriors on battleboards flanking their high-crowned king—maybe *they* were coming to make peace. *Haa! Haa!* Is that it, Umukoro? Is that what Temitope promised after leading the charge to our shore on his flying death craft? My boy, your naivety is showing, and while your sire in all his wisdom instigated the Royal Code of Defense to guard against such a voracious foe, ultimately saving our island, you would have us lay down our arms and be duped by the cannibal invaders straight into their boiling cauldron!"

"I am not your *boy*, Xavion, and what you fail to mention, time and time again, is how we first rejected Chaka's envoys when they came here with a plea to assist us, sending them off with a useless pile of polyps instead. And then, when they were beaten down, you went over to raid them, but lo and behold, you were received kindly by King Chaka, who offered you breakfast along with a renewed peace offering, and what did you do? You slew his firstborn son before his very eyes. No wonder, then, that he sent his navy before him as a precaution, as he came once more to try our comity, undoubtedly concealing his weapon in the event we acted with duplicity again—which we did, as my father waved him ashore with a high-circling hand before we shot arrows at our slow-approaching guest. And to say naught of your bloodlust, Xavion, which has no end. How intent you were to kill the last remaining dynast of M-11, Princess Iniko—a grom, just like me—had I not intervened. I am indeed at odds with you, brutish man, and cannot accept your methods. But that's all a foregone conclusion now that we've lost everything of value—our goodwill, most especially."

I exhale heavily and then reply amiably (in a bid to assuage his mother), "You have every right to be upset, my prince, but in all sincerity, Kendi's death was an accident, and one which I deeply regret. Mind you, they were intent on eating us, and so we had to flee, and that's when the mishap occurred. Alas, that incident more than any other precipitated this war that ended so tragically for both sides. But let us not rewrite the events of history: the Elevens' long-standing contempt for us, spurring us to instigate our Code of Defense; their severe treatment of other-islanders before us, forcing them into service or murdering them outright like they did Babacar; their duplicity, every step of the way, on trade, but most importantly, let us not forget it was they who brought this war to our shore, and not vice versa, and in the end, we prevailed against them while sparing their noncombatants and then some. And here, my prince, is the inestimable value that remains: we've indeed won at great cost, but we're

now sovereign rulers of the sky realm and shall continue to be, if only by the sheer force of our will—it's the only way."

"We're in a shitty predicament, Xavion, and you know it. You warmongers on both sides have slaughtered each other to reign over a vanishing world, and now we don't have the collective manpower left to forestall the rising Mothersea. *Touché*, old warrior. We would've been better off a federation of surfers."

With that, he eyes his mother broodingly and takes his leave.

The queen, her deadlights barren, her countenance drawn and sallow, regards me sheepishly, and then she looks down at her victuals and resumes picking at them, ever so minutely, with her seashell spoon.

"Stow your worries, my good lady," I entreat tenderly. "He'll come 'round, eventually. It's been too soon, and we're all still in shock and mourning. I'm only concerned for our future. There's a pressing need to lead our island in defense against the Mothersea, now that the threat of invaders has been quelled."

"I understand that part, Xavion, and I welcome your guidance as we transition forward," she at last makes bare her feelings. "My husband distrusted M-11 for good reason. I only wish he would've double-downed on that conviction instead of circling up a hand in a fleeting grasp at reconciliation. King Chaka has precipitated our utter ruin, and I am so, so put out."

She places her spoon gently down beside her omelet, lowers her head and trembles in a paroxysm of weeping.

I slowly but dutifully rise from my chair, stand behind her and gently squeeze her shoulders. "*My lady* …"

She places a hand over mine and responds with a snivel, "Thank you for the omelet, Xavion. I'm sorry that I've lost my appetite."

"I understand, my lady—believe me. It's the least I could do after all you've been through. Your Highness, I've brought something extra special for you."

I unfurl a sharkskin satchel over the table, revealing a small treasure of jewelries and pearls. "These were Queen Sassandra's before she threw herself upon the shield of San Jiao. I could think of none other than you that should have them, both in memory of her valor and in ours—which proved greater."

She regards the gleaming horde, plucking from it Sassandra's iconic *rivière* of rare pink pearls. Lifting the exquisite heirloom before her gullet, she suddenly twists around and throws her arms around me. "Oh, Xavion!" she quavers. "These are precious!"

I embrace her, gently rubbing her back until she erelong regains her composure and we separate. She returns the necklace to the little heap of treasures, sits up erect, wipes the tears from her cheeks with her palms and fingertips and then continues with renewed confidence, "My loyal keeper, I trust that you shall set to work right away. There's much to do ere the next storm hits. Aye, it's all too soon, I know—and you've barely had time to rest, but I honor your resilience even as we mourn. I need you now more than ever, my victor. You must rally all able-bodied islanders and take stock of our assets—see where our landholdings should first be reinforced, being especially mindful of the dikes surrounding the palace. As you know, they're failing. I shall stay here with Umukoro; we shall clean house and resume a new norm as best we can. Aye, he'll come 'round, and then he shall be crowned and you knighted Royal Steward."

"My lady," I offer with a slight bow and downward motion of my hand, "until supper."

Taking my leave, I reflect upon her words and silently opine, *A 'royal steward' I have been—the new sky empire shall require more.*

———

Another night passes with the swell dropping off southeastward with the storm. I sleep soundly in knowing that our landholdings

will have several suns to dry out, or perhaps more, now that we're transitioning into summer.

Come daybreak, I grab my longspear and quit my abode for the containment facility. This is the first time that it's kept detainees since it was initially constructed under Tai Yun's reign, and so I'm keen to make sure it's holding up as it should after our recent upgrades.

As I draw upon the skookum house, I notice Adisa standing at the bars of her cell, staring at me as if she were watching me. The sight of her looking at me blindly is something eerie, and so I continue to Bobo's cell.

The uprooted farmer is likewise staring at me from behind his bars. He signals me closer and then confides in hushed tones that he's been waiting all morning for me, or for someone who could fetch me, because he has some very important information to relay. He says he's whispering so that the other inmates won't overhear this crucial matter that only I should know about, and then he beseeches that we repair someplace more private to talk.

I ask him to wait a moment and then proceed to Iniko's enclosure, where I find her sleeping in a corner.

Returning to Bobo's cell, I undo the latch, which is situated in a block of heartwood that he cannot reach around. "Come, Bobo," I announce firmly, "you must work for me on the perimeter!"

Glancing back at Adisa, I see that she is looking in our direction, as if watching us, and so I add for effect, "Try to run, Bobo, and I shall forthwith toss you into a pit of quicksand!"

As the husbandman plods out in front of me in a great playact, I pretend to prod him forth with the butt end of my longspear, and thus we trudge along until we're well out of sight of the village.

Erelong, we arrive at the north end of the island, which has been cut massively short by the Mothersea. We turn eastward and proceed along the waterside until we come to an old shack originally constructed for salt driers. Entering the dilapidated structure, we

seat ourselves on a pair of shipwood benches obliquely facing one another, and then we alternately eye each other and the ominous view before us. Where the Mothersea has claimed North Point, she courses this way and that in an ochre morass of contrariwise currents and ephemeral whirlpools. The changeable display of perils stretches out for as far as the eye can see and appears unnavigable, no matter the pilot or watercraft. But the turbulence serves our present purpose well, for it masks our sounds with its pervasive coursing.

"You know," I remark to the husbandman somewhat despairingly, shaking my head at the runaway breach, "there used to be a surf break out there called Hen Combs—a big-wave spot that peeled off North Point in both directions, when it *was* still a point. At low tide, it was pretty hairy because it broke so far out in Okonkwo's zone, but I've surfed it many a time at high tide, and while the incoming current was sometimes a battle, there were days when it all came together, with long, glassy lefts reeling far into the lee and monstrous right peaks just plowing through the deeper water outside."

"We knew of Hen Combs," replies my hale but meek captive. "Actually, we could see it on big days with the naked eye."

"Shows you just how big it could get, eh?"

"Aye," he rejoins, then sighs, "but for localism."

"Eh?"

"No trespassing and all the rest—it seems like such a waste in retrospect, doesn't it? This would've been an epic spot for a big-wave event—a confederate game, perchance. Wouldn't you agree?"

"Aye, well, we were trying to orchestrate a competition before everything went to shit, but being the furthest island out made it difficult to land a contest venue. The Ones and Twos weren't too crazy about coming all the way out here to compete, for starters."

"Yeah, well, I would've liked to see a confederate contest here, or at some of my heavy-water gems like Moronyis, Zuberi or Akata, <sigh> if it were not for King Chaka." He shakes his head in regret. "But it's too late now—all our spots are gone forever."

"Your King Chaka," I, too, snicker in disapproval, "and the inter-island wars … *tsk-tsk-tsk*. What would you expect? We didn't accept you here, not just because your king was a swaggering blowfish and a dangerous man. We didn't accept other-islanders here because, as you can see, we simply cannot afford to. Once the Mothersea began rolling over, our landholdings were also daily diminishing, and just as you fought to keep M-1 through M-10 out of your island, we strove to keep all of them, and you, from swamping us here. The creep of war came all too soon, and so we abandoned our big-wave guns for longspears just like everyone else."

To which the husbandman retorts, "Just like everyone else? Did you view us as equals trapped in the same crab bucket? Look, I fully understand why you despised my leaders and defended yourselves against them. But my people—the color of our skin, our beliefs—you chose to erect these as meaningless divisions between us, and by that, I am truly saddened. Your judgment of the average Elevener could not have been poorer, nor more shortsighted. We were, we *are* no different than you at core; while here you've food enow for everybody and terra firma enow to sleep upon, we've been reduced to naught."

"Is this why you've brought me here, Bobo? To hear your litanies? My time is exceedingly valuable and you are trying my patience."

"Nay, nay. It's your Prince Umukoro, Xavion. Just hear me out! Late last night, he visited Princess Iniko under the cover of darkness. She had her lantern burning, and so I could distinguish his figure cast before her cell. Adisa, on my other side, was dead silent in her lockup. Was she asleep? I don't know, and I dare not ask her, for I'm intent on feigning my own ignorance of what has transpired.

"As it were, the young'uns began conversing in hushed tones, but not quietly enow o'er the dead air and slack tide to prevent my overhearing. Umukoro had come to apologize for the loss of Iniko's family, blaming your Royal Code of Defense and Preservation for

the Chakanian demise. He said that only if he'd had his way, none of this would've happened.

"Iniko responded that her name meant 'born during troubled times,' and that for as long as she could remember, she'd been unhappy on M-11. But neither was she fond of Meridian 12 because of the false rumors you spread about us being cannibals and such."

"I'm well aware of these children's recalcitrance, husbandman. Did something of substance come about from their tryst, or are you merely trying my patience?"

"You're right to call it a tryst, Xavion, because Umukoro proceeded to comment on Iniko's well-toned physique. He said he found her captivating.

"She thanked him for saving her life against you, Xavion, but she despaired at the greater turn of events, saying that her sire's discharging his secret weapon was merely an act of self-defense. *'You people are the savages!'* she raised her voice in anger.

"But then the prince, after regarding the adjacent cells warily, took a different tack, inquiring sweetly if she was hungry, to which she replied she was, having had grown tired of the worms, grubs and seaweeds we've been fed.

"The prince then departed, clandestinely without a lantern, only to return a short while later with some sea turtle eggs, avouching he saved them from his supper in the event she should like them.

"In reply, the princess openly mused about how she wears sea-turtle shell armor, but does not know how to swim."

"Is this such grave information, husbandman?" I snap. "It is of little import to me—I already know the prince is fond of her. Perhaps you're just trying to leverage the favor of your release by feeding me with these saccharine stories."

"Nay, Xavion—just hear me out! Along with the eggs, Umukoro gave her the *rivière* that had belonged to her mother, saying you gifted it to Queen Itoro, but that the heirloom should instead be bequeathed to Sassandra's only remaining progeny.

"Iniko answered that she intends to conceal the pearls within her armor and that she shall forthwith return the favor by gifting the prince her gold cross necklace, which she said was given to her by her older sister, onetime princess Adeze. She explained that the M-12 authority has been wrong about the cross the whole time, for it is a magic talisman of good that brings everlasting life. She then reached out and placed the necklace over Umukoro's head, and in tying the cord behind his neck, she drew them close together and delivered a kiss upon his quavering lips.

"In return, the prince promised an even greater tiding: the intention to make her queen of Meridian 12. At that, he took his leave, and as he stole away into the night, I could see him reaching up to untie his new necklace—in order to keep the whole escapade a secret, of course."

"*Haa, haa,* Bobo, I see, I see—this is news indeed. Now tell me, why are you revealing this to me, your sworn enemy?"

"Nay, Xavion." Bobo frowns, shaking his head in regret. "I told you already: you're not my sworn enemy. M-12 was the sworn enemy of the Chakas, but not mine enemy, nor were you the sworn enemy of the majority of my fellow islanders. King Chaka treated us badly, you see, as did his feather-bed daughter. Let me tell you, I brought them the best foods on the island and toiled in my labors, but I and my family—we were never rewarded for it, but were merely indentured servants like most everyone else who were not close to the royal family. And while the princess is right about the cross—and you wrong—my belief in it is not enow to suffer any further from her family's legacy. They placed themselves above Jesus Christ, you see—the undead one from the black book in whom they preached. But while Jesus Christ was said to be a benevolent Lord and King, the Chakas were harsh and mean and kept us under strict control. We had to be mindful not to walk in the king's shadow, lest we get struck over the head by Fela or Temitope for doing so. And then

when war broke out across the archipelago, surfing was prohibited to everyone except for the royal family."

"Aye, Bobo, we had that same rule here, only Tai Yun rarely surfed. He said he had more important things to do, but I think he'd just grown weak from lack of practice."

"Is that so? But let me tell you, my friend, I shall obey the Chakas no more and am glad to witness their demise. I cannot see any good that will come of Umukoro's momentous promise to that little wench last night and would far prefer to live under your rule than that of Queen Iniko."

"My rule?"

He regards me smugly. "To think these spoiled children would usurp Queen Itoro and reign in her and Tai Yun's stead is as absurd to me as it is frightening. I wish not to return to the hardscrabble subservience of M-11, knowing the freedoms your king has long provided your people—freedoms I believe you, as his dutiful royal protector, will continue to honor. But beyond that, the pressing needs here to fortify your landholding against the Mothersea are clearly not in the capacity of these mischievous grommets to properly dictate."

"Aye, Bobo—in all these things you are correct! *Haa! Haa!* And you are right, that we must keep these matters an utmost secret until I can confirm the weight of their bearing. While I trust in your report, you best pray, for your own sake, that you're not lying, for if you are, I shall deposit you into a sand trap forthwith!"

"No need for that, old friend. My concern for M-12 is wholly aligned with yours. But we must be extremely careful of these little imposters. By right of succession, they may yet strike a bid at sudden power."

"Aye, well, until now I've forestalled the prince's ascension, for even I, retainer of the royal family, recognize its profound folly. But tell me, what of Adisa and the others? Are there any more threats harboring among the refugees, or are the remainder composed only of these long-oppressed commoners you speak of? Surely, Adisa is close to the House of Chakinian, aye?"

"Our survivors, including Adisa, are all good people—all save for the cosseted princess. I only ask that you try to tolerate our beliefs, and Adisa, well … she can be particularly eccentric at times. You know how seers are. But she's harmless."

"Yeah." I chuckle, "I know what you mean."

"But you'll find that we wish to live here in peace and are more than eager to help grow your landholdings. It is only Iniko and her secret entente with Umukoro that pose a significant danger—both now and for all future. She hails from a family who demand obedience by threat of sword, unlike here where good counsel reigns supreme. I do not see her accepting the M-12 authority—on the contrary, she shall seek to thwart it by marrying Umukoro."

"*Haa, haa*, Bobo, your argument is compelling. I shall investigate further. For now, I shall convey you back to your cell—after you've done me this great deal of manual labor, as it were."

"Aye, my good captor, and I shall feign exhaustion."

"Worry not, good husbandman. To your cell, I shall deliver fresh crabs and seaweeds, but to Iniko, I shall send expired sea slugs."

He regards me with a shit-eating grin, and then we repair to the village in our well-practiced playact.

———

After depositing Bobo at the skookum house, I continue down to the windward *praetorium* where a meeting is scheduled regarding the new coralworks initiative. Those slated to be on the project greet me at the garrison. As we begin to formally assemble, Umukoro and Shao Ying suddenly enter, garnering our attention.

The oracle wears a tiger-striped, sharkskin skirt and white scallop shells over her breasts, and her hair is braided to match the ridge

patterns of her double-mollusk top. She continues down to the water and fills her divining conch before returning to the *praetorium*.

The floor is already moist on account of the elevated water table seeping up though the sand, but nonetheless, the comely sibyl utters an incantation, humbly beseeching the Mothersea to grant us a sign, and then she pours the seawater from her conch in a slow, even stream that penetrates cleanly into the wetsand, boring a little hole. Suddenly, a great swath of sand collapses around the hole, followed by a rapid welling of water up into the sand trap.

Those around me gasp at the cataclysm in miniature, and then the oracle relays the bleak portent, "The Mothersea has augured continued misfortune in the sky realm. Long ago, she sent us up from the water, but she's since changed her mind and wants us back. Queen Itoro has fallen ill, and so I shall continue making sacrifices in her stead at the leeward *praetorium*."

"What exactly have you seen?" asks Umukoro.

The oracle raises her voice in a low monotone, "Everyone should clean and press their proudest rotunda attire and prepare to fuse with the Mothersea in a great hecatomb."

"What?"

"Reintegration, my prince. We shall erelong be returning to the Mothersea."

As the garrison erupts into a commotion, Umukoro falls to his knees, squeezing wetsand out between his fingers while bemoaning, "*No, no, no ...*"

As the oracle saunters out, the befuddled prince launches into a mumbling jeremiad against her vision quest, ending with the words "I'm going to consult with Adisa, seer of the sky realm."

"No!" I warn, but he's already fled the garrison.

The assemblage, with myself at the lead, chases after him. As he hastens past Shao Ying, I warn ahead, "He's going to consult with Adisa, the witch!"

On hearing this, the oracle grips her sharkskin skirt in thick folds, lifting the garment knee-for-knee, as she tries to move more expeditiously behind him.

When we reach Adisa's cell, Umukoro's already asked her a question.

The dreadlocked mystic of the dark arts, her eyes pointing in slightly different directions as she gazes out blindly from behind her whalebone bars, responds to the prince, "Aye, so ye 'ave at last come ta ye senses, 'ave ye? Der be a savior named Jesus dat come, risen from da dead he walk an' lift yer soul from da sinkin' ground an' drownin' sea all 'round, yea. And all ye here—ye dat nay believe—ye shalt be cast into da sea fer nay takin' up da cross in Jesus's name. Da Modersea be a sick an' cruel 'un ta take ye back wen da sky realm be so close at hand. Hold ta da golden cross, yea, an' ye shall be lifted ta life eternal wid Jesus an' his sire up in da heavens above we's."

Shao flounces up to the bars, releases the folds of her skirt and points sharply down at the sorceress of dark arts, upbraiding her thus, "And where is this zombie who shall convey us skyward?! Where is his flying craft? We weren't made with wings!"

"An' nay we's made wid flippers, lass. 'Ave we's be ben breedin' wader, me lady? Eh-eh? Nay, we's be destined fer da heavens above we's. Da Modersea be a lovesick dam, she be. She wen gone cull ye like all da oder-islanders before we's. She be a false moder, mateys. Our true fader be up der in da sky realm, we's knows it by da air we's bredin', eh? Jesus wen come an' lead da way."

"Charlatan!" scathes the blond sibyl. "Fake, blind seer! How dare you speak such blasphemy here! The end of the sky realm has been a long time coming! We've no future here and must prepare for reintegration with the Mothersea! It is our Destiny!"

"Den go an' get preparin' fer yer eternal dead, ye's. Only Jesus Christ given eternal salvation, yea."

"You lying witch!" Shao shoots back. "You abominable cannibal! You won't trick us into eating the flesh of your zombie Jesus or

anybody else! Your ways have shamed and angered the Mothersea, leaving her little choice but to withdraw her sky realm foothold and pull us back into the undersea in chastisement. While we've been here, dutifully making hen sacrifices and following her *every* indication!—*every* augury in the sand!—you and your bloodthirsty king have been over there preparing concoctions of dainty little crackers from the flesh of dead men and drinking their blood from a single conch as instructed by your vile black book!"

The quarrel between the oracles grows nastier by the interval, while Umukoro stands practically between them, regarding them with an air of shock. Massively frustrated and apparently not knowing who, or what, to believe, he calls out, "Ren Mai!? Ren Mai!?" while looking this way and that for the reclusive warrior.

"What is it, Umukoro?" implores Jomo. "Why do you seek Ren Mai?"

"I want to know what he believes! Where does he go? Why is he never here? Maybe he's found a way out, like a giant crab hole through which he escapes. Ren Mai?! *Ren Mai?!*" The befuddled grommet goes running off in the direction of North Point, clearly at his ends.

"Be careful up there!" I shout to him and then command the rest, "Everyone! Back to the garrison! We must hem out the details of the new reef project, as we were about to do before the prince launched this pointless interruption."

———

The meeting in the garrison proves promising. While our register of Ocean Masters has been reduced to just Ren and myself, we've a robust team of secondary operatives to assist with the replant effort, which shall commence as soon as the leeward *praetorium* is resupplied. I know that, in due time, Bobo and Umukoro can also join the extraction effort. Bobo's a good seeder, and Umukoro, while presently acting like a typical grommet, is a capable enough waterman.

Unfortunately, Umukoro makes a further show of his rebelliousness by going surfing in plain view of the meeting. Surfing the subpar, knee-high peaks equates to an utter mockery of the importance of our coral restoration forum. However, I know that he's genuinely put out by the quarrel between the visionaries and is merely trying to blow off steam. Without a doubt, Shao Ying can be a doomsayer of a sibyl, but her visions are not always accurate, especially when others employ a concerted effort toward a contrary outcome. As for Umukoro's supposed tryst with Iniko, if it turns out to be true, it will not be difficult for me to end.

———

The details of the project now set, I repair to the royal residence to brief the queen and check on her condition. Not finding her in the summer veranda, I call out, "My lady?"

San Jiao approaches from the door leading to the private apartments and informs, "The queen has taken ill, and I'm tending to her in her chamber. She asks that you wait here an interval."

"Of what manner of ailment does she suffer?"

"Overmuch trauma these recent days, I would say. But her heartache is accompanied by a very real fever. I prithee, stay an interval— she wants to see you when she's ready."

"As you were," I offer with a nod.

The boardshaper repairs back to the penetralium.

At length, I'm conveyed to Her Majesty's chamber, where I find her propped up against the headboard of her canopy bed, half-sheltered behind a curtain of rare red silk hanging from the bedposts. She asks San Jiao to fetch some warm seawater, affording us an interval of privacy.

"Xavion," she weakly impetrates, raising a limp hand, "I prithee, come forth."

I draw unto the edge of her featherbed and sit askew of her, and then while taking her hand in mine, I offer tenderly, "My lady, I did myself the honor of calling at the soonest opportunity."

She's but a sallow shadow of the monarch I'd known just yesterday, with sucked-in cheeks and dark rings encircling her eyes, her very orbs having lost their luster. A strip of cloth, wet with sweat, rests upon her forehead, while the downy pillow set behind her is further dampened by her fevering.

"My lady, upon hearing you were off-color I have come forthwith after the coral reef meeting. Have you a fever?"

"I have indeed fallen into disposition, my marrow, *<wheeze!>* but I'm glad you've come. How *<cough!>* *<cough!>* how's the project going?"

"My lady, I see that your chalice is empty. I must fetch more water."

"Aye, Xavion, my throat is sore, *<cough!>* but no need—San Jiao is tending to that."

"Your Highness, I am duly troubled to see you like this. You must continue your repose, and you mustn't hesitate to call on me if you need anything at all."

She squeezes my hand. "I shall, Xavion, thank you for your concern. It *<hack!>* it is dear to me."

After a pause in which I know it is difficult for her to continue speaking, I inform her that the reef project shall commence first thing on the morrow and that those not participating have been assigned to replant the dikes, first around the royal residence and then around the greater hamlet.

She wagers a half-smile, replying, "Thank *<cough!>* thank you for taking care of that, Xavion. I must vouch *<cough!>* vouchsafe that I've grown exceedingly dispirited in recent days, and *<hack!>* today

especially, when I discovered that the *rivière* you'd gifted me has gone *<cough!>* gone missing."

"My lady!" I squeeze her hand more fervently. "What do you mean 'gone missing'? Has it been stolen or merely misplaced?"

"I—I must've misplaced it *<cough!>*. There's only been me and Umukoro here and San Jiao. They *<cough!>* *<hack!>* they've looked everywhere but *<kerrupth!>* but cannot find it."

Her cough grows nigh uncontrollable, and she seems to be having difficulty breathing. I rise and call out, "San Jiao! Water, please!"

"I'll—I'll be okay," Itoro bids stoically as she struggles to maintain her composure amid the repetitive hack swelling up in her bosom.

At last, San Jiao rushes in to tend to her.

I end with the promise, "I know it pains you to make voice, my lady, so I prithee, remain silent and fret not upon these things in which we've spoken. I shall erelong conduct a search and return that which I've gifted you. You have my steadfast word."

She brings my hand to her heart while circling her free hand betwixt us, which is the deepest gesture of solidarity, and so I circle my free hand betwixt us, as well.

I tenderly break away and then offer a nod in conjunction with a downward swing of my hand, from my forehead toward the floor, in a curtsy befitting of good men before royalty. "Until then, my lady."

———

With a knowing nod, Bobo alerts me that Iniko has fallen asleep. I nod back and then proceed to the princess's cell and quietly undo the latch. With strong arms and swift movements, I cover her mouth and snatch her. She kicks and tries to scream, but I hold a death grip over her lips with my good hand—a clutch too powerful for her to even nibble. Only when I reach the cleaved North Point do I release my clasp, whence she screams out for help.

"Shout all you want," I laugh. "Nobody can hear you over the great sweep of the Mothersea!"

I fondle around her breast armor and, after a time, find my prize concealed beneath one of her shoulder straps, tucked away in a padded sheath meant for an arrowhead. "And what have we here?" I feign surprise, wresting out the *rivière*.

"King Umukoro gave me that!"

"*King* Umukoro?" I shake my head.

I lift her over my shoulder, proceed down to the waterline and deposit her onto the prince's new shortboard that I've prepositioned there.

"What do you think you're doing?!" she squeals. "I can't swim!"

"Who said anything about swimming? Or does the pampered princess not even know how to paddle a surfboard?" I laugh as I cast her off into eddies, which are flowing swiftly seaward with the dropping tide.

She tries to paddle the thruster through the turbulence but gets tossed off the side, from where she continues to grasp the rail in desperate measure as she flounders out into the darkness. "*Umukoro! Help me, King Umukoro!*" she screams forth from the blackness.

"The prince is asleep!" I holler back. "But say hello to Okonkwo!"

She vanishes with the last of her falsehoods into the void.

Chapter 11
OVER THE SUNRISE HORIZON

The sunrise casts a gleaming path o'er the tawny water and into the leeward *praetorium*, where I, Ren, and others on the new replant project are gathered to assemble our equipage.

Umukoro comes rushing in without warning, nearly impaling his foot on an anti-shark skewer lying in the sand. "Where's Iniko?!" he demands, looking at me. "What have you done with her?!"

"What?" I muse. "Where hath she gone?"

He draws closer, and so I extrude my burly biceps, checking his advance. The extraction team has meanwhile stopped what they're doing to watch the exchange.

"Adisa said you kidnapped Iniko late last night!" he accuses me directly.

"A blind woman told you that?" I laugh.

"Aye, the princess is gone! What have you done with her, Xavion? You must tell me at once!"

"Very well, Umukoro, I've nothing to hide, but perhaps you do? Your deceiving princess was caught stealing your mother's most prized jewelries, and so acting as royal protector, I banished the marauding thief."

"Banished?! Alone?!"

"By watercraft, aye."

"But she can't swim! Where did you do this? And you lie that she stole my mother's jewelries! How could she? She's been locked up in a cell!"

"Aye, and so the truth comes out: why did *you* take the pearls that I gifted your infirm mother and return them to the enemy?"

The assemblage murmurs with confusion, and so I seize upon their concern, adding, "What are you trying to do here, Umukoro? Undermine our rule by consorting with a foreign dynast?"

"Keep away from my mother, you monster!" he snaps. "How long ago did you force Iniko off and where?!"

I close my eyes and rub my temples histrionically, as if trying to remember, at length answering, "I don't know, it was sometime late at night, I guess. I pushed her off North Point, I think. Now behold what we're doing here, wayward prince, while you went surfing during the planning of this crucial project. We're fighting for our survival, while you've been fornicating with an enemy thief. The time for decisive actions has come, but you continually prove yourself unfit and unworthy to assume the mantle of king. As such, *I* am pressing ahead with the pivotal matters of our island, and if a prisoner of war goes around thieving, so be it—I shall toss her forthwith into the sea!"

He clenches his fists and casts a black look upon me and the assembly. But my fellow Twelves remain behind me, unwavering.

"You're monsters—all of you!" he scathes and then goes bolting out of the *praetorium* in a northbound heading, calling out the princess's name all the while.

With the momentous exchange still fresh, I procure the *rivière* and parade it before the others. As they vie for a closer look, I hold the necklace up high, remarking, "Observe the lovely pinks, the rarest gems in all the Mothersea! You can dive ten board lengths and still not find them."

The assemblage soughs in astonishment.

"I shall now return this lovely bijou back to its rightful owner, Queen Itoro, but shall return shortly."

———

I deliver the necklace to the bedridden queen, telling her that it was stolen by the enemy princess, after which I check on the dike replantation effort surrounding the palace.

Umukoro suddenly comes sprinting through the village. He stops abruptly before me, and bracing himself over his knees while panting heavily, he strains to speak, "As king <*gasp!*> I shall have you <*wheeze!*> locked up for insubordination!"

I glance up at the palace and then answer in a low tone so that only he and those working around us would hear, "Keep your voice down, reckless one—your mother is unwell. You're yet too young to know what you speak. Imagine! To immure your family's loyal protector and strongest warrior!"

"You—you shall pay for this!" he stutters indignantly.

"Is that so? Show everyone the cannibal cross, grommet—the one that Iniko gave you to wear."

The bystanders gasp.

"Aye," I continue, "show us how you've been corrupted by the M-11 belief. Reveal all the saucy details, wayward prince, about you and King Chaka's daughter, who seeks to dupe you into marrying her so that she can convert us all into crackers for her and your future young'uns' consumption, just as she'd been weaned."

The workers recoil in revulsion and then start casting aspersions down upon the prince, saying things like, "*How could you be so gullible?*" and "*What would your sire say?*"

But the indignant grom has a retort of his own, proclaiming, "Xavion is trying to woo my mother to usurp me as king!"

The crowd is equally as roused by his claim, but in censure of it, iterating that it cannot be true and ultimately backing me—longtime protector of the M-12 monarchy.

Umukoro turns away, shaking his head in anger and disappointment. It goes without saying, our relationship is irreparably strained.

———

Since my dispute with the prince two days ere, the swells have returned from the west and are growing larger by the interval, and in looking out over the summer veranda, I can see why: a black wall is climbing the sunbed horizon, portending a great storm on the rise. Meanwhile the water table has swollen so high that the villagers trudge ankle-deep through brackish water—a reservoir now covering most of the island. The reef transplant project has been suspended as we work day and night to reinforce our dikes, which are failing to bind to the porous wetsand, even as we plant them. New sand traps are everywhere opening, and these quickly flood, becoming quicksand, leaving only a few principal byways safe for crossing. To make matters worse, word arrives that the rotunda must be evacuated of its refugees, for it is sinking and water is invading its interior.

After wading through the village, I reach the rotunda to find the entrance sunken beneath the floodwater and the undersand beneath. Nightmarish screams reverberate from within the shipwood cupola, and in the horrifying chorus, I can distinguish the cry of Qi Dong, who's become trapped inside the dome alongside the refugees.

I send Ren to fetch San Jiao's axe and then wait atop the cupola for his return. A woman and a child, who managed to escape the edifice prior to my arrival, sit next to me while clinging to one another fearfully.

After a long interval passes without Ren Mai's returning, the building succumbs to a sinkhole—there's no other way to explain the speed with which it submerges, once it falters. As it descends, a fervent banging sounds beneath our seats accompanied by a cacophony of high-pitched screaming. Pressurized air whistles out through the

dome's minute cracks followed by the report of numerous muffled detonations, and then only silence.

I grow nauseous, for by the sound of it, it appears as if a massive increase of air pressure within the dome, as it was submerging, exploded the heads of those trapped inside.

Our cause now lost, I slip down into the inundation with the sole surviving young'un seated over my shoulders. I take his matron's hand and convey them back to the royal palace, depositing them on the steps leading to the summer veranda. I yank a board display down from a wall post and then launch myself o'er the flooded surface of the island.

Arriving at the skookum house, I find Bobo and Adisa trapped at the tops of their cells. I instruct the husbandman to hold my board firmly through his whalebone rafters so that we shan't lose the craft, and then I dive down and unlatch his gate.

Resurfacing over the containment cells, I tell the farmer that his barrier is now open, at which he takes a breath and dives, emerging beside me a short interval later. I instruct him to stay with the board so that I can fetch Adisa, who requires me to physically swim her out of her entrapment.

Once freed, we place the sightless sorceress atop the board and convey her back to the palace.

The summer veranda has become the final fallback with the remaining survivors gathered there, all save for Ren Mai, who has disappeared, no one knows where.

Sheltering in the sunroom, we watch the ocean rise in ever-recurring waves, until the swells begin scraping the underside of the second-story floor upon which we take harbor. The sky lowers menacingly with darkly churning clouds, and erelong a steady rain begins to fall.

Our position in the summer room growing dire, I band together with San Jiao and several other able-bodied persons to transport all

manner of paddleboards and other essential voyaging supplies from her compound back to the palace.

When we return, a cloudburst strikes as we're making final preparations, sending waves into the sunroom unimpeded until, alas, the palace begins to falter. We make a haphazard attempt at finalizing our escape flotilla, lashing boards together and supplying them as best as we can before casting rudely off with the remaining survivors. No sooner than we push off from the second floor does the edifice collapse in the Mothersea's overload.

We're scudded eastward with the violent surge sweeping over the island, immersing it in its totality. I endeavor to pilot the flotilla while towing the infirm queen on a float tethered behind my board. San Jiao is navigating a battleboard beside the queen, and beside her, her husband Jomo is prone paddling a big-wave gun. Bobo, Adisa, Umukoro, Shao Ying, and the two survivors from the dome round out our escape party of ten.

Stripped down to my loincloth, my formidable iron blade strapped fast to my side, I intend to survive this ordeal as best as I can. The Mothersea has put us out, aye, but the leader in me refuses to capitulate and instead regards this as my greatest test. There's long been a myth in the Meridians—a legend of a thirteenth island, far to sunrise. Nobody's ever seen it, and the few who went searching for it never returned. But it was on one of the maps in a shipwrecked galleon, if tales of yore hold any merit.

I'm an opportunist no different from the Mothersea and never wince at the threat of death, for it is in these moments that I feel truly alive. I accept her challenge, without reservation, in conveying as many survivors as I can o'er the sunrise horizon.

———

After a half-day's scudding in the storm, the rollers surging ever higher, we encounter a viscous herd of bulls. Jomo is taken when a

beastie jaws into his legs and drags him off the tail of his board. I'm unable to intervene with my knife because he's several board lengths abeam when the event transpires, and it's over quickly.

Even as San Jiao is wailing over the loss of her husband, the last refugee grommet is swallowed by a bull shark directly from his board, which is lashed alongside the infirm queen's craft. While I'm taken aback by the ferocity of these events, the queen is put into a state of immutable shock. I attempt to console her, but she just stares silently back at me, as if through me. I'm left with little choice but to lash her to the middle of her craft where she will be more secure, and then I retrieve Shao Ying and sit her squarely beside the disabled queen as an attendant.

"Hold tight!" I cry as I plow ahead o'er the surging seas, towing the improvised scow behind my stand-up towboard while leading the remainder of the flotilla away from the feeding frenzy. Umukoro and San Jiao are flanking my either side on battleboards, while behind the queen's scow, Bobo is towing Adisa. The last refugee woman cannot be found. She must have fallen overboard.

———

Our first day at sea has been long and arduous, and as the sky turns gray in the gloaming, we find ourselves numbering only three: Shao Ying, Umukoro, and me. Bobo and Adisa drowned when they were hit by a rogue breaker and became entangled in their tow rope, while the good Queen Itoro at last succumbed to the overflowing Mothersea, even as Shao Ying propped Her Majesty's head upon her lap in an effort to keep the water from Her Highness's face. Sadly, San Jiao has also been taken by the Mothersea, having become separated from us and completely disappearing.

Umukoro and I mourn over his mother amid the towering seas, and then with utter dismay, I free her legs from the timbers and inform the others that we must return her to the Mothersea. While

holding her by her neck in the water, my fingertips playing upon the *rivière* I'd gifted her, I let Umukoro hug her one last time. Shao Ying utters an obsecration for her safe passage beneath, and then we consign the good Queen Itoro to the deep.

While Umukoro's deeply pained by his mother's passing, I cannot help but castigate him, "And to think you went surfing while we were endeavoring to build a new reef! Behold what remains of your rebelliousness! An ocean of waves, waves of oceans! Here you shall catch your last breaker, Umukoro!"

He regards me tearfully in the rain.

Realizing that my ire shall get us nowhere, I tell him to resume paddling alongside me so that we can keep what remains of our fleet properly righted in the waves that are now hitting us broadside.

———

In the last wink of twilight, Shao Ying, still sitting behind me on the raft I'm towing, peers over the timberheads, looking at her waning reflection in the water.

"Get to center!" I shout back, for her action is causing the craft to list.

"The sign is here," she utters, barely audibly. "We now return to the Mothersea to be reborn as turtles, sharks, seals, or whatever we shall be, each according to our natures."

"*No!*" I cry as she plunges headlong into the water, but ultimately, I honor her final word and don't dive in after her.

Umukoro, meanwhile, has procured from a compartment within his battleboard the gold cross necklace that Iniko had gifted him, and dangling the icon before his eyes, he prays aloud for our salvation.

I paddle vehemently toward him, turning my tow raft about, and then snatch the necklace from his clutches and throw it into the water. "Now I know why the sharks have been eating us, imbecile!"

My curse falls on deaf ears, however, for he's already diving for the icon, whose cord of coir is slowing its descent.

To my great disappointment, he emerges on the other side of his battleboard with the cross and remains there where it is more difficult to reach him.

"Away with that evil thing!" I condemn.

"No, Xavion!" he counters with anguished voice. "It was given to me by the girl that you cruelly murdered! What's happened to you, Uncle X? Why have you grown so mean? I used to look up to you, but now you terrify me. This is all I have now, this belief in a greater man than you—a man named Jesus, a kind and forgiving man who seeks to save me, because you've let me down. This memento is all I have, and I keep it as a reminder of what separates you from me."

I shake my head angrily and dejectedly. "How can you say that I've let you down? I've guarded and protected you ever since you were a wee little one, and I'm saving you even now! And where is this Jesus, anyway? Is he here, like me, paddling incessantly while battling all manner of calamities upon the Mothersea? I've always wanted only what's best for you, Umukoro, and it pains me that you've been so denying of me and my mentorship."

"You said you'd teach me to surf big waves, Xavion, but in the end, you've sought only to teach me to hate."

"Don't say such things, wayward prince, for you know not what you speak. You can see out here, when all else is lost, the way of the warrior prevails. We're the last survivors of M-12 for good reason, and if you'd just trust in my guidance, I shall yet see us through this!"

"All hope is lost, Xavion. We must pray for salvation from Jesus Christ and let him guide us." He jerry-rigs his battleboard next to me, to the raft I'm towing behind, as if he intends to assist in my duty.

I shake my head in disappointment and jaw my lip in frustration. "Damn if I let the demon powers assist me! Belay such notions and drop that omen you carry, boy! Get on the scow behind me, and I

shall convey you forward. You're crazy from weakness. It's getting dark, and you need to rest. There's another island out here—there must be! Where do the coconuts come from, if not the Meridians? And what of the map once seen by your sire—the galleon map with the thirteenth island? We're not alone in the world, Umukoro— there *must* be others out there like us, and you still have me, if only you'd be a good disciple and do as I say!"

"I'm keeping my cross."

"You're getting on the raft."

"Not without my cross."

"Then go find another board, you snake!"

The dimwitted grom tightens his pendant cord around his neck until it's nigh choking him, and then he unfastens his battleboard and starts paddling away, into the night.

I shake my head, deciding to let him go, and then with my paddle, I fling his towboard back onto the raft.

Gauging from the primary swell direction, I regain an eastward bearing, and sure enow, the prince is not long in returning a few board lengths abeam. The only reason he's able to stay abreast is because I'm still towing the makeshift scow on account of much needed supplies lashed over its foredeck and stashed away in its aggregate compartments.

———

After a long night of voyaging, the prince passes out over his battleboard, and so I lash him to my carry-raft and tie his board abeam. The swells have long since stopped breaking at their crests, but are still high and heaving, and as such, I'm unable to remove his choker amid the vaulting seas. My fingers are deeply pruned, and I simply cannot undo the cord he's tied so tightly around his neck, while using my knife would be too dangerous. The pendant itself is held fast to the coir rope by an iron loop that appears to have been

melded shut without a breach from where to sever it. What's worse, the cross has sharp edges, nigh cutting my fingertips when handled; even Umukoro's neck is showing signs of abrasion. I'm only choking him further with my futile attempts, and so I decide to let it rest.

Erelong, I, too, lose all strength, and as I begin nodding out, I make a final effort back to the scow, lie down beside the prince and wrap my arm through a stowage loop. Not a moment later, I pass out.

Chapter 12
NEW SKY KINGDOM

I'm awakened by a blinding light backed by a reverberant roar and a great downdraft of air.

"Xavion!" Umukoro screams, kicking madly as he's lifted into the light, and then suddenly I'm surrounded by alien men wearing white helmets with red flashing lights and yellow plastic visors drawn before their faces. They force me into a harness, the sudden shock of the happening and my own weakness rendering me a puppet at their control, and then I'm hoisted swiftly up into the side of a great, hovering bird whose wings whirl overhead in a circular blur. As if in a nightmare, the sky people convey us in their whirlybird deep into the night. I shudder at their every movement as I try to comprehend their advanced technology and intention. They offer what looks like a plastic bottle full of water, and seeing Umukoro quaffing it, I wrest it from his clutches and eject it from the skyship.

"They'll poison you!" I scold.

Two alien men seated in front are manhandling short staffs betwixt their legs while pressing sundry pukas before them that emit colorful lights and strange sounds when touched.

<Bleep!-Bleep!-Bleep!> <Blip!> sounds their skycraft under the deafening roar of its wings as the aliens shout at one another, saying things the prince and I don't understand …

"It's a miracle we found them in these seas!" one calls out.

"Even more of a miracle they survived!" cries another.

<Scratch!> <Bleep!>

"By God's grace!" a third hollers. "It's a good thing we didn't wait for the government to act while they sat on their hands in endless debate!"

<Bleep!> <Blip!> <Scratch!> sounds the interior of the skyship.

An alien seated in front grabs what looks like a conch attached to a cord and starts yapping into it, "Two natives from the no-contact tribes have been successfully extracted! *<Scratch!>* They were found floating on rafts about forty kilometers southeast of the sunken islands! Returning to base! ETA forty-five minutes!" *<Scratch!-Bleeeep!>*

Umukoro and I are given soft coverings by a female alien who speaks to us in what sounds like a different tongue from the others, but still we have no idea what she is saying, such as when she vociferates, "We're an islands mission NGO! Congratulations! You've just been saved!"

"They can't understand you!" another alien shouts. "What you gonna to tell them next?! *<Bleep!-Blip!-Bleep!>* All about global warming?"

The female continues to us, "I know you cannot understand me! But know that you've been rescued! *<Blip!-Blip! Bleep!>* By good Christians with deep pockets! And while we've been prohibited from contacting your islands directly, now that they've all sunken *<Bleep!> <Blip!>* you'll soon prove to the world that our search and rescue mission was not only legal but was the right thing to do! The *Christian* thing to do!" *<Scraaaatch!>*

"Tell them they have my apology!" a male-sounding one yells back from the front. "Modern man and his pollution is a crying shame! But our crew here *<Screech!-Scratch!>* *<Bleep!>* we're all good! We work through the hands of God *<Blip!>* and have lifted you up into his kingdom!" *<Bleeeep!>*

The female hovering over us suddenly takes notice of Umukoro's gold cross pendant, and her eyes grow wide with fascination. It had shifted behind his hair, and so she repositions it to his front, but not before nipping a fingertip on one of its edges. "Where'd you get this?!" she vociferates while sucking on her bloodied finger like the cannibal she is. *<Blip!> <Blip!> <Reeeee!>*

"He's wearing a golden crucifix!" she calls out to her crew, who appear shocked by what she's saying. "Imagine that," she utters, as if in soliloquy, "pricked by gold." Reaching into her bag, she pulls out a small strip of seal gut and affixes it around her nipped finger. And then, reaching into her bag once more, she procures the black book with the gold cross skewers—*the human cookbook*!

My eyes widen in terror as she holds the book before us and starts uttering things that sound vaguely familiar. I struggle mightily in my seat, then realize they've lashed me fast with straps.

"Contain him!" *<Scratch!>* an alien cries out from the front as he manipulates his control stick.

I grab my iron blade from the side of my loincloth. The aliens fall back in fright.

With a quick slice at my restraint, I release myself from the trap and then go to free the prince, but three aliens attempt to stop me, and in the fray, I lose control of my knife, and it falls into a crack betwixt the seats. As the skyborne cannibals close in on me, I push myself back to the threshold.

The prince reaches out for me, grabbing my hand just as I'm falling back, while the aliens take hold of my other hand and together they try to pull me back into the spaceship. But I'm determined to live.

I yank my hand free from the aliens and then pull hard at Umukoro's hand in an effort to take him with me, but his seat strap holds him fast and he's screaming in pain at being stretched. And then *he* fights against *me*, trying to pull his hand away.

"They'll eat you!" I cry. "They'll eat you, Umukoro!" Alas, he's determined to stay …

I release my grip and fall through the sky, shouting up at the grom one last time, "*Never surrender!*"

Faster and faster, I fall through the night, circling my arms wildly 'round in a desperate attempt to swim through the air, and then after twisting around and turning upside down, I penetrate head-first into the water. The splash jars my shoulder, and I'm driven far beneath the surface. When I finally emerge to take a breath, I see the spaceship circling around while shining its blinding light upon the Mothersea.

I dive again, keeping well beneath the surface for a long interval until the light passes over me, and then I repeat this tactic of hiding underwater and furtively coming up for air four or five times before the whirlybird at last moves on to another area in search of me.

As I swim in the opposite direction, the spacecraft eventually lowers its nose in defeat, turns off its searchlight and darts out of sight.

I feel bad about Umukoro and cannot fathom why he would abandon me and our Meridian ways to go with the alien cannibals instead. I'm deeply hurt by that. I did my duty to protect him, as I always have. But then I realize, now that he's a young man he's made his own choice in life, and so I can no longer be responsible for his fate. I try to stop feeling bad for him and myself especially. I swim hard and long as I struggle to drive away these thoughts and feelings, and then finally, after a very long interval, I hear something other than the splashing of my arms, the bubbling of my breath and the screaming of my past. I stop to listen.

Waves! The sound of breaking waves, crashing upon a shore!

Sure enow, as I draw upon the tumultuous sound, I perceive the Mothersea striking terra firma—*an island! Rising up before me, blocking out the stars on the horizon!*

I swim with renewed fervor, negotiating through a reef pass and into a wide lagoon. As I continue shoreward, I'm startled by a pro-fusion of skewers rising up out of the water all around me, some of which appear to have human heads impaled to their tops. *What kind of island is this? Another cannibal kingdom?*

But when I draw upon one of the fearsome spikes, it appears to be some manner of driftwood that has been planted into the seabed. The growths become more abundant as I reach the shore, rising up in gnarled clumps like exposed coral heads with hairlike green tops, or so they appear in the crescent moonlight.

I follow a wetsand path through this strange, half-submerged garden until I come upon even taller posts resembling smoothly chiseled beams rising high into the sky, with spiky tops not unlike Adisa's dreadlocks, while just beneath their overflowing crowns I behold great clumps of pearl earrings. Suddenly, I kick into some-thing round, sending it rolling over the ground before me.

Is that ... ? I squint to see in the bluish, crepuscular light of the clearing heavens, at last gaining the gumption to pick it up.

A coconut! So this is where they come from! I look up again at the clumps hanging beneath the high crowns, knowing now that pearls they are not.

I'm very thirsty, and my throat has contracted from saltwater, slightly choking me, so I reach for my knife.

"We'el!" I curse, remembering that I lost it on the spacecraft.

I take a deep breath, and then ease, realizing my great fortune: not only have I discovered the lost landholding of yore, but it's full of fresh coconuts and strange growths of all shapes and sizes rising up from the undersea and rooted in solid terra firma. In addition to the sustenance I've found, the tremendous coco-spires planted everywhere around me amount to a natural field of dikes anchoring the landholding against the affront of the Mothersea—something we never could've dreamed on Meridian 12. Perchance the coconuts are natural dike kernels in themselves, but given our daily scavenging activities back home, we never gave them the chance to grow.

With my legs aching and my body swollen all over, I sit down over my coconut and reach for a nearby shell fragment, with which I begin husking my first bounty. I can't help but think of Umukoro, and for a moment I stop husking. *If only he'd stayed with me!* I realize it will be different not having him to care for. I feel a twinge of remorse, but in knowing that I did everything in my power to save him, I take a long, deep breath, lower my head and then continue husking, trying to forget …

———

My first dawn on the island—*Xavion's Island!* The landholding is vast and green with spectacular life forms I've never seen, from the tall coconut spires to giant crabs to multifarious insects and birds of all formation, color and sound.

Venturing through the cornucopia of new sights, smells and noises, I arrive at a narrow, sandy beach on the other side of the point cradling the lagoon. A dark, shape-shifting mass just offshore evinces a school of fish, fresh for the taking. Exploring the beach further, I find a lengthy patch of shells and coral fragments that've washed ashore, mostly bleached white by the sun. A small shark's jaw with numerous teeth still intact rests amid the jumble, and so I set to work in the shade of the coconut spires, constructing a rudimentary spear with my newfound saw.

———

Meandering knee-deep through the shallows, about to spear my next fish, I'm suddenly frozen by the sound of the whirlybird, roaring over the coco-spires.

I retreat to the beach as the black spacecraft appears overhead. It stops mid-air and slowly starts pivoting around so that the aliens onboard can get a better look at me from the threshold.

Planting my back foot into the sand, I lunge my shaft hard up at the spacecraft. The vessel starts to pull away as my projectile streaks into its open side, and while I cannot ascertain if I've struck one of the cannibals or not, the whirlybird nonetheless continues arcing off.

I dash beneath the coco-spires, my heart pounding in my chest as I spy the demon bird through the canopy, until at last it fades with its terrible roar over the sunbed horizon. I did not spot Umukoro onboard. They must've already eaten him, poor grom.

————

Nightfall. I now feel more secure on my new island. I know that I have all I need to survive, including the ability to fashion weapons and abundant cover from which to repel the sky demons, should they return. I'm almost certain they will.

As I'm constructing my first shelter from driftwood and dried out, fanlike things that I've found on the upper reaches of the beach, a king tide comes in, washing through the short stacks of green tops and up around the trunks of the lofty coco-spires. But by now, I'm well versed in the wily ways of the Mothersea and so have chosen to make camp near the center of the island, well above the recurrent surge. Rising higher than any tract of terra firma in the bygone Meridians, this central landholding appears the perfect place to build a royal palace, and then, at long last, I shall seat myself as King.

Chapter 13
THE SINKING ISLAND

Years have passed. I was once called Prince of Meridian 12, but now I simply go by Umukoro, penultimate survivor of the sunken archipelago of which only one other, the warrior Xavion, made it through—if he's still alive. I now return with the missionaries in search of him, for the sea level has continued to rise, threatening the island he escaped to after he fell from our rescue helicopter.

Foul weather is coming in fast, a superstorm that very well may inundate his island: a previously uninhabited landholding that I've successfully lobbied the United Nations into renaming Meridian 13 in honor of my lost world. The debate over its status of a no-contact island has come to an end, because we now know from my example that, should it sink, it is better to save its sole inhabitant than let him perish with his unique, "untouched" culture.

But beyond a humanitarian mission that has finally been green-lighted by the powers that be, this is a *Christian* mission no different from the one that saved me—and by "saved," I mean not only my life but also my eternal soul.

Princess Iniko and the Elevens were right about Jesus Christ, as was I, while Xavion was blinded by his own ignorance, which is unsurprising given his penchant for brutish, warlike behavior. Yet, as my onetime loyal protector, I am happy to finally be returning his favor, namely, saving his life, and then some—it is my duty, as a good Christian, to save his soul from eternal damnation.

The first sign that he is still alive on the island is a clearing at its center with an expansive encampment, where a fire, undoubtedly for cooking, remains smoldering. He's amassed a considerable cache of spears, arrows and other weapons, which are stacked into neat bundles and leaning up against the dwellings he has constructed.

I'm about to tell the pilot to pull up and search the beaches along the perimeter, when a flurry of arrows come shooting up from the foliage. One of the projectiles whizzes past my face and strikes the helicopter blades with a loud *pop!* that sends the craft listing sideways momentarily before the pilot regains control.

"*Stop, Xavion!*" I scream down in our native language to the foliage below, but I am met with a renewed flurry of arrows that seem to emanate from several different directions.

<BLEEP!> "*Stop, Xavion!*" I implore once more, this time through a megaphone. "*There's a superstorm coming, and you won't survive it without our help!*"

A spear suddenly rockets up, striking the undercarriage and causing the pilot to pull the helo awkwardly back.

"It's too dangerous!" my advisor warns through our headsets, to which the pilot adds, "There must be a whole tribe of hostiles down there! We need to pull out, now!" *<Bleep!-Scratch!>*

Another wooden projectile comes flying up from the canopy, narrowly missing our blades.

"Wait! Just a moment!" I yell into my receiver and then down again through my loudspeaker at the unseen adversaries *<BLEEP!>* "*Please stop, Xavion! <REEET!> It's me, Prince Umukoro! You protected me as a grommet! I prithee, come with me! <BLIP!-BLIP!-WU-REET!> We're here to help you! It is safe and all shall be forgiven!*" *<BLEEP-SCRAATCH!>*

And then Xavion appears, striding out into the clearing while holding two arrows above him in the form of a cross. He points the arrows sharply up at me, screaming out in castigation.

I glance out at the side of the helo, where a thick red cross is emblazoned over the white carriage, for we've requisitioned the Red Cross organization's aircraft to aid in the emergency rescue operation.

As my fellow missionaries look on, Xavion turns around, raises his loincloth and defecates. More projectiles suddenly shoot up, clearly from multiple locations away from him, with an arrow narrowly missing me and a fellow missionary before landing in the pilot's lap.

"That's it—we're outta here!" *<Scratch!-Bleep!>* the pilot announces over radcom as he pulls sharply away.

As we're veering off, Xavion lowers his arrows and gazes coldly up at me before marching determinedly back into the jungle.

Retreating over the mangrove swamps on the south side of the island, we observe a heavy sea surging high into the bay and washing clear into the palm tree forest almost up to Xavion's encampment.

As we track further away from M-13, the full extent of the superstorm becomes evident, with a massive wall of darkness curling over the island.

In zooming ahead of the cyclone, trying to outrun it, we hit heavy rainfall and a violent patch of turbulence. *<Blip!> <Screech!> <Squawk!> <Scraaatch!>* sound atmospherics over the radcom as the pilot communicates through it, informing the base that he has the aircraft under control and providing them with our ETA.

I look back again, as the storm completely engulfs Xavion's island. And then in a flash of lightning, the emerald holm appears once more, like a dot of green amid a sea of darkness, before disappearing forever in the distance.

I grip my choker and shudder, and while I cannot see the crucifix pendant, I run my fingers along its sharp edges, feeling it deeply until the blood is drawn from my digits.

I begin to cry, the tears streaming down my cheeks and blurring my vision of the rain as it glides across the windshield.

I relinquish the cross and bury my face in my hands, enveloped in an ocean of blackness.

GLOSSARY

abaft—*adv. & prep.* (*naut.*) nearer to, in or behind the stern of a ship or watercraft.

abeam—*adv.* (*naut. & aviat.*) situated parallel to a ship's length; opposite the middle of a ship or watercraft.

aft—*adv. & adj.* (*naut.*) at or toward the rear of a ship or watercraft.

agone—*adv.* (*archaic*) ago.

alow—*adv.* (*archaic/naut.*) below; downward; beneath a level; below deck.

amphibians—*n.pl.* (*Mer./naut.*) (see also **squids**) members of Meridian archipelago navies specially trained in shoreline combat operations; sailors who specialize in **battleboard** warfare.

anti-shark spikes—*n.pl.* (*Mer.*) (*var. of* **anti-shark skewers**) sharpened wooden stakes measuring up to one meter in length that are inserted into dedicated slots along the rails of a surfboard or watercraft to ward against aggressive or attacking sharks.

barrel—*n.* (*surf*) the curl or tube of a water wave.

battleboard—*n.* (*Mer.*) (*var. of* **warcraft**) a Meridian Island surfboard between eight and ten feet in length that is designed for combat operations. Battleboards are shaped from **hardwoods** and have a sharply tapered tail, enabling them to be quickly erected into the sand as a shield. Battleboards contain a narrow slit through the deck at eye level from where the warrior can spy the enemy while using the board as a shield, and some battleboards have anti-personnel spikes similar to **anti-shark skewers** emplaced along the rails. Like a modern-day tank, battleboards are designed for both mobility and resilience in frontline combat and are capable **paddleboards** and surf crafts.

beastie—*n.* (*Mer.*) a large and ferocious shark.

benison—*n.* (*literary*) a blessing.

betwixt—*prep. & adv.* (*archaic*) between; in between; in the space separating two people or things.

big-wave gun—*n.* (*surf*) (*var. of* **big-wave gun**) (*colloquial* **"gun"**) (see also **rocker**) a surfboard specifically designed to be ridden in extra-large surf, big-wave guns are typically between seven and twelve feet in length and resemble elongated spearheads, with a narrow nose (front) and tail (back) to enable the rails (the sides) to have closer contact with the waves.

black book—*n.* (*Mer.*) the Bible.

blowfish—*n & n.pl.* (*Mer. slang*) (*pejorative*) a fish species, including bubblefish, globefish, sugar toads and sea squab, which when threatened or alarmed can inflate their bodies like balloons, making themselves appear much larger than they normally are. In the Meridian Islands, to call someone a "blowfish" is a patent insult, for it means that someone is inflating themselves (their ego, stature or persona) to appear much braver, grander or more threatening than they actually are.

bog—*n.* an area of low-lying, waterlogged or muddy ground, frequently surrounded by a body of open water, which is too soft to support a person.

bombora—*n.* (*Aus.*) (*colloquial* "**bombie**") a wave that breaks far offshore, usually over a reef or rock, and oftentimes in shallow water. Bombora waves tend to be large and shifty due to the unmitigated flow of the open ocean around them.

bottom turn—*n.* (*surf*) the initial turn a surfer executes at the bottom of a wave. •*v.* while surfing, to turn at the bottom of a wave, either in the trough or further out in front of the wave.

bulls—*n.pl.* (*Mer. colloquial*) bull sharks; "bulls" are large and aggressive sharks that tend to feed close to the shore in shallow water and are responsible for the majority of nearshore attacks on humans. While their average adult size is 7.6 feet, a maximum size of 11 feet is not uncommon.

caught inside—*v.* (*surf*) when a surfer is stuck or "caught" in the **impact zone** of a breaking wave. Typically, a surfer is caught inside by a **set**, or a series of waves larger than the intervening waves.

Central Meridians—*n.pl.* (*Mer.*) Meridian Islands 5 through 8, lying at the center of the chain. The Central Meridians maintained the seat of the **Meridian Confederacy** and hosted the archipelago-wide summits, surf contests and games.

comber—*n.* a broad wave that slowly sweeps in, "combing" the seafloor, namely, rolling for a long time before breaking.

Confederacy of Islands—*n.* (*Mer.*) (*var. of* **Meridian Confederacy**) the political, social and cultural body of the Meridian Islands, with each of the twelve islands participating as member states, but maintaining their autonomy and right to self-rule. The "Confederacy," or "Federation," used to assemble in the **Central Meridians** (specifically, M-5, M-6 or M-7) every two hundred **suns** (two hundred days) to discuss interisland disputes, trade and current events and to organize the interisland games, which happened once every three hundred suns. The summits came to a tumultuous and seditious end as the islands began to sink.

coralworks—*n.pl.* (*Mer. colloquial*) activities or ventures related to growing, transplanting, replanting and protecting corals and reefs.

craven—*adj.* cowardly. •*n.* a cowardly person.

crumbler—*n.* (*surf*) a wave that crumbles at its crest, as opposed to curing or tubing; a weak wave.

cutback—*n.* (*surf*) (see also **roundhouse cutback**) a cutback is performed when a surfer U-turns on a wave 180 degrees (or thereabouts) in order to return to the steeper part of the wave, which drives his forward momentum. As such, cutbacks are typically performed on or near the shoulder, or the more gradually sloping end portion of a breaker, which is usually situated toward the terminus of the wave's visible horizontal line. A cutback can also be employed to turn back along the wave toward another section, or as a means of slowing or stalling, such as when a rider begins "setting up" for a **barrel** as it approaches him from behind. •*v.* while surfing, the action of turning oneself in conjunction with one's board back toward the direction whence one has come.

deg-deg!—*Excl.* (*Mer.*) a phrase, possibly of Somali origin, meaning "hurry!" or "hurry up!"

derrière garde—*n.* (*Fr.*) a group of soldiers who advance behind the frontline soldiers (or forward guard).

dike—*n.* (*Mer.*) an underground fence or embankment made from **dike staves** strategically placed to prevent **landholding** terrain shifting, erosion and sand loss due to water saturation. Dikes are typically placed in concentric circles (like the swirls on a lollipop) around their target areas, but can also be placed in a straight line, such as along the seacoast, to help shore up **terra firma**.

dike staves—*n.pl.* (*Mer.*) (*var. of* **sand pickets**, **pickets**) (see also **dike**) **hardwood** stakes measuring between one and three meters in length that are placed beneath the ground as abutments to prevent **terra firma** from slumping, listing and foundering. The pickets resemble the stakes of a wood-picket fence, but are driven completely beneath the surface in concentric patterns around structures or areas that need to be shored up. Because the Meridian Islands are composed entirely of sand, the islands are highly susceptible to the negative effects of water saturation, and so dike staves were developed to help counteract this major threat.

double-up—*n.* (*surf*) a wave that has two distinct concaving sections, or curls, stacked along its face, which coalesce at its top half, forming an extra-thick and heavily falling lip. Double-ups tend to form hollow tubes, but can be difficult to **duck-dive** and catch due to their sheer power and steepness. •*v.* the occurrence of two waves, back to back, that coalesce together as they break, forming one extra-thick and powerful breaker.

duck-dive—*n.* (*surf*) a maneuver performed by a surfer while paddling toward an oncoming wave, or whitewater, in order to move beyond it. To successfully duck-dive, the surfer pushes the nose of her board underwater (as if doing a push-up, only forcing the nose down) while simultaneously pushing her foot or knee against the tail portion of her board in order to carry the entire craft beneath the oncoming water obstacle, thereby emerging safely on its other side, ideally with minimal loss of forward momentum. Duck-diving large or heavy waves can be difficult and sometimes impossible if the surfer is hit by the falling lip, destroying the endeavor. •*v.* the action of conveying oneself in conjunction with one's surfboard beneath an oncoming wave or line of whitewater.

dynast—*n.* a member of a ruling family; one who maintains political power via their hereditary bloodline, or whose existence potentially continues the political succession of a dynasty.

Elevens—*n.pl.* (*Mer.*) (*colloquial* **Eleveners**) the inhabitants of Meridian 11; the M-11 tribe; those who live under the Meridian 11 fiefdom. •*n.* **Eleven; Elevener.**

enow—*pro. & adv.* (*archaic*) enough.

ere—*prep. & conj.* (*poetic/archaic*) before.

erelong—*adv.* (*poetic/archaic*) before long; soon.

featherbed—*n.* a bed that has a mattress stuffed with soft feathers. •*v.* **feather-bed**—to protect someone too much and make things easy for them; to pamper someone with excess privilege, especially economically.

floater—*n.* (*surf*) a trick in surfing where the rider maneuvers to the top of a cresting wave and then "floats" (rides swiftly and lightly) over it and connects again with the wave's smooth surface on the other side of the crest, or otherwise successfully drops back down to the base of the wave and continues riding. Floaters enable a surfer to ride directly over a section of whitewater or tube that he or she might not be able to get around otherwise. Due to the more unpredictable nature of whitewater, floaters are best attempted with a surplus of speed to help the board power over the churning surface.

fore—*n.* (*naut.*) the front part of a ship or watercraft. •*adj.* situated or placed in, toward or near the front.

free-surfing—*n.* (*surf*) the act of riding waves for recreation, as opposed to for competition, work, transportation, etc.

garrison—*n.* (see also **praetorium**) troops stationed in a town or fort; the building they occupy. •*v.* to occupy in this way.

grommet—*n.* (*surf*) (*var. of* **grom**) a young surfer, approximately seven to fifteen years of age, who is obsessed with surfing and will eagerly surf at every opportunity, no matter how poor the conditions may be. Groms always remain in the water for an inordinate amount of time.

groundswell—*n.* (*naut. & surf*) a broad, deep rolling of the sea in the form of ocean waves, groundswells are created by distant storms, gales or seismic disturbances and are typified by longer **intervals** or distances between each wave. Groundswells are noted for their likelihood of having greater size and power than shorter **period** swells, such as **windswells**.

gullet—*n.* the passage at the throat where food goes down into the stomach; the esophagus.

haa—*Excl.* (*Mer.*) hello; welcome; used as a greeting, especially as a sign of recognition, comity, and to begin a conversation or to establish communication or such as when shouted from a distance. •*n.* an utterance of "*haa*"; a greeting. •*v.* to say or shout "*haa!*"; to greet someone. In the Meridian Islands, to say or shout *"haa!"* while circling one's hand over one's head is an indication that one comes in peace, and also can indicate capitulation (or surrender) in a dignified and deferential way.

hardwood—*n.* high-density woods from dicot trees that are typically found in temperate and tropical forests. Examples of hardwoods are teak, mahogany, oak, maple, alder and walnut.

heartwood—*n.* wood at the center of a tree, such as at the core of the trunk or the center of a branch. Heartwood is technically a dead wood and is darker, denser and less permeable than the sapwood surrounding it on the outermost portion of a stem or branch. Because it is watertight and more durable than sapwood, heartwood is the preferred wood for surfcraft production in the Meridian Islands.

howzit—*int.* (*surf*) (*colloquial*) always employed as a question, *howzit?* means "how are you?", "how are things going?" or "how are the waves (or ocean conditions)?" While the phrase has a Hawaiian pidgin origination, its use in the Meridians is likely only coincidental to that.

innard—*n.* (*Mer.*) the place within or just behind the penis or vagina where urine is stored; bladder.

interval—*n.* (*Mer.*) a segment of time in the Meridians, from short (a few seconds or minutes) to long (approximately ten to thirty minutes); (*surf & naut.*) (*var. of* **period**) the distance between individual waves or single ocean swells as measured in time. Wave intervals are commonly measured in seconds, such as between five and twenty seconds for wind-generated waves, but for **tidal waves** and tsunamis, waves can have an interval of anywhere from five minutes to one hour. Generally speaking, the longer the wave interval (the higher the count in seconds), the larger and more powerful the wave will be when it finally breaks upon a shore, reef or obstacle. For example, an open ocean wave measuring three feet in height but with an interval of twenty seconds will likely create a taller and more powerful breaker than a four-foot swell with a five-second interval.

impact zone—*n.* (*surf*) the area where waves are breaking or unloading most of their force by crashing down.

landholdings—*n. & n.pl.* (*Mer.*) (*var. of* **landholding**) (see also **terra firma**) land, particularly the extent of land owned by a Meridian Island tribe, the limits of which are ultimately determined by the size of the island; ground, solid or otherwise, as it can be owned by a Meridian tribe or individual.

lee—*n.* (*naut.*) (*var. of* **leeside**) the sheltered and therefore calmer side of an island or object, as opposed to the **windward** side, which is more exposed to the prevailing wind, sea action and inclement weather. On Meridian 12, the leeside is the east side (or "sunrise" side) of the island, for the predominant ocean action, wind and weather arrive from the west-northwest, hitting the opposite side—its windward side on its western shorefront—at a more direct angle.

leeward—*adv.* (*naut.*) on or toward the sheltered side of an atoll, island or other landmass, protected from the predominant wind and ocean waves and sometimes offering protection from certain hazards posed by tidal forces. •*adj.* downwind. •*n.* the side sheltered from the wind.

lineup—*n.* (*surf*) the area where surfers wait to catch waves; the lineup is a more or less a predictable area (which can shift over time) where waves start to break, and the surfers sitting on their boards "in the lineup" are gathered in and around this most favorable area from which to catch waves. •*int.* "the lineup" can also refer to the individuals who are gathered in this grouping of surfers, such as "*Who does the lineup consist of?*" to which one might reply, "*Oh, the lineup are all the regular crew,*" or "*It's a lineup of four gnarly locals.*"

macking—*adj.* (*surf*) (*slang*) very large in terms of wave size.

malefic—*adj.* (*literary*) harmful, injurious or destructive, especially by nonrational or supernatural means; having malignant influence.

Meridian Confederacy—*n.* (*Mer.*) (*var. of* **Confederacy of Islands**) the political, social and cultural organization of the Meridian Islands, to which each of the twelve islands participated as member states but maintained their autonomy. "The Confederacy" or "the Federation" used to assemble in the **Central Meridians** (in this case, either M-5, M-6 or M-7) in a great summit once every two hundred **suns** (two hundred days) to discuss current events, interisland disputes, and trade and to organize the interisland games, which occurred once every three hundred suns.

Meridian Islands—*n.pl.* (*Mer.*) The Meridian Islands (M) is an archipelago of twelve islands that exists in the **sky realm** (above water), on **terra firma** (land) set upon the **Mothersea** (the ocean). The islands are composed entirely of sand and are treeless, with Meridian 12 being the only island with a coral reef (on its **lee-side**). The **Central Meridians** (islands M-5 through M-8) house the seat of government—the **Meridian Confederacy**—which hosts summits to discuss and organize current affairs, but which has no real power of plebiscite over each island, which are autonomous. The **Outer Meridians** (M-1 through M-4 and M-9 through M-12) lie on opposite ends of the chain, and their inhabitants tend be more ruggedly individualistic than the Central Meridian Islanders. The Meridian Islands practice free trade and take part in archipelago-inclusive assemblies and games—contests that test athletic feats, warrior abilities and specialized skills such as spear-fishing and surfboard construction. Meridian natives navigate their nearshore waters and between neighboring islands using a variety of surfboard-shaped watercrafts including **paddleboards, stand-up paddleboards (SUPs), sailboards** and **big-wave guns,** all of which are made from great beams of **timber** salvaged from shipwrecked galleons in bygone times. Their belief system is centered around the conviction that they hail from the Mothersea, their creator, with a small percentage instead believing they are descendants from the sky realm, whose "demon beings" have in times past shipwrecked along their shores. Other than these two genesis theories, Meridian Islanders believe that they, as a group, are alone in the world, with no other people or landmass outside of their archipelago. As such, they can be classified as a no-contact tribe, if we are to apply the termi-nology of the outside world, which they have no direct knowledge of. The story of *Meridian 12—Surfing's Lost Outpost* follows the fate of the archipelago's tribes as the Mothersea begins to rise, with special focus on Meridian 12, the last island nation to survive.

mire—*n.* muddy, boggy or swampy ground, too soft to support a person; sludge.

moons—*n.pl. (Mer.)* nights; (*singular*) one moon equates to one night.

Mothersea—*n. (Mer.)* the ocean as perceived by Meridian Islanders, from which all are born, sustained, and to which all shall return; the ocean as personified as the one supreme Goddess; the creator.

narwhal—*n.* a small whale with a long, straight tusk at its front, which is actually an overgrowth of one of its teeth. (In this book, regarding the unique **battleboard** of Temitope as shaped by Ekon of M-11, it appears to be a **big-wave gun** with a longspear affixed to its nose, while its ability to "fly above the surface of the water" upon a "formidable iron blade attached to a submerged turtle shell wing" evinces it is something akin to a modern-day hydrofoil surfboard or foilboard.)

Ocean Masters—*n.pl.* (*Mer.*) the highest-ranking watermen and waterwomen in the Meridian Islands, as officially certified by a monarch; royally ordained "knights of the sea."

off-the-lip—*n.* (*surf*) (*var. of* **off-the-top**) an intermediate to advanced surfing maneuver where the rider angles steeply toward the top of the wave and then turns sharply off the "lip," or the cresting upper edge of the wave. •*v.* while surfing, the action of driving the nose of one's surfboard up past the crest and then suddenly reverse turning back down the wave, effecting a whip-like "snap" off the top.

oracle—*n.* (see also **seer, sibyl, visionary**) a human medium who can receive messages, insights and predictions of the future from god, gods and/or supernatural powers; (*Mer.*) each Meridian Island has an oracle who acts as the high priest or priestess and through whom the **Mothersea** or other supreme entities are believed to speak.

other-islander—*n.* (*Mer.*) someone from another island in the Meridians other than one's own; one from a rival tribe, including refugees and émigrés; an outlander.

outflow chamber—*n.* (*Mer.*) lavatory; garderobe; a room equipped with a fixture into which urine is discharged.

Outlying Meridians—*n.pl.* (*Mer.*) (*var. of* **Outer Meridians**) Meridian Islands 1 through 4 and 9 through 12. Situated toward the opposite ends of the chain, the Outlying Meridian tribes were, by necessity, more self-sustaining than those of the **Central Meridians** and therefore characterized by a more autonomous, "territorial" mindset among their inhabitants. The outermost Meridians, islands 1–2 and 10–12, were known to have the best big-wave spots, but due to their isolation (and the relative lack of big-wave riding skills possessed by the Central Islanders), the outlying tribes had difficulty in organizing archipelago-inclusive big-wave contests and events.

paddleboard—*n.* (see also **stand-up paddleboard**, which is propelled very differently) a watercraft, resembling an unusually long surfboard (nine to fifteen feet in length) or kayak, which is used specifically for paddling prone (in the lying-down position) or kneeling and is most commonly employed for paddling great distances, for physical fitness and for racing.

pearling—*v.* (*surf*) while surfing, when the nose of one's surfboard hits the water at too steep of an angle, causing the front half of the board to suddenly submerge underwater and throwing the rider forward over the nose of the board. The main reason a surfer pearls is because their body weight is centered too far forward, especially when they are riding down a steep wave and fail to make the necessary counter adjustment by shifting their weight over their back foot before reaching the trough. However, even an over-vertical wave can be successfully descended via an "elevator drop," or freefall, so long as the rider is properly shifting their body weight over their board while employing advanced wave knowledge by accurately "reading" the wave as it is breaking.

penetralium—*n.* (*literary/archaic*) the innermost part of a building; the interior of a building; the most secret room in a house; an inner sanctum.

perchance—*adv.* (*literary/archaic*) perhaps; by some chance.

period—*n.* (*var. of* **interval**) (*naut. & surf*) the distance between individual waves or single ocean swells as measured in time (seconds, or minutes for tsunamis). Knowing what the wave period is will provide a learned surfer or mariner with a much better understanding of oceanic conditions than having wave height data alone.

port—*n.* (*naut.*) (see also **starboard**) the left-hand side of a watercraft when one is facing forward on the craft. •*v.* to turn a watercraft to port, or to the left.

praetorium—*n.* (*archaic*) (*var. of* **garrison**) historically speaking, a praetorium is an ancient Roman general's tent within an encampment; in the Meridian Islands, the *praetorium* is a forward operations center consisting of a shack or sturdier **timber** structure such as a garrison, depending upon its purpose. It is designed to house equipment and personnel, such as day workers, for a specific, local project, or is built as a military prerogative to house soldiers for a nearby engagement. It is built directly upon **terra firma** or sand with no added flooring, and typically has a large opening at its main **threshold** in front.

prithee—*Excl. & adv.* (*literary/archaic*) please (used in conveying polite questions or requests); also, short for "I pray thee."

puka—*n.* (*var. of* **puka shell**) a small, tough, bead-like shell with a naturally occurring hole at its center, rendering it an ideal shell for jewelry making; (*Hawaiian pidgin*) a small hole or pit in something.

quiver—*n.* a case for holding and carrying arrows; the arrows in a quiver. •*n.* (*surf*) a collection of surfboards, usually prized by its owner, with a register of boards suitable for a wide variety of wave conditions.

rivière—*n.* (*Fr.*) a necklace of precious stones, pearls or shells of all the same species. The jewelries on a *rivière* wrap in continuation all the way around the neck and are either all the same size and shape, or graduate smoothly in size, with the largest gemstone situated in front.

rocker—*n.* (*surf*) the lengthwise, bottom curve of a surfboard from its nose to its tail, as can be observed in the concave curvature of a surfboard's profile, or side angle. If the board has a lot of rocker, the curvature will be more acute, like a banana. Less rocker will produce a flatter bottom, like a sheet of plywood. For a variety of reasons, a surfboard's degree of rocker has a massive influence on how it will ride. The more rocker, or drastic the bottom curve, the less planing surface the board has with the water, making it slower and looser, but better formed to negotiate steeply curving waves and for making sharp turns, and so "more rocker" is better suited for more advanced surfers and experienced **shortboard** riders. "Less rocker," equating to a flatter bottom, provides more planing surface and therefore more inherent speed, inertia and stability, but less maneuverability in steeply curving wave sections, and is therefore better suited for longboards and beginning surfers. Some boards, however, such as **big-wave guns,** and elfin boards termed "fish," often contain a variance of rocker, such as less rocker at the tail and center, but more toward the nose.

roller—*n.* (*surf*) a wave that rolls or moves toward the shore for a long time before breaking.

rotunda—*n.* a circular domed building. In the Meridian Islands, the rotunda is the religious center, where fowl sacrifices are performed and where people pay homage to the **Mothersea**. It typically consists of a mother-of-pearl mosaic worked into the ceiling of its cupola, depicting waves, sea creatures and humans emerging from the sea. The edifice itself is constructed of **shipwood**, is subsidized by the island's monarchs and is maintained by the island's **oracle** and her familiar(s).

roundhouse cutback—*n.* (*surf*) (see also **cutback**) a maneuver performed when a surfer U-turns his board at least 180 degrees in order to return back to the curl, or the steeper part of the wave, and then turns 180 degrees again at the curl, completing what amounts to a figure-8 along the wave's face. More than a mere cutback, a roundhouse cutback adds a radical and often complex follow-through turn at the most critical part of a breaking wave. •*v.* while surfing, the action of turning oneself in conjunction with one's board back toward the direction whence one has come and then back again the other way, essentially drawing a figure 8 or S-pattern upon the face of a wave before continuing forward.

Royal Code of Defense and Preservation—*n.* (*Mer.*) (*var. of* **Code of Defense, the Code**) a comprehensive policy of military strategy, island defense and environmental protection instigated on Meridian 12 by King Tai Yun at the time of the Central Meridians' sinking and the subsequent downfall of the **Confederacy**. Enduring for the remainder of Tai Yun's reign, the main tenets of "the Code" consisted of fierce territorialism, armed rejection of trespassers, distrust of outsiders (foreign monarchs especially), war readiness and ongoing geological support and defense by means of concentric sand **dike**-line construction, coral transplantation, **landholding** conveyance (**terra firma** relocation) and **Mothersea** offerings.

royal guard—*n. & n.pl.* (*Mer.*) (*var. of* **royal guards, royal guardsmen, royal guardspersons, guardsmen**) the military, or warrior force, of Meridian 11 under the reign of King Chaka, consisting of a naval division, a corps of frontline "grunts" (conscripted fighters) and a specialized unit that guards the monarchs.

sand pickets—*n.pl.* (*Mer.*) (*var. of* **dike staves, pickets**) (see also **dike**) **hardwood** stakes, measuring between one and three meters in length, which are placed beneath the ground as abutments to prevent **terra firma** from slumping, listing and foundering. The pickets resemble the stakes of a wood-picket fence, but are driven completely beneath the surface in concentric patterns (like the swirl of a lollipop) around structures or areas that need to be shored up. Because the Meridian Islands are composed entirely of sand, the ground is highly susceptible to the negative effects of water saturation, and so sand pickets were developed to help counteract this major threat.

sand trap—*n.* (*Mer.*) in the Meridian Islands, a sand trap is a hollow area of ground partially filled with sand. It forms by a sudden collapse of ground, like an imploding sinkhole, and is one of the ways in which a pit of quicksand is initially formed. The difference between a sand trap and a pit of quicksand is that a sand trap is usually the result of dry or moist sand collapsing, and so geologically, it typically resembles a pit or ditch, while quicksand is already a fully matured bog whose viscous surface is level with the surrounding land. However, if enough water accumulates inside a sand trap, such as from seepage or a downpour, it will transform it into a pit of quicksand. Sand traps are hazardous because, while the crater may be dry, the sand itself is often too loose and unstable to support a human, drawing him or her into a swallowing glove of pebbles that can be equally as engulfing as quicksand.

seer—*n.* (see also **oracle, sibyl, visionary**) (*Mer.*) a prophetess; a woman who is believed to portend the future through supernatural insights.

set—*n.* (*naut. & surf*) two waves or more that move in sequence and that are bigger than the ordinary waves, or which rise higher than the prevailing ocean conditions.

shipwood—*n.* (*Mer.*) the **timber** or beams of a ship. In the Meridians, all shipwood comes from old shipwrecks such as sunken galleons. The salvaged wood is preserved over many generations and is used in the construction of a plethora of things ranging from surfboards to spears, stairways, rotundas and monarchial palaces. Its greatest assets lie in its hardiness, being formed of **hardwoods** and **heartwoods**, and in its water-resistant quality, which is begot from its high-density and waterproofing treatment prior to its use in galleon construction.

shorebreak—*n.* when waves break directly onshore, such as directly onto the sand, with unmitigated power. A shorebreak can easily knock someone over and thrash them about in its own shoreline **impact zone** or suck them out to sea as the water recedes again between waves or **sets**.

shortboard—*n.* (see also **thruster**) a high-performance surfboard, typically with three fins (sometimes as many as five) and a pointy nose, which is highly maneuverable. Contemporary shortboards average between 5'5" and 6'6" in length (trending toward 6'0" and under), are narrow (17"–19" wide), thin, lightweight and have a lot of **rocker**, especially in the nose, and therefore are designed for more experienced riders who know how to "pump" the board (swing it from rail to rail under their feet) to generate speed.

shoulder—*n.* (*surf*) the part of a wave on the side of the curl that has not yet broken (unless it is a "closeout," or a wave that curls up and breaks all at once along its entire length, in which case the wave has no shoulder). In good surf, the shoulder will gradually flatten the further it stretches out "down the line," or away from the curl, causing the wave to peel off more evenly and thus providing for a longer, more predictable ride. However, to be riding too far out on the shoulder is relatively banal and easy and, as such, is often the mark of a novice surfer. A more advanced rider will often **cut back** on the flattening shoulder in order to return to the steeper part of the wave closer to the curl, where the breaker is more challenging and dynamic than along the safety of its shoulder. Most surfers' (aside from longboarders and beginners) ultimate goal is to be riding within the curl itself, *not* out on the shoulder.

sibyl—*n.* (see also **oracle, seer, visionary**) a prophetess; a woman who can speak the prophecies of God; (*literary*) a woman who is able to foretell the future.

sire—*n.* (*archaic*) father; male ancestor; a respectful form of address for a nobleman or king. •*v.* for a male to beget or procreate as the father.

skookum house—*n.* (*colloquial*) jail; detention center.

sky realm—*n.* (*Mer.*) the world above the surface of the **Mothersea**; the realm of air and sky, as opposed to the realms of undersea and **undersand**. The Mothersea has delivered humans (the Meridian Islanders) from out of her aqueous womb to inhabit the sky realm, where she has placed them upon islands (**terra firma**). She has sent them above as pilgrims in a bid, or experiment, to occupy the sky realm, thereby giving her a foothold in both realms of water and sky. But owing to her jealousy in wanting her children back, and/or due to her anger over their wayward behavior, she has begun swelling up over terra firma in a "lovesickness," reclaiming her children (mankind) in the process; (*pejorative*) the realm whence the alien beings (the "demon beings") of yore came in ships and inflicted the Mothersea's children with terrible diseases; the unknown world beyond where the demon beings live; the realm of Jesus as glorified by the **Elevens**, which can only be reached by practicing cannibalism (real or symbolic), worshipping Jesus and then dying.

sorceress—*n.* (see also **witch doctor**) a female magician, wizard or witch who is believed to have magic powers ("magic" as it pertains to genuine spellworking and the supernatural, as opposed to conjuring tricks and legerdemain).

squids—*n.pl.* (*Mer. slang*) (see also **amphibians**) members of Meridian Island navies; •*n.* (*derogatory*) a "squid" can connote a low-ranking sailor lacking in experience.

stand-up paddleboard—*n.* (*var. of* **SUP**) (see also **paddleboard, sweepers**) a watercraft resembling an unusually large and wide surfboard that is piloted by a rider in the standing position who propels the craft forward with a long paddle, much like a canoe paddle. Its most common utilization is for recreation, exercise and wave riding, while in the Meridian Islands its main purpose is for interisland transportation, fishing and hauling things over the water.

starboard—*n.* (*naut.*) (see also **port**) the right-hand side of a watercraft when one is facing forward on the craft. •*v.* to turn a watercraft to starboard, or to the right.

summers—*n.pl.* (*Mer.*) years; the mode by which Meridian Islanders determine an individual's age, i.e., "*a woman aged forty summers;*" (*singular*) one summer equates to one year.

sunbed—*n.* (*Mer.*) (*var. of* **to sunbed, sunbed horizon**) west. •*adj.* westward; toward the west; facing west. •*adv.* in a westerly direction. •*v.* to travel west.

sunrise—*n.* (*Mer.*) (*var. of* **to sunrise, sunrise horizon**) east. •*adj.* eastward; toward the east; facing east. •*adv.* in an easterly direction. •*v.* to travel east.

sunrise veranda—*n.* (*Mer.*) (*var. of* **summer veranda, summer room, sunroom**) a partially enclosed veranda on the second floor of a royal palace that faces east. A sunrise veranda contains an open balcony overlooking the eastern sea and is where monarchs monitor their eastern seafront, dine with family and friends and hold meetings with other powerful figures or delegates, usually over a snack offering or meal. The royal palace of each Meridian Island is situated along either the eastern or western seacoast, depending upon the particular history of the settlement and the interisland concerns of the ruling monarch(s).

suns—*n.pl.* (*Mer.*) days; (*singular*) one sun equates to one day.

sunset veranda—*n.* (*Mer.*) (*var. of* **summer veranda, summer room, sunroom**) a partially enclosed veranda on the second floor of a royal palace that faces west. A sunset veranda contains an open balcony overlooking the western sea and is where monarchs monitor their western seafront, dine with family and friends and hold meetings with other powerful figures or delegates, usually over a snack offering or meal. The royal palace of each Meridian Island is situated on either the western or eastern seacoast, depending upon the particular history of the island and the geopolitical concerns of the ruling monarch(s).

SUP—*n.* (*var. of* **stand-up paddleboard**) (see also **paddleboard, sweepers**) a watercraft resembling an unusually large and wide surfboard that is piloted by a rider in the standing position who propels the craft forward by means of a long paddle.

superstorm—*n.* an exceptionally powerful and destructive storm that affects a large area.

surf line—*n.* (*naut. & surf*) where breaking waves are encountered along a shore or reef passage; (*Mer.*) where the whitewater from breaking waves expires along a shore.

surf zone—*n.* (*naut. & surf*) the area of breaking waves, including the **shorebreak, impact zone** and **bombora**; where waves are actively encountering a shore, reef or stationary obstacle.

sweepers—*n.pl.* (*surf*) (*slang*) (*derogatory*) (*var. of* **janitor**) those who ride **stand-up paddleboards**, their activity giving the impression they are sweeping a broom over the water.

swell—*n.* the heaving movement of the sea; rolling waves in the ocean that do not break until they encounter a reef, shore or obstacle; a large, discernible wave or succession of waves moving across the ocean.

tallyho—*Excl.* (*Mer.*) a Meridian Islander's cry of rapture or excitement. •*n.* a cry of "*tallyho!*" •*v.* utter a cry of "*tallyho!*"

tawi-manu—*n.* (*Mer.*) a weapon resembling a canoe paddle whose wide end is lined with protruding shark's teeth and/or sharpened sea mammal bone fragments.

terra firma—*n.* (*Mer.*) (see also **landholdings**) an island; land; solid ground, as distinct from sea and sky.

threshold—*n.* a point of entry; a piece of wood or stone forming the bottom of a doorway and which is crossed over when entering a room or house.

thruster—*n.* (*surf*) (see also **shortboard**) a revolutionary surfboard design invented by Australian competitive surfer Simon Anderson that has three equally sized fins, or near equally sized fins, configured in a nabla formation (an inverted Greek delta), with the two outer fins situated just forward of the center fin, which is set closest to the tail. Thruster shortboards range from five to seven feet in length, with around six feet being the contemporary average. They are designed for radical maneuverability and reliability in performance, and as such, the thruster is the preferred board for intermediate to advanced riders.

tidal wave—*n.* an exceptionally large and destructive ocean wave created by a seaquake, powerful storm, volcanic eruption or by the effect of a massive object either sinking rapidly, rising to the surface or displacing large amounts of seawater, such as with a meteor strike or seacoast landslide of epic proportions; an unusual rise of water upon a shore that is not a rogue wave or storm surge.

timber—*n.* (see also **shipwood**) the wood used in ship construction; wood beams with which wooden ships such as galleons are built.

Twelves—*n.pl.* (*Mer.*) the inhabitants of Meridian 12; the M-12 tribe; those who hail from the kingdom of Meridian 12.

Twos—*n.pl.* (*Mer.*) the inhabitants of Meridian 2; the M-2 tribe; those born on Meridian 2.

undersand—*n.* (*Mer.*) buried sand; the ground beneath **terra firma**; the final resting place of Meridian Islanders who are not returned to the **Mothersea**.

visionary—*adj.* (see also **oracle, seer, sibyl**) fanciful; not practical. •*n.* (*conversely*) a person who has great imagination and wisdom in the planning of affairs intended for the future; the seeing of visions in a dream or a trance; (*Mer.*) a high priestess who, while serving as a medium to supreme beings, can augur the future.

vulgarian—*n.* a belligerent oaf.

warcraft—*n. & n.pl.* (*Mer.*) (*var. of* **battleboard**) Meridian Island surfboards between eight and ten feet in length specifically designed for combat; (*colloquial*) any watercraft employed in frontline combat operations.

we'el! —*Excl.* (*Mer.*) a phrase, possibly of Somali origin, meaning "bastard!"

wee little one—*n.* (*colloquial*) an infant or toddler aged between zero and three **summers**.

wetsand—*n.* (*Mer.*) moist ground; wet **terra firma**; land or sand made infirm and unstable by water saturation; where the beach meets the **surf line**.

whence—*adv.* from where; from which; as a consequence of which.

windsurfer—*n.* (*var. of* **sailboarder, sailboard**) a person who rides a surfboard that has a sail attached to its deck by means of a mast; someone who goes windsurfing; a surfboard that contains a sail with a boom, with which the rider holds and manipulates as the wind propels him or her along the surface of the water.

windswell—*n.* (*naut. & surf*) an ocean **swell** created by the wind transferring its energy along the surface of the water and with an **interval** of ten seconds or less. A windswell is often the result of a locally occurring breeze or storm, while a groundswell (ten to twenty plus second interval) is originating from, or has originated from, a more distant meteorological disturbance.

windward—*adv.* (*naut.*) on or toward the unsheltered side of an atoll, island or other landmass, unprotected from the predominant wind, ocean waves and tidal forces. •*adj.* toward the wind. •*n.* the side not sheltered from the wind; the side facing the wind. On Meridian 12, the windward side is the west side or **sunbed** side of the island.

witch doctor—*n.* (see also **sorceress**) a tribal magician; a person who is thought to have magic powers, especially in the use of traditional medicine(s), and who can heal people, prevision the future and protect against the magic of other witch doctors or sorcerers; (*Mer.*) (*pejorative*) someone who practices black arts or magic to invoke evil powers (or entities) for wicked purposes.

young'un—*n.* a youngster; (*Mer.*) a child aged between three and seven **summers**.

MERIDIAN 12

Itoro—queen; her name means "praise." She is forty-two summers of age.

Jomo—farmer; husband of San Jiao.

Jue Yin—warrior; retainer to King Tai Yun and secondary guard of his royal family (behind Xavion). Her name means something akin to "sensitive."

Nsia—sixth-born princess (and only remaining princess of M-12). She is eight summers of age.

Nyoto—lead warrior nicknamed "arrowmaiden" due to her prowess at the bow. She is twenty-four summers of age.

Qi Dong—low-ranking warrior lacking in experience.

Ren Mai—a highly skilled but reclusive warrior who often goes by "Ren."

San Jiao—chief engineer and surfboard shaper ("boardshaper"), married to Jomo.

Shao Ying—oracle who studies the interplay of sand, water and wind to predict the future. She is thirty-two summers of age. The name of her familiar(s) is unknown.

Soko Yun—lead waterman and warrior who often goes by "Soko."

Tai Yun—king; aged approximately sixty summers. He is a deep thinker who no longer surfs on account of its inherent dangers.

Umukoro—prince; he is aged fifteen summers and is an avid surfer.

Xavion—lead retainer to King Tai Yun. Xavion is the chief guardian of the royal family and the official mentor of Prince Umukoro in warrior and waterman training. He sometimes goes by "X."

Yang Ming-Hua—an expert spear-fisherman who usually goes by "Yang." He is twenty-five summers of age.

MERIDIAN 11

Adeze—onetime princess of Meridian 11. Upon her death, her younger sister, Iniko, succeeded her as princess.

Adisa—oracle; she is completely blind.

Bobo—chief farmer; he is humble in nature.

Cadiz—warrior and delegate to King Chaka. Cadiz claims to be of mixed ancestry, with a mother from M-8 and a father from M-11, but he is likely a mercenary from another island.

Chaka—king; approximately fifty summers of age.

Ekon—surfboard shaper ("boardshaper") and chief engineer; his name carries the connotation of "strong." He is married to Fela.

Fela—lead warrior, married to Ekon.

Iniko—Princess of Meridian 11 after the death of her older sister, Adeze. Iniko is sixteen summers of age. Her name means "born during troubled times."

Kamali—protectress of the House of Chakinian (King Chaka's royal dynasty).

Kendi—prince; King Chaka's firstborn (and only) son. His name means "loved one."

Ojore—lead warrior; adjutant to Fela.

Sassandra—queen; King Chaka's second wife and the mother of their only son, Prince Kendi, and Chaka's surviving daughter, Princess Iniko.

Temitope Mukondi—chief retainer to King Chaka and guard of the royal family. The androgynous-looking Temitope has invented and mastered a type of foilboard.

Other

Babacar— (in)famous warrior/adventurer from Meridian 2.

Okonkwo—a male tiger shark feared for its immense size (twelve plus meters in length) and penchant for surprise attacks. Okonkwo frequents the open ocean between M-11 and M-12 and sometimes cruises around M-12's North Point to feed.

Royal guard—the total conscripted fighting force of Meridian 11. Originally numbering around twenty members, the royal guard is believed to have swelled during the Meridian diaspora to somewhere between forty and sixty plus warriors.

More Great Titles From Phantasea Books

The Good Christian, by Quinn Haber and Dr. Steven Meyers

Islands on the Fringe—A Year of Micronesian Waves and Wanderers, by S. Jacques Stratton

Old lanai (Illustrated) —A True Ghost Story from Hawaii, by Warren S. Croft and Quinn Haber

The Heart of a Traveler—Reflections from the Fathomless Edge of the World, by Ari Marsh

The Volcano Trilogy—A Philippines Surfing Odyssey, (in one book) by Quinn Haber

CA$H CRAFT—The Musings and Meditations of an Income Investor, by Rancroft Beachley

I Fell in Love with an Aleutian Vampire (Illustrated) —The WWII in Adak Commemorative Edition, by Quinn Haber and Lt. Jake Harper

Surfing Guide to Ilocos Norte Philippines, by Rey Cajudoy and Quinn Haber

Echoes from the Sun: A Modern Quest for the Fountain of Youth, by Ari Marsh

Tonkin, by Quinn Haber

The Somali Pirate Trilogy, (in three books) by Quinn Haber and Noor Fayrus

Also by the Author
Experience Pipeline—An Interactive Adventure Book, by Quinn Haber (Casagrande Press, ©2008)

Author's Music on Bandcamp
QARK—Skyworld
QARK—Open Circuit

PhantaSea Books, Honolulu, HI